# The Key and the Scythe

## Tales From Eve's Hollow

### Charles Bedlam

*For my Blackbird*

# CHAPTER 1

## THE CRACKED MIRROR

The clock of the headmistress's office struck 12:30 PM as Estelle paced before tall white bookshelves. She wore the Madame Katherine's University uniform of a maroon pleated skirt, white button-down shirt and gray sweater. She strode back and forth on long dancer's legs, hands on her hourglass waist, staring straight ahead.

She ran her fingers through her silky black hair and examined her makeup in a handheld mirror, ignoring the blood smeared on her pristine collar. The black eyeliner she wore complimented her deep green eyes, but she lacked a shade of lipstick to cover the dark red cut on her lower lip.

The office's dull gray walls made it feel like a prison, even with the decorative plants hanging by the windows and motivational posters hung up. A slate colored desk sat before the glowing panes and behind it sat Ms. Volkova, a lanky white haired woman in her fifties clad in a black turtleneck dress. She glared at the young woman over half-moon eyeglasses.

"Perhaps you'd be more comfortable if you took a seat," Ms. Volkova said. "I'm sure your father will be here soon."

"It won't make a difference," Estelle said. "He'll get here, give you a check and I'll walk out of your office just to see you again on Monday. This is a waste of time."

"Estelle, this is the third fight you've been in this month! I know you think we're attacking you, but we are trying to help you. This isn't how a young woman should behave."

"How should I behave? Timid? Obedient? You want me to let those little bitches say what they want about me?"

"Language, young lady!"

Estelle's eyes grew wide as she leaned over Ms. Volkova's desk.

"I meant what I said. If you want to discipline anyone, go after Nina and her little posse. They're the ones who are making my life hell. I wouldn't have to fight if you'd get them to stop."

"It's not that simple. We all know she's been acting out since her sister died- and I assure you no one blames you for what happened to Natasha."

"If that were true, I wouldn't be in your office. It was over a year ago and they still stare at me. They still whisper. What about you? Do you blame me?"

Ms. Volkova held her breath and cast her eyes at a file on her desk. Estelle scoffed.

"You're such a bright woman," the headmistress said after clearing her throat. "Putting your high GPA aside, you're a talented pianist and an accomplished ballet dancer. Your future looks bright and you can do anything you want, but your behavior will hold you back. Is that what you really want?"

"What I want is to get out of this city and away from you people."

The headmistress grumbled and they locked eyes for several quiet moments. A knock at the door broke the uncomfortable silence.

"Come in!" Ms. Volkova said.

The door opened and heavy footsteps entered behind Estelle. She had known their weight her entire life; the shadow that loomed in her wake every day. She turned to face her father. Damian Grigori was a burly man in his early fifties, standing six and a half feet tall. He kept his hair slicked back, gray forming at the fringes and fading to jet black. The deep lines in his face lead to a bushy mustache and his dark green eyes matched Estelle's. He wore a forest green suit with a black tie and bore a thick, golden square ring on his right middle finger.

"Mr. Grigori," Ms. Volkova said. "I appreciate you making it over. I know how busy you are."

"Yes," Mr. Grigori said. "Apparently, my daughter stays busy as well. How bad is it this time?"

The low timber of his voice resonated like a drum in Estelle's ears. He spoke as if a retired military official, standing straight with his eyes locked forward like search lights. Ms. Volkova cleared her throat and straightened her glasses.

"A girl called Estelle *that word-* which resulted in your daughter fighting two other ladies in the restroom, causing extensive damage. A broken sink and mirror. One girl is fine, but the other is being treated for lacerations on her face."

Estelle's father sighed and his hand disappeared into his inside breast pocket. He drew a checkbook and a pen, scribbling out the form before ripping it out and sliding it to the headmistress. She hesitated to take it, looking up at Mr. Grigori, but never for more than a few seconds.

"It may not be a matter of money anymore. I'm afraid... the situation at the lake keeps resurfacing."

"What's that girl's name again? The sister?"

"Nina- She feels..."

Ms. Volkova's eyes shot toward Estelle, who observed the conversation with quiet tensity that threatened to snap like an overstretched rubber band.

"Go to the car," her father said.

"If this is about me, don't I deserve to be here?" Estelle asked. "You always preach responsibility, then lock me away to make choices about my life!"

"Silence!" Her father squinted, his bushy brows arching. "If you made responsible choices, I wouldn't need to do it for you."

"You haven't even heard my side of the story!"

"You'll have the chance to explain yourself- at home. Go to the car."

"But-"

Towering over her like a brick wall, Mr. Grigori's form was imposing; his dark green eyes shone with a slight twitch.

"*Go.*"

Estelle snatched up her leather satchel and tore through the door, passed the secretary and rushed into the crowded halls of Madame Katherine's. Her heels clicked on gray and white tile as the young women in the corridor cast sidelong glances and whispered to one another.

The class bell rang as she entered a locker room, the other students filing out behind her. She waited until she was alone to change out of her uniform. A tight blue dress with the straps relaxed around her shoulders was her favorite outfit. She wore a long-sleeved black shirt beneath, charcoal gray leggings and black boots that came to her knees, meeting the end of her dress.

She stuffed the balled up uniform in her bag and examined her wound, leaning on a sink. She smiled to herself, proud of the yellow tape surrounding the broken porcelain a few mirrors down. She touched a finger to her lip and a dot of fresh blood pushed its way out. Yellow and purple blotches of a bruise presented themselves across her cheek, ruining her flawless ivory skin. She turned on the water and washed her face.

When she looked up, she stepped back so fast she nearly toppled over. Eyes bulging from her head, she beheld her reflection.

"What the hell?" she said, touching her face.

Her flesh felt smooth, but her counterpart touched a sagging, wrinkled cheek. Her gray-green eyes sank into the sockets and her dark hair faded to silver at the roots. The haggard woman smiled at Estelle with stained, darkened teeth.

"I remember when I looked like you," she said, her voice rattling. "I was so beautiful. So perfect, even though I didn't think so."

"Wh- what are you?" Estelle's voice quivered.

"I'm you. And you..." The strange woman's voice fell to a whisper. "Need to wake up."

"What kind of trick is this?"

"The best kind. Where you get a treat at the end. But first..." The woman's voice shrank, then erupted into a screech. "WAKE UP!"

The sound raked the inside of her ears and she cried out, shrinking back and covering her head.

"Estelle?" came a voice from the door.

The woman's head snapped to the locker room door. There waited her best friend, Kamaria. Hailing from Cameroon, her dark chocolate skin contained a natural golden glow and she wore her long black hair in small braids that draped over her shoulders and down her back. A cherry lollipop hung between her lips, head tilted and brows furrowed.

"You okay?" Kamaria asked, rushing to her.

"Just..." When Estelle looked back at the mirror, her reflection returned to normal, but the glass bore a long, fresh crack running from top to bottom. "Can't believe Nina got me in the face."

Kamaria entered the locker room and cupped Estelle's cheeks, examining her bruise.

"You got Clara worse. I saw her with the nurse on my way to calculus. Her face is all swollen and bandaged. She must have really pissed you off."

"Everyone pisses me off- except for you and Marcel. You should have seen them staring at me in the hall."

"Why don't we talk about something positive?" Kamaria's eyes widened as an eyebrow arched. "You made it into the Age of Music concert- what are you doing to celebrate? That spring dance is coming up."

Estelle made a fake gagging sound.

"I'd look corny all dolled up."

"You'd look like royalty! How many numbers do you get when we go out?"

She smiled bashfully. "I'd just like a quiet night at the house with Marcel."

"Girl, you're going to get him in trouble. Why not just get a fancy hotel room? You have enough money."

"It's not about the money. That's why I like him. Marcel isn't like the others who want the clout or a one-night stand. He sees passed what I am. I want it to be in the house I grew up in."

"I get that, but still. We both know how your father feels about people who look like us. It's a wonder he even let my brother tutor you."

"Well, it's a good thing he's going out of town," Estelle said with a sly smile.

"What if your maids say something?" Kamaria crossed her arms and leaned on her hip.

"There are only two in the house right now and one of them is like a sister to me."

"Don't you feel guilty about all that scheming?" Kamaria asked with a laugh.

Slinging her bag over her shoulder, Estelle grinned. "You're not guilty if you don't get caught."

Deep purple mixed with lofty pink and rays of sunlight as evening set in. Estelle and her father rode in the back seat of his tinted SUV with Oscar, one of his henchmen, driving. Oscar was a man in his early thirties. He wore black jeans and a leather coat as dark as his hair, which he kept styled as if he lived in the 1920s. His dark blue eyes kept searching for Estelle's in the rearview mirror.

Estelle kept her vision trained on the flashes of shop windows and the people dressed in heavy clothes to guard from the bite of the winter wind. Her father had not said a word since they drove away from the university and came as a surprise to the young woman when his deep voice shook the air.

"Why must you get in trouble the day before I leave?" Mr. Grigori asked. "Don't you have any idea how important these connections are? How am I supposed to run our empire when I have to pull you from the bed you made?"

"You're not even going to ask me what happened?" Estelle asked, unsurprised.

"Ms. Volkova was very thorough."

"That hag wasn't even there!"

Mr. Grigori rubbed his temples and stared straight ahead.

"Fine. What happened?"

"Nina and two girls from the wrestling team cornered me in the bathroom. What was I supposed to do? Let them beat me up? You told me to ignore her, but she won't stop. I've already fought her before... might as well keep going until she quits."

"You swear there was no way you could have walked away? Even if she called you 'crazy?'"

Estelle's lips pursed.

"There was no way," she lied.

"This is going to continue escalating. You may think you're defending our name, but all everyone will see is Damian Grigori's belligerent child. I want what's best for you. You're destined to take over when I retire and you can't do that unless you learn to control yourself."

Estelle mumbled something.

"What was that?"

"I said 'did you ever even ask if that's what I wanted?' I don't want to be around those people and their expensive parties and boring stories."

"You don't want the responsibility. But you love what money can buy you."

"It's not about the money. I just want to live my own life. Why can't Oscar or Hugo take over for you?"

"You're my daughter," Damian said with an exaggerated sigh. "The mantle has been passed from father to child for three generations. It's supposed to be you, but... to be honest, you're getting to be more trouble than you're worth."

The sun disappeared behind the buildings, and the street lamps blinked on. They came to a row of brightly colored shops. The SUV came to a stop at the face of a light blue jewelry shop, a neon yellow diamond light shining in its window.

"Go inside and get your mother's bracelet," Damian said, handing Estelle a credit card.

She took it and left the car, weaving through foot traffic and entering the shop. The glass display case divided the interior in two, forming an upside down "U." The left case contained a myriad of gold, silver and platinum rings, lockets, bracelets and charms. Similar items filled the right case, each embedded with precious gems. Rubies, emeralds, amethyst, topaz and others sparkled beneath display lights. The prize of the shop, its front case, showcased multiple glittering diamond themed pieces.

Despite the rare starlight stones, another caught Estelle's eye; an oval sapphire pendant the size of her thumb and set in silver. Its smooth surface caught light in such a way that slivers of purple and indigo flashed. A grimace came to her face due to the *$1499.99* price tag. She stared passed her reflection and jumped back when the sales associate called to her.

"May I help you, miss?" he asked. "Something caught your eye?"

A short, plump man with a bushy gray beard stood before her, inspecting the young woman.

"What's that, there?" Estelle asked, pointing to the oval. "Second shelf next to the ruby charm."

"Ah! The violet sapphire is very rare. A true prize that would look stunning on you."

The man slid the case open and removed the radiant gem, placing it on a cloth. Estelle bent forward, observing it. Studying. Obsessing. As she moved, the piece shifted to show its violet streaks. The words fell from her mouth before she could think.

"I'll take it," she said, clutching her father's credit card.

The man praised her for the choice and boxed it with a turquoise bow. Estelle met him at the cash register.

"I'm also picking up an order," she said. "For Damian Grigori."

The man's face fell into a frown.

"The gold bracelet," he said, realizing who stood before him. "Regrettably, the order is delayed."

"Wasn't it delayed last week? What's the problem?"

"We have a shortage of workers at the moment. I'm very sorry-"

"What do I have to do to get good service around here? This is supposed to be one of the most reputable jewelers in the city."

"I'm truly sorry, miss. Perhaps a discount on-"

"Wasn't it my grandfather who kept this business from going under? This is the thanks my family gets? My father is waiting outside. You can tell him why he doesn't have my dead mother's bracelet."

The salesman stared at Estelle, bewildered and mouth agape. He stammered, but before he could form words, a telephone rang in a back room.

"P-please don't leave, miss. I'm sure I can make this right. One moment... Please."

He let himself in a small door that appeared too small for his frame. Estelle gave a groan of disgust and paced before the diamond case, allowing her mind to run wild with fantasies of what pieces she would wear and with which outfits.

"*Take it,*" a quiet voice said.

Estelle wheeled around, but found herself alone in the shop. She shook her head and tried to peek through a small square window set in the backroom door. She could just make out the top of the man's head. Her eyes glided to the white box containing the violet sapphire.

"*It should be yours. Take it, Estelle.*"

She hesitated at first, but opened the box. The sapphire caught the light and shone as if pried from a heavenly crown. Estelle shook her head again, replaced the lid and turned to leave. She did not know what stopped her after two steps, but she spun, stowed the box in her jacket pocket and returned to her father's SUV.

"It's delayed another week," Estelle said.

"Must I do everything myself?" Damian said, reaching for his door handle. Estelle grabbed his arm.

"He already got an earful from me. Trust me, he's more

than sorry. I told him how important it is and he begged me not to upset you."

"What does a man have if not his word? I'll set him straight."

"Father, please. Our families have known each other for years... times are hard."

"Not to mention your heart, boss," Oscar said. "It's not good for you to get worked up. It'll just be another week, and I'll personally visit every day to make sure it's on time."

"Fine," Damian said, scoffing. "Take us home."

## CHAPTER 2

---

## SHADOW IN THE MUSIC ROOM

Following a restless night, Estelle sat before her decorative African blackwood bureau and stared at herself in the mirror as she brushed her hair. Her spacious room lacked the lavish decorations of other rooms in her manor. No glamorous chandelier, elaborate paintings or expensive vases.

A bureau sat against the East wall and a tall canopy bed at the Southern. A row of dressers and bookshelves framed the white door, bearing school books, romance novels and a myriad of silver and gold trophies for concert performances and ballet. Long white curtains swept the floor as bright sunlight filtered through them, giving the green walls a humble glow.

A woman in her thirties, dressed in a black maid's uniform joined Estelle, leaning against the bureau. Straight auburn locks sat upon her head and deep brown were her eyes. Her round face and petite frame gave her an aura of innocence and her soft laughter fluttered like a gathering of butterflies.

"Not so loud, Irina!" Estelle said, covering her own mouth. "You told Father I was still asleep, remember?"

"I'm sorry," Irina said. "That's just too funny. They came at you three-on-one and you still won? Nina should give up already, the stupid girl."

Estelle looked away from her reflection, and her friend motioned for the brush.

"I understand her, though." Irina drew the brush through Estelle's black hair. "If I had a sibling... and that happened to them, I'd want someone to blame too."

"It's not like she was the only one there. She fought with her boyfriend that night."

"About you."

"That doesn't prove anything."

"You don't have to convince me, Stelly."

Estelle groaned. "Come on, don't call me that. I'm not six anymore! Six-year-olds aren't normally murder suspects."

"How long were you under investigation? A year?"

"Fourteen months. Everyone in this city thinks I killed Natasha."

"Didn't they drop the charges?"

"Do you think that matters to anyone here? The accusation alone was enough to tarnish Father's precious family name."

Irina draped Estelle's hair down her back and placed her hands on the woman's shoulders, massaging her neck.

"Family is the only thing we have in life," she said, stern as an oak. "I know Mr. Grigori isn't perfect, but he only wants what's best for you. He's just from a different time, you know?"

"That's not a reason to treat me the way he does."

"But-"

"He forced me to fight at ten years old. Controlled where I went and who I spoke to until I got to university... I still think he had something to do with the landscaper's son. I spend one night with him and suddenly his family is moving to Scotland? Should I go on? Should we revisit that year's Easter?"

Irina sighed. "You're not wrong. But Mr. Grigori has gotten better over time."

"I just want to get out of here. Away from this place and away from him."

"You don't mean that. Where would you even go? You've lived in Hiemson your whole life."

"California or New York, maybe. I'm sure there's no shortage of opportunities for dance or music. If I go West, I can get away from everyone who knows my name. I'd rather die than stay."

"Look at everything you have here, though. You have money, influence, you live in one of the largest houses in the city- you're basically a princess."

"Ugh, don't call me that!"

The two laughed, and Irina hugged Estelle from behind.

"I just don't want anything to happen to you," the maid said. "I don't mean to be so overbearing, but you're like a little sister to me."

"I know, and I appreciate being able to confide in you. There are very few people I can trust."

"Hurry and get dressed. Mr. Grigori wants to talk to you before he leaves. I did the laundry this morning, so your favorite dress is on the bed."

Irina departed. Once Estelle had clothed herself, she waited for the knock at the door. When it came, she bade her father to enter. That day Damian wore a sienna colored suit with a taupe vest. His gold ring caught the sunlight streaming through the windows. He stood angled away from her and she had the sense that he looked to the window behind her rather than at her. He could not wait to get away, she surmised.

"I'm leaving for France," Damian said in a grumble. "I trust the house to be in one piece when I return."

"I don't have friends anymore," Estelle said, shrugging. "So no parties. When will you be back?"

"In four days. Can you manage to stay out of trouble in that time?"

"You act like I go looking for it. Those girls attacked *me*. You'd think my father could show some sympathy."

Damian exhaled sharply.

"Do you need me to take care of it?"

"I can handle it."

"How?"

Estelle hated when her father asked her "how?" It usually meant that he had the answers to her dilemma and anything she said otherwise would be incorrect or insufficient. She had long since given up trying to align her thoughts with his.

"I'll show her she can't beat me. I'll hurt her so bad she'll never even look in my direction again."

"What would you do to accomplish this?" Damian snickered. "Beat her in the streets in front of everyone? You have no tact. You're reckless and emotional. The great power we wield does not pair well with your temperament."

"You're the one always saying 'one should never squander great power.'"

"That means learn how to wield it. Don't just claim it when you need an escape. You're talented and smart. Your grades are above average, you excelled in all your electives. You have endless opportunities before you. Yet you choose to shirk your duties, miss competitions, and besmirch the Grigori name."

"I'm sure I could do anything with my skills. And you'd be standing over my shoulder every step of the way. Is a little freedom too much to ask for?"

"Meaning what?"

Estelle stomped over to her window. She peered across the acres of glistening snow and silver topped trees.

"All my instructors and tutors were hand-picked by you. I can't do anything without you watching. It's suffocating, Father. You've never even asked me what I want to do with my life. You just assume."

"I expected you'd want a part in the family business. I'm getting the sense that isn't the case."

"I want to play in the great halls across the world. Maybe join a dance group. Maybe both?"

"You know I could get you in the regional ballet."

"That's what I'm talking about! I don't want to get there because of your connections. I want to know I'm good enough on my own."

She turned toward Damian, whose brows met in contemplation. He massaged his mustache and checked his wristwatch.

"Fine," he said. "I can admit that I follow you too closely at times. Show me I can trust you and I'll back off."

"How can I do that?"

"First of all, go visit your grandfather today. More importantly, stay out of trouble. If I return with no bad news, I'll allow you more freedom. Now, is there anything else before I leave for the airport?"

Estelle shook her head. Damian turned to leave, but stopped at the doorway. He looked over his shoulder and the woman held her breath. For half a second, her father's left eye took on a red glow; a quick flash that she would have missed with a blink.

"I can go to any corner of the globe and still see you. If you do anything displeasing... I will know about it. Do not betray my trust."

∼

The hanging wall clock sounded at 1 PM but its chime went unnoticed, suppressed by a wave of fast pace piano notes. Estelle's fingers sprang back and forth across the ivory keys as she grit her teeth.

A tall brown-skinned man stood beside the glossy, black instrument, studying the woman with earthy, umber eyes. He kept his hair short and a thin goatee circled his full lips and fell to a fuzzy bush at his chin. He wore black jeans and a purple button-down shirt with the sleeves rolled up, allowing lean forearms to be exposed.

"It's after one," Marcel said. "You know you can stop, right?"

With a final series of minor chords, she let the notes resonate and disperse. When she looked at his almond-shaped eyes, she blushed and smiled.

Golden sconces lined the white walls, stopping at velvet red curtains that hung down to a polished wooden floor. The piano sat at the base of a ceiling high window, its edges catching the afternoon sunlight.

"I just got caught up in the music," Estelle said. "I get carried away."

"That's why I think you'll do great at the concert in a couple of months."

"I'm still so nervous. There'll be over three hundred people there. What if I mess up? What if they don't like the song I choose? What if-"

"Stop that," Marcel said, taking a seat on the bench beside her. "Those thoughts will sabotage you. You're more than good enough. It matters if they like what you play, but it matters more if you like it. To let your emotions flow through the keys. Like you just did."

"How did you-"

"You always play Suggestion Diabolique when you have a fight with your dad. Is everything okay?"

Estelle lingered on the black and white keys, striking random notes and letting them ring.

"I finally worked up the courage to ask for more freedom."

"How'd that go?"

"I mean, he didn't yell at me this time. He seemed more understanding than usual."

"We all know the rumors about him, but I think they're exaggerated and that the man has a heart. I honestly thought he'd kick me out when we first met, but here I am."

Estelle scoffed.

"Did you forget who you're talking to? I know him better than anyone on Earth. Your skin isn't the problem, it's your monetary worth. If you had millions of dollars or a business empire, he might actually let us date."

"What did he say when you spoke?"

"He wants to know he can trust me."

"I take it that means I should not stay over tonight?" Marcel asked in a whisper.

Estelle pouted, and he ran his fingertips over her hand.

"You can sneak in when everyone's asleep. Just for an hour or two? No one will know."

"Is that what you want?"

Marcel entwined his fingers with hers, each falling victim to the other's gaze. Footsteps from the hallway gave them pause and their hands tore apart as a maid peeked in passing. Estelle rose from the piano and made her way across the white room to a whiteboard against the wall. She pretended to read the notes on music theory until she was sure they were alone again.

"I love when you ask me that," Estelle said, turning to a nineteenth century oil painting of an orchestra on the wall. "Everyone around me is only ever concerned with what I can do for them. What I really want is to take the trip."

"You're still willing? Leave all this behind and come back to America with me?"

"I want that more than anything, Marcel. To begin a real life with you and not one I have to hide from anyone."

The corners of his mouth rose, plumping his cheeks. Confidence, clarity and wisdom were in his eyes. She would have run into his arms if she could have when he joined her at the painting.

"Do you think that will really make you happy?" he asked.

"Why wouldn't it?" she asked, frowning. Marcel's voice dropped to a whisper again.

"We talked about it before. You want to get away from the shit-talkers and your dad, but the past still has ways of following you; no matter how far you travel. It would break my heart to see you with everything you want, but still not at peace."

Estelle crossed her arms and her eyes narrowed.

"If you don't want to be with me, you don't have to dance around it. Just say what you want to say."

"I mean it. What if we go to L.A. or New York and you're still seeing him around every corner? Or if someone says something wrong and you think they're talking about your past? You do have a tendency to fly off the handle."

Bubbling heat rose in her face and she clenched her teeth, but took a deep breath.

"I've only ever defended myself. Were I in a place without such instigation, I wouldn't need to." She turned away from him. "I thought you, of all people, would understand. Sometimes... sometimes I feel like death would be the best escape, but-"

A heavy hand clasped Estelle's arm and so hot was the touch it was numbing. All light vanished from the room, replaced by a hellish red glow from outside the windows. Estelle was spun around and taken by both shoulders. Where

Marcel just stood, she beheld a towering shadow, glaring down upon her with radiant purple eyes. Its hands dripped with blood and glowing molten chains dangled from its wrists.

"Do you wish to die?" it said in a deep, hollow voice. It was like the echo from a deep well.

Panicked, she twisted and pulled to get away, but the shadow held like a vise. Forced to stare at it, her breath shortened to shallow gasps. Her green eyes bulged from her head and no matter how hard she tried, she could not willingly look away.

"I-I'm-"

"Wake! Wake or die!"

Its chains rattled and its essence spread upward like shaded wings as it shook her, repeating itself.

"Why are you doing this?!" Estelle cried.

Heart thumping, the woman grabbed the creature's wrists, her hands smoking and her skin blistering. She fought her way free, shut her eyes and pushed the shadow's arms back. When she prepared to run, the music room returned to its normal state and Marcel sat bewildered on the floor, staring up at her. Estelle's mouth hung open and, mortified, she fled from the room.

# CHAPTER 3

# THE OPEN GRAVE

The early evening sunset gave the chapel's stained-glass windows a consoling glow and cast its decorations as black silhouettes. Estelle huddled in the warmth of her fur coat, seated on a pew with her face dug into a turquoise scarf. Her mind dwelt on Marcel's shocked expression and the visions that invaded her sanity. After the shadow disappeared, so did the burns on her hands.

The chapel was small and made of dark gray stones whose cracks let slip a chilly draft. Three colorful windows lined either wall and two columns of six pews stretched toward the altar with a red carpet covering the hardwood floor. A silent nun lit candles at the three-tiered altar before bowing her head in prayer to a large wooden crucifix a small distance beyond. Estelle flipped through the pages of a bible, reading random passages and finding one that gave her pause.

"The Lord is not slow to fulfill his promise," she said. "As some count slowness, but is patient toward you, not wishing that any should perish, but that all should reach repentance."

"That is a lovely verse," said the nun, a withered woman

with hazel eyes. "Something troubles you, my child. Perhaps I can help?"

Estelle rolled her eyes, but allowed the woman to sit with her.

"How may the light serve you?"

She was silent, but looked over to the nun, fiddling with the tassels of her scarf. She opened her mouth to speak several times, but no words came. She cleared her throat and shut the book.

"I think I've found happiness," Estelle said. "But I lack the freedom to claim it... because I don't deserve it. Everyone knows I don't. I'm sure you feel the same way, right?"

"Why would I?"

"Don't you know who I am? Who my father is?"

The nun shook her head.

"I'm Estelle Grigori. Daughter of Damian Grigori? Our family owns Blue Well Energy?"

"I'm afraid I don't watch much news," the woman said, shrugging.

"That would explain the state of this place."

"I've dedicated my life to studying holy texts to do the Lord's will. I find the media brings preconceptions that interfere with my mission. I don't care who you are or what you've done, miss Estelle. I'm only here to help."

The young woman sighed and toyed with the tassels of her scarf again.

"I'm... not a good person. I don't care that I'm not, but I've found someone who also doesn't care. He's- everything anyone could ask for. Calm, compassionate, loving. There's not a bad bone in his entire body. How could I have found love with him when I'm so aggressive? So angry all the time? He sees through it all and loves me for me. I know I'm going to screw it up."

"If it's retribution for your past you seek, I believe you may find it. It's like the scripture said; it doesn't happen as fast as we want it to, but the Lord will forgive you. It seems to me that you also need to forgive yourself for whatever it is you did."

"Easier said than done."

"Yes. It is. But that's the point. It's not supposed to be easy. There are hurdles to cross and many look to God for strength. Or find strength within themselves. I believe anyone can be redeemed."

"Some, sure. But mostly, people love to sin. They love sex, violence, drugs. No one really changes, they just stuff it all down and play the part society wants them to. Once a sinner, always a sinner."

"There are plenty of people who have repented. Whether the urge is there or not, they choose to become good people. I know you said you're a bad person, but there is good in you as well."

Estelle scoffed. "I know what I am, lady. You should watch the news more. You'd understand why forgiveness is not possible."

Estelle shoved the bible in the nun's lap and left the chapel without another word. She bundled herself in her coat as the icy air raked across her face. The setting sun left the sky a smooth expanse of purple and deep blue, leaving the tombstones around her as dark, square splotches. She traversed a shoveled path between tall, leafless trees until she came to a large headstone bearing two names:

*Ivan Grigori*
*1897-1977*
*Loving Father, Brilliant Businessman, & Devoted Member of*
*the Community*

⌇

*Annabella Grigori*
*With the Angels, Where she Belongs*
*1900-1946*

Estelle knelt and brushed the snow away from the base, staring at the names. A freezing wind blew her hair back and despite the tiny ice particles slashing at her cheeks and nose, she bowed her head and clasped her hands together in a momentary prayer. Digging into her coat pocket, she drew the violet sapphire she had claimed the previous night. Deep were its hues of blue, reminiscent of the moonless night above.

"I know it's been a while," Estelle said. "These past couple of years have been really hectic. I aced almost all of my classes and I graduate this spring. With my grades, they say I can do anything. I'd love to dance... like you, Grandmother. Father makes it impossible for me to think, and I wish I was free of him. Free of this burdensome life I'm trapped in. He makes me feel so worthless."

The call of a fish owl seized her attention, hidden in the tangled branches. Following the soft hoots came the crunch of multiple boots in the snow. Estelle looked over her shoulder and shot to her feet.

A short, plump girl with dark blue eyes and a mess of curly brown hair shoved beneath a winter cap stood flanked by two others. To her left was Clara, a tall, stocky girl with dark wavy hair and bear-like arms bulking the sleeves of her coat. Multiple bandages covered the right side of her face and she scowled, turning pink from either her temper or the frigid air. Clara's frail younger brother, Roman, stood to the right, hesitance in his dark brown eyes.

"You know this cemetery is holy ground, right Nina?" Estelle asked.

"What do you care?" Nina said. "The only thing that matters is you pay for what you did to my sister."

"We'll take that pretty little jewel, too," Clara said.

"You're not taking a damn thing. Like I keep telling you: Natasha's death was an accident, and I had nothing to do with it. Just because I was investigated doesn't mean I did it."

"That doesn't mean anything! Your father knows people who can make these things go away! But Daddy's not here to save you."

"There's nothing to hide, you dumb little bitch! Your sister was drunk out of her mind, fell and hit her head. Just because you can't deal with grief doesn't mean you get to blame me!"

"I was on the phone with her that night. She hung up because she said someone was coming down to the lake."

"What makes you think it was me?"

"You're the only one who hated her! We've all seen you flirting with Niko and you know he and my sister wanted to get married! It had to have been you." Nina's eyes grew black like a shark's. "It had to."

Silence fell as the wind ceased, and the owl called once more.

"So what now?" Estelle asked. "I already put Clara's face through a mirror yesterday."

A grim shadow fell across Nina's face. She slid her hand into her inner coat pocket and revealed a long, clean butcher's knife. Both Clara and the young boy drew blades of their own, staring Estelle down like hungry wolves.

"You get away with everything... Not this time!" Nina said, lunging.

Estelle caught her wrist, but staggered back with the tip of the blade aimed toward her abdomen. As they grappled, Clara ran forward, delivering a slash to Estelle's left arm. The cut stung and heat rushed to the wound. In the blistering cold, her blood was hot. She pushed Nina into Clara and stumbled back, gripping her bicep. When she pulled her hand away, her white wool gloves were stained deep red. She nearly tripped over a tree root as her assailants closed in. Clara rushed forward, and Estelle fled.

The snow made it difficult to run, coming midway up her calf. The scrambling trio behind her shouted and hollered like coyotes. They chased her across a gloomy, gray expanse between headstones as a starry night covered their city. The wind bit harder, and Estelle could no longer feel her face. They pursued her into an old part of the cemetery where the graves fell victim to a dense thicket, disappearing beneath frozen roots.

"You're not getting away!" Clara said, wheezing over the wind.

Nina and her friends twisted their way through the small forest. Pain in Estelle's her arm paired with fatigue and slowed her movements as low branches tricked her into thinking she was caught. She moved slower and panted, but pressed on, clutching her bloody arm. She came to a small clearing of various half-dug graves and turned to watch the treeline. Nina and Clara's voices rang out, the echoes preventing her from telling how far away.

There came rustling from branches in the dark and Estelle spun to see, but could not. A sliver of moon hung low that night, leaving her in a realm of dense shadows. Clara's voice came closer and Estelle stepped back, waiting for the hulking girl to emerge.

"There's a clearing back here!" Nina said, not thirty yards away.

Estelle clenched her sapphire in her fist, sticky with blood, and prepared to face whatever would come. Twigs snapped and snow crunched. Shadows moved through the tree line, and she backed up a few more paces. Because of the anxiety and adrenaline of the situation, Estelle failed to realize the tree root curving out of the ground. Her heel caught it and she tumbled backward, falling into an open grave she knew could not have been as deep as it was. The woman screamed and flailed and darkness swallowed her.

With a sharp inhale, Estelle awoke. Her body ached and her arm burned, though she still clasped her violet sapphire. She could see nothing in the black hole, and her heart raced alongside her mind. She willed herself to sit up and feel the ground. The dirt and rock felt warmer than the Earth should be in the dead of winter. She touched walls of firm, thick roots and pulled at one to see if it could support her weight. She slid the sapphire into her dress pocket and began climbing.

The rough roots ripped her gloves, but they held firm as she placed one hand above the other. Sweat dripped from her chin and her wounded left arm ached as if bees stung at it. Leaning her head on the wood, she took a moment to rest, conserving energy for another fight with Nina and Clara.

A short rumble and a gurgle came from beneath, causing her to lose her footing. She grasped the wall and righting herself, gasped. She peered down into the depths and her eyes widened when a dim, red glow formed. It grew brighter and more vibrant, filling the hole with the putrid stench of sulfur.

Estelle climbed faster, ignoring the pain of her bleeding wound. The hole rumbled again, and she lost her grip, falling several feet before grappling another root. As she hoisted herself up, something gripped her wrist. It was a hand; a rotting, half-skeletal hand. It held so tight that Estelle thought her wrist would snap. She wrenched herself free and pushed upward. The higher she climbed, the more hands emerged to greet her. They grasped and tore at her arms and legs, eventually ripping her coat and scarf from her body.

"Leave me alone!" she said with a shriek. "Leave me alone!"

She began clawing, breaking and biting the hands as she climbed. Knowing surely the pit would claim her, she yelped when her hand fell upon a dusty, solid ground. The roots continued after feeling around and, with a final kick, she dragged herself out. Panting like a deer who had escaped a lion, she fell against the base of something tall and made of rock.

"Please," she said to herself. "Please let this be a dream."

She grasped the outside of her pocket and felt the lump that was her gem. She drew it and clutched it to her chest, her breath shuttering. She examined her surroundings. She was still in the forest, but the snow disappeared and the trees stood as ash-gray husks. Instead of a night sky filled with stars, Estelle beheld a sky dyed dark and red as the blood on her arm.

The stone structure she rested against vibrated, and she crawled away like a frightened cat. Tiny scarlet symbols wrapped around what revealed itself to be a pillar. Crosses, slashes and dots were no recognizable language, and they rose ten feet high, tapering at its peak. It curved to lean over the hole, joined by three more and evenly spaced, as if to represent the cardinal directions. The pit gurgled again, and she ran from it, weaving between the dead trees.

The exhausted woman came to an old stone path lined with wooden park benches and rusted iron lampposts. She paced up and down the path, seeking any signs of life. There came the call of crows in the distance, and strange moans from somewhere far off. A presence manifested behind her, and when she turned to it, she fell back and found her body paralyzed.

"Don't hurt me," Estelle said, covering her face. "P-please."

Two apparitions appeared before her. One made of soft white light with a shining star at its throat and a second, larger figure robed in dancing shadows. It bore deep purple eyes that fixed unblinking on her- the creature from her vision.

Estelle pushed herself back as they stepped closer. Her temples throbbed and her breath was as difficult to catch as the wind in a sack. Pressure overcame her body and her heart danced against her ribcage. Pushed to the brink of her mental limits, she lost consciousness.

## CHAPTER 4

———

# WEB OBSIDIA

"Estelle," a man's voice said. "Estelle, wake up."

The woman awoke with a start, grappling the park bench and digging her nails into the wood. She whipped her head around. When her sticky, red hand stuck to the bench, she clutched her left arm. With no recollection of how, the slice Clara gave her healed.

A snow-white crow perched at the opposite end of the seat and she shrank back when she realized it. She searched the area for the voice, but no one occupied the dark, twisted woods. Fifteen or twenty more crows of jet black curiously observed her from the ugly branches, calling to one another every so often. She wearily stared at the white bird.

"Hello Estelle," it said, speaking without moving its beak. "Check your pocket."

Her eyes grew wide, and she reeled, falling from the bench. Steadying herself, she focused on recalling what came before. She remembered freaking out with Marcel, then being chased through the woods by Nina and her friends.

"This is ridiculous," Estelle said under her breath, shaking her head. "Birds don't talk. This must be a dream."

"This bird talks," the crow said. "And this is no more a dream than when you beat that girl for your mother's bracelet. Now, read the letter in your pocket."

Estelle's eyes widened again and her breath became caught in her throat. The woman squeezed through fear for curiosity's sake, and searched the pockets of her blue dress. In one was her violet sapphire, but she found a folded piece of dirty paper in the other. She opened it and the writing seemed singed into the page. She read the message, a low quiver in her voice.

"'Estelle, I know it's going to seem hopeless and impossible. You have a monumental task ahead of you. You are the last good part of us and you have the chance to escape Eve's Hollow for the life you want. You must find five keys, each possessing a shard of your soul. Reassemble them and gain access to the Dimension Door. Only then will you be complete. Only then will you escape Eve's Hollow. Stay strong, brave and compassionate. You WILL succeed. Go to the *Kern Museum*. That's where your second key is, along with your Guardian. The crow has the first. Get to the Supernova Swordsman and complete your soul. Escape Eve's Hollow.'"

Estelle pondered the letter for a moment, looking from it to the crow. Beneath its talons was a thin sterling silver key with a round piece of quartz fashioned into its bow. As she focused on it, a gentle, angelic song came into her mind. Then it left as fast as it had come.

She flipped the paper over, finding a printed map on the other side. A series of different colored blocks were labeled as different districts, numbered one through seven. Whoever left her the map also drew red lines signifying obstructions; impassible roads, toppled towers or whole sections scribbled over in red ink. According,the paper, she was in the turquoise-colored District 1: Garnet Grove. Apparently, she was meant to journey to District 2 in orange territory where *The Kern Museum of Natural Sciences* was located.

She let her hands fall to her lap, took a deep breath and scanned the dead trees. Taking in what should have been lush woods, all was dark and leafless, the ground worn and cracked. The menacing shadows creaked and moaned with the breeze, the branches swaying like claws reaching upward. The air smelled of stale rot, making her nauseous.

"Kern," the crow said. "That's where we must go. Now, forward."

"What is this?" Estelle asked. The crow did not respond. "Why am I here?"

It stared at her with blank eyes.

"Where did this letter come from?" It said nothing, and she scowled. "Will you tell me anything?!"

"Forward."

"Can you at least tell me where I am?! What good is a talking bird if it says nothing useful?"

"Eve's Hollow," the crow said. "It's a place of redemption. Like Hell."

"What are you talking about? I was just home! I have a date with my boyfriend tonight, for God's sake!"

A wild shriek in the distance scattered the black crows. It was chilling, furious and inhuman. Estelle threw herself beneath the bench, clutching one of its legs as her heart rate elevated. She shut her green eyes and wished in her mind to wake up somewhere else. *Please, please let this be only a bad dream*, she thought. She opened her eyes, the crow on the ground with her, staring and waiting. The shriek came again, but further away.

"Beware the monsters." The crow hopped closer to her. "The Punished- immortal demons of the Hollow. Creatures, apparitions, evil humans. Beware this place."

Eve's Hollow? The name held no meaning to her. It

sounded cold and foreign, especially coming from a strange bird. Estelle reluctantly stood as she tried to stave off irrationality and the fear it courted. She watched the crow take flight down the stone path, then took the quartz key. Rocks clattered beneath her feet as she hugged her arms, searching for warmth whilst coming to terms with how alone she really was.

She arrived at a stone wall encasing a small courtyard with a simple granite fountain in the center. The woman walked through an opening in the wall and crossed to the other side where a sidewalk began. The crow, perched on a guard rail, flew to Estelle, and rested upon her shoulder. She shooed it away. She crossed a parking lot and followed the street, passing between two steel pillars. It led to the top of a long hill, and from there, Estelle saw the towering shadows of skyscrapers. Some were short but crimson clouds shrouded tops of others.

Estelle leaned back as she descended the hill so as not to fall forward. The crow waited at the bottom as she stepped onto the main road. One hundred yards ahead was a tall, luminous sign. As Estelle approached the towering message, she squinted to read.

"'Eve's Hollow welcomes you to the city of Web Obsidia. Population: Eight-point-six million.'"

Loneliness and morbidity hung heavy in the wasted outskirts as a pinkish haze blurred the road ahead. Distant in the veil, beady orange lights danced. The more she focused, the more of them she counted. There must have been dozens. Angry moans and growls of madness rolled atop the fog.

"What are those?" Estelle asked the crow.

"They are the Punished," it said. "Once aware of you, they are relentless. Forward, Estelle."

The crow took flight, guiding Estelle to the city border as fast as her feet would take her. Further down the road was a neighborhood. Broken sidewalks lined the streets, stretching into a grid before her. The rusted, crumpled cars strewn about were like worn, jagged sculptures. Shattered windows marred the dilapidated buildings. Seeing lights in a handful of other windows, Estelle questioned whether they indicated people inside.

Estelle passed a stone sign reading *G.G Middle School*. A stirring in the woman's spirit stopped her in her tracks. As she gazed at the broken school, apparitions appeared. Pale ghosts of children running and playing on the dirt property as if the world around them was not wretched.

"What kind of trick is this?" she asked. "Everyone knows ghosts aren't real. What is that? Some kind of projection?"

"They are very real," the crow said. "And thankfully, benign. Some spirits take offense to the presence of the living, and others pay us no mind."

Estelle laughed.

"So- what? The fall killed me? Now I've come to Hell where I belong?"

"The fall did not kill you and you do not belong here. No longer beyond completing your trials, at least."

"What trials? Why am I here?"

"You asked for it."

"No, I didn't!" Estelle's angry shout echoed off the face of the middle school. "I'm supposed to be with Marcel tonight! I'm supposed to perform in the Age of Music Concert! I'm supposed to graduate this year! I DID NOT ASK FOR THIS!"

The reverberations of her voice lasted several seconds before the air became still. Shouts and groans came from behind the school, the specters continuing their playtime, unaware or uncaring. In a fluster, Estelle pressed on.

~

Hours passed as Estelle and her crow made their way north. The sky transitioned to a dull wine color and cool air swept through the streets. The crow flew forward several yards and waited for the brooding woman to catch up. With rows of tall apartment buildings flanking her, she took to the center of the broken street to avoid darkened alleys. She would jump at the sound of scurrying rats or the occasional feral dog.

Estelle's heart refused to calm down as distant screeches and bellows echoed sporadically. The dirty, rusted lamp posts were mostly dark, but some here and there burned with cloudy yellow bulbs. Ever present was a dry, decomposing scent, that Estelle tasted in the back of the throat.

Echoes of a man's laughter lingered in the alleyways; when the woman arrived, she saw firelight dancing silently on the brick walls. Weary of what may be between her and the voices, she crept forward. Her crow landed before her, stretching its wings to the sides.

"We must go to Kern," it said. "Continue North."

"There're people back there," Estelle said. "I'm tired and hungry and sweaty. I need to get home before Father does or he'll have my head."

"It would be quicker and wiser to continue, then."

"How am I supposed to make it to the stupid museum if I die of starvation? And it wouldn't hurt to learn more about this place, since you obviously have nothing useful to say."

Storming passed the crow, Estelle made her way toward the firelight. Running her hand along the brick walls in the dark, she came to the small pyre of three men. To the left was a tall, thin man with bulging eyes and thinning gray-blond hair. Sitting in the center, roasting some sort of meat over the fire, was a heavyset man whose belly protruded from his white and gray plaid shirt. His bushy black beard hid his face. To the right, carving a mongrel animal was a younger man in his early thirties wearing an eyepatch. The carcass smelled hot and musky, though her stomach grumbled at the scent of it cooking. Disheveled and filthy, they stared at Estelle, frozen like a deer in a quiet forest.

"I don't mean to intrude," she said. "I don't know where I am and I've been walking for hours."

"What's that got to do with us?" the fat man asked.

"I was wondering... if I could have just a small bit of food, I'd be grateful."

"Yeah?" said the bug-eyed man. "What are you giving us in return?"

Estelle briefly considered parting with her sapphire as her stomach pulled in on itself.

"I don't have anything," she said. "I woke up in the woods and I don't know how I got here."

The men looked at one another.

"Could she have come on that war train with you?" the fat man asked. "The Matterhorn?"

"Not if she 'just woke up,'" the younger man said. "It came through six months ago. It's not due for another year. Maybe she's a monster? Like the Pale Lady."

"Nah." The man with bulging eyes stepped toward her. "If that was the case, we'd be dead already. Now that I'm looking at her though... she is a sexy little thing."

He licked his lips, and Estelle stepped back.

"Hey," the fat man said. "Didn't Rainer say something about a wanted girl? Wearing a blue dress?"

"I think you're right. But how do we know she's the right one?"

"Let's just bring her in. If she's the right one, we'll get raised up something nice."

Bug eyes smiled at her, his teeth brown and cracked. He gestured her forward, then reached out to grab her arm.

"Come along, girl. We wouldn't want to ruin that pretty face."

"Let me go!" Estelle said, wrenching her arm free and slapping the man.

He lunged forward with both arms extended. She grappled him, twisted her body and flung him over her shoulder. His friends roared with laughter as he groaned.

"Please don't tell us you need help!" the fat man asked, snorting.

Bug Eyes rolled on his stomach and pushed himself up. Estelle's boots skidded on shards of broken glass and she took up the longest one and holding it like a dagger.

"On second thought," the woman said. "I'll be on my way."

Bug eyes jumped up and his friends joined him, forming a half circle, backing her against the wall. Estelle slashed at the air with her makeshift knife, but Fat Man grappled her wrist while the younger took the other, forcing her to drop the weapon. Bug Eyes, with a crooked smile, ran his grimy fingers down her smooth cheek.

"D-don't you know who my father is?" Estelle asked. "He'll have you killed for this."

"Well, he ain't here, is he?" Bug Eyes asked, tracing the lines down her neck to her collarbone. "Maybe we can have a little fun before we turn her in."

"We should take her back to the group!" Fat Man said. "Don't let your bullshit get us in trouble."

"That machine test takes forever. I bet they haven't even noticed we took off."

Wheezes, grunts and incoherent shouting came from the streets.

"Let's get out of here," the younger man said. "I'm not getting torn apart by Punished just because you can't keep it in your pants."

"You're both cowards," Bug Eyes said. "We haven't seen a girl this lovely in years and you want to give her up because of some voices a mile away? Why did we join Crius if we were going to stay weak, pathetic beggars? What's the point if-"

The ground rumbled and there came a heavy buzzing in the air. A flash ignited beyond the buildings, so bright Estelle glimpsed it through cracks in the walls and windows.

Using the distraction to her advantage, Estelle delivered a stiff kick to Bug Eye's groin. He crumpled to the ground, and she pulled the younger man toward her, sinking her teeth into his hand. He screamed, then let go, and Estelle threw her fist into Fat Man's face as hard as she could. He stumbled, holding his eye, and she took off through the alleys.

Keeping low and hopping over down-turned trashcans and rubble, she eventually found her way back to the street, where she collapsed on a stoop. From the rooftop flew down her white crow.

"Where the hell were you?" she asked, sneering and panting. "Didn't you see what almost happened to me?"

"You think my advice is useless," the bird said. "What was I to do?"

A heavy sigh left her nose.

"You could have caused a distraction. You could have put those little feet to use. You could have tried *something!*"

At the sound of the men's voices, she leaped to her feet. Their rushed footsteps came from the alley and they questioned each other on where their quarry went. Then screams came. The monstrous roars of the Punished drowned out the men as flesh ripped and bones popped. Estelle watched the alley, backing away, too fearful to turn her back lest she be taken by surprise.

"Come on," the crow said, taking flight from the stoop. "Forward!"

As she stepped away, the gurgling growls and screams increased. Estelle followed the crow, pushing from her mind the squelching and cracking. She broke into a jog, keeping focus on the white speck waiting atop an overturned food cart. Upon reaching it, she froze, mouth agape.

Radiating from a large intersection was a charred ring of blood and body parts. The ground was singed, slicked with red, and many of the bodies were recognizable, yet mutilated. Survivors on the border of the explosion stumbled aimlessly as their very lives burned away. Some of them wore dark brown coats with the remnants of a bright yellow symbol. Estelle clasped her hands over her mouth and turned away in horror.

"What...," she said. "What happened here?"

"An explosion, apparently," the crow said. "Best not to linger too long. Make your way to Kern."

"Why don't you say anything else?!" the woman snapped. "Look at this! This is- *horrific!*"

"Lower your voice."

"No! I'm not doing anything until you answer my questions!"

The breeze blew a piece of paper against Estelle's leg and she took it up. Its upper half was burned away, leaving cinders before the message continued. The only legible script was the last few lines.

"'-lose this opportunity. She will arrive any day now, Rainer,'" she read aloud. "'The time to act is now. My machine is nearly complete and requires only a few rudimentary tests. All that's left is the true battery. I'll see you after you test the Cross Portal. Signed T.M.A. Caution: Do not plug the generator in before chemical-'"

"We must go. Now." The crow was persistent.

"I'm not moving." Arms crossed, she glared at the star-white bird. "Not until you tell me how to get home."

Ragged breathing came from the shadow of a nearby alley. The crash of boxes and bins fell into the street, sending rats fleeing to sewer drains.

"The Punished are coming," the crow said in a panic. "Leave now, Estelle."

She stood her ground. A cold sickness formed in the pit of her stomach, but she was determined, even if it was in a foolish way. In actuality, her feet itched to rush away, but she would get an answer.

"I guess they're going to get me," she said, shakily. "I'm not moving until you tell me something. *Anything.*"

An uncomfortable "caw" left the crow's beak.

"Estelle, you are a Seeker," it said, conceding. "You are meant to reconstruct your soul and move toward a better life. Guardians protect Seekers and the Supernova Swordsman is your Guardian."

"That wasn't so hard, was it?"

Estelle looked toward the alley to witness a pale, sick-looking woman shuffling into the street. Her skin sagged and appeared dehydrated, cracking at the tight points around her mouth, eyes, and joints. She muttered things to herself Estelle could not make out, her head twitching and her hands clenched and shaking. Estelle knelt to avoid being seen.

"Behind you!" the crow shouted.

Before she could react, cold, dried hands spun her around. Estelle, in horror, beheld the Punished; A rotting shell of something that used to be human, grinning at her behind stringy, greasy hair. Its eyes were sunken, with lips worn away, exposing jagged, broken teeth. Most unsettling of all were the dim orange lights staring through empty sockets.

"Ashlyn will reward me!" she wheezed. "Protect the Hollow! Kill the Blamed!"

The creature wrapped its creaking fingers around Estelle's

throat. She tried to pry them loose, but could not. As she struggled to take a breath, the crow flew in with swiftness, throwing its talons into the Punished's face. She howled in pain, allowing Estelle to break free and crawl away. Directly in front of her, upon the ground, was a hunting knife with a burned blade, its handle wrapped with dark brown leather. The Punished swatted the crow away and jumped at Estelle. The woman closed her eyes and held the knife before her, letting the rabid creature impale itself upon the blade. She tried to attack Estelle despite the wound, but the orange light in her eyes died, leaving them wholly black. Estelle panted, staring at the knife stuck in the creature.

"Let's go," the crow said.

"I...," she said, trying to breathe. "Just... just a minute."

As she watched in disbelief, the body convulsed. Estelle would not have believed it if she did not witness it. The bleeding wound healed, encasing the knife's blade. The beast sat up, and stared at Estelle through ebony holes. She scooted back as the eyes reignited.

"I remember you!" she hissed through rotting teeth.

She crawled forward as Estelle moved further away.

"Die for Ashlyn!"

Estelle rolled away from the attack and turned to see the disembodied voices finally manifest. A group of twenty or more Punished limped toward her; a crowd of gray-skinned, moaning, flame-eyed shades of human beings. They could not run, but all the same, they were not slow. Estelle's crow took flight and she followed.

Though Estelle maintained a good distance from the group, she could not lose them completely. They shouted insults at her and worked in tandem to maintain the chase, calling out her location just before she turned down a new street. She slowed to a jog and wiped sweat from her brow.

Her heart beat against her chest as she turned another corner, coming to a long stretch of road. The crow led her along that path, only for the Seeker to find it obstructed by a huge, raised drawbridge.

"You can fly and you brought me to a dead end?" asked Estelle, pulling at her hair.

The bridge sat upon a massive canyon, a hundred yards deep and the same distance across. Estelle looked back down the street. Her pursuers increased in number and were excitedly hurrying toward her. In a serendipitous incident, the heavy drawbridge shook and whined before beginning a labored descent. It was not even halfway down before the crow shouted to her.

"Go, Estelle!" it said.

She climbed the rough structure, slipping here and there, but continuing forward. At a quarter of the way across, the Punished had caught up to her. A man missing his arm and the stabbed woman were the closest, crawling like agitated spiders.

"Get back here!" the woman said. "I'll tear you apart!"

More leveled out, Estelle hurried toward the gap. Just as she was able to handle the incline without her hands, the bridge stopped moving. The steep hill did not deter the Punished, and they were nearly upon the exhausted woman. She climbed to a crouch on the steel at the end, the distance ten feet wide.

"Jump!" the crow shouted as it flew by.

Before the Punished forced her, Estelle crouched, gritted her teeth and took the leap. Her hands caught the lip of the other side and her feet swung as she held on with all her strength. She gasped as the bridge rose again, increasing the gap so the Punished could not follow her.

As she climbed up, she looked into the chasm below, glimpsing a massive shadow in the deep. It shifted and fell out of sight before she descended the bridge. The monsters behind her cried out in rage, loud as an air-raid siren. At street level, a shadowy figure stepped from the control booth where Estelle arrived. She shifted to step forward, but stopped when the person raised a hunting rifle, aimed at her head.

# Chapter 5

## Beware the Warden

Held at gunpoint, Estelle raised her open palms. Behind her, on the other side of the drawbridge, the rage filled screams of the Punished rode the breeze across the chasm. A few took to leaning over the guardrail, reaching hopelessly to attack. Estelle's crow landed on the ground beside her.

"Are you human?" an old British voice said. "Did I make a mistake by helping you?"

"We only seek to pass through," the crow said. "We're heading north and mean no harm."

"What sorcery is this, lass? You look too clean to be a normal survivor. And the talking bird? What are you? Some apparition? Or a dark witch?"

"My name is Estelle Grigori, from Hiemson. I- I don't know how I got here. I've been lost for hours."

"Hiemson? Never heard of it. Your hygienic appearance suggests you're not from here- at least these parts. You're not armed, from what I can tell, so this is either a haunting or a trick to rob an old man."

"What am I going to take, your medication? I don't even have anything to rob you with."

"Please keep an open mind, sir," the crow said. "This woman is a Seeker, given passage to the city to atone for passed actions. We're trying to reach the Kern museum, avoiding confrontation as best we can. Do us no harm and allow us to pass."

The tension eased, and the stranger lowered his rifle. He stepped from the shadow of the booth, revealing himself to be in his sixties. A wide-brimmed hat hid his silver hair, and his mustache and beard created a bushy triangle beneath a thin, hooked nose. His dark blue eyes peered beneath thick eyebrows with both insight and experience. He wore an old, tan leather overcoat with a half-tattered satchel hanging from his side.

"A Seeker?" the man said. "Like the old legends... I've heard that Seekers come with familiars of some kind. I suppose to guide them."

"She hasn't been one for listening, I'm afraid," the crow said. "Take that small group of Punished."

"You call that small?" Estelle asked. "They would have torn me apart!"

"That's why I urge you to listen to me more." The crow faced the man. "We thank you, sir."

Estelle walked passed the gentleman in the coat and started down the road.

"Wait," said the old man. "A warm bed and some food couldn't hurt. I live at the Catalina- a few miles up the main road. It's safe- as long as you don't make trouble, young lass."

"Really?" Estelle asked. "A second ago you were ready to put a hole in my head."

"One can never be too careful on these streets. But I believe if you meant me harm, you'd have taken your shot by now. Traveling at night isn't the best idea. I'd recommend resting until daybreak."

"That is agreeable," the crow said.

"Just like that?" Estelle asked her familiar.

The response to her question came in the form of the crow flying to the man's shoulder. He chuckled at the bird and pet its head with a finger. He beckoned Estelle, turning on his heels to leave. They passed an orange sign with gold engraved letters; *Welcome to District 2: Kollektra. By the People, for the People.*

"Thank you," the Seeker said. "For helping me."

"You're very welcome- Estelle, correct? I'm Baron Ransley, at your service."

The sky grew darker as they traveled northward, to a deep mahogany with slivers of flashing orange through patches of black clouds. They passed several Punished corpses, lying like twisted husks scattered in just about any direction.

"What makes them get back up?" Estelle asked. "I killed one on the other side of the bridge. She came back to life."

"I've seen it happen," Ransley said. "I couldn't tell you why. There are many things that make little sense in this city, which explains my demeanor earlier. Apologies for that."

"No offense taken," the crow said. "I would advise my Seeker to embrace the same caution. She is overly willful."

"I'm right here, you stupid bird," Estelle said, beaming at the crow.

"I meant what I said. Eve's Hollow is no place for rash decisions."

She scoffed. "I have no words for how horrid this place is. Where even is Eve's Hollow? It's no city I've ever heard of."

"Well," Ransley said. "This place has had a complicated and depressing history. A long time ago, millions of people came here to create new lives for themselves. This whole thing started with the literal dream of a girl."

"A girl?"

"Ashlyn Isle," the crow said.

"The woman who attacked me said that name."

"She was born with extraordinary power," Ransley continued. "Some have said she's a goddess in human form- or a devil. As the story goes, she created this realm with her mind. Supposedly a dream city once upon a time."

"Who dreams of a red sky?"

"It didn't always look like this, apparently. It was once a place of joy, wonder and prosperity. People excelled in science, knowledge, art, merging societies and melting ideas together. Ashlyn allowed people to enter this place and, they began to build. The citizens brought culture, making it a mosaic of ideas from many, many worlds."

"Where did all the people come from, exactly?"

"Everywhere. Through the growth of the city, they learned that there are hundreds of Earths existing at the same time. When Ashlyn created Eve's Hollow, she opened doors to those worlds."

"How do you know all of this?" asked the crow. "It seems to be very specific knowledge."

Ransley pulled his satchel from his side. He undid the buckle and drew a large, heavy book. Its old chipping leather and the pages creaked as he handled it. Handing it to Estelle, she read its title, printed in gold letters.

"Historical tome of Eve's Hollow, volume 3. Publication year: 1403."

Estelle opened the book and read silently for a time, her brow furrowing in certain places.

"'In the year four-ninety-five, Ashlyn enacted what would be known as The Great Inversion. At two-oh-three in the afternoon the sun bled, turning the sky red. Supernatural fog invaded the streets of Grace's Landing. Evil entities emerged, beginning a ruthless slaughter of Eve's Hollow's citizens. The dead rose up in a rage to attack the living. They were determined to retake Ashlyn's city; protect it and herself from the greed of the parasites that took without regard. The Blamed. Terror and carnage ensued for five years before settling into what is currently known as 'The Dark Peace.'"

Estelle closed the book and handed it back to Ransley.

"That really happened? It sounds so... ridiculous."

"You've seen the Punished with your own eyes."

"Still, there must be some explanation. Maybe it's a mutation. Maybe some kind of virus."

Ransley laughed.

"Encounters with monsters leave little room for skepticism in my experience. This book is my only reference for what could have been before. I don't know how true it is, but I have no choice but to believe it. I've seen things out here far worse than the Punished that vindicate the story."

The sudden sternness of Ransley's voice reminded her of her father. As he spoke, he kept his eyes trained ahead and his posture rigid. Even when replacing his book, he stared forward as if seeing some far off destination.

"How long ago do you think it was?" Estelle asked. "If the city fell in 495, what year is it now?"

"Twenty-nine-ninety," the crow replied.

Estelle looked around with a forlorn pity. Each building was so tilted and weak that it was a wonder they stood at all. The unkept streets were peppered with potholes and sections of the sidewalk were crumbled and covered in dirt. The morbid atmosphere, punctuated by the occasional pile of human bones, sent her thoughts to Marcel.

"This place has been like this for two and a half thousand years?" Estelle asked.

Ransley did not respond at first.

"I suppose if I granted a miracle," he said, gesturing around. "Like this. And people never thought of the toll it took on me- I might be upset as well. Not that I condone this, but I sympathize."

Estelle kept getting sidetracked, staring at the large husks of buildings around her. Most notable to her was a multitude of curving shadows that connected several of the skyscrapers. She could not make them out completely.

"I live up ahead," Ransley said, pointing out a tall black building with silver windows. "That's the Catalina."

As she stared up at the majesty of the dark tower, a peculiar occurrence took place above. Hollow black suffocated the burgundy sky for a few seconds. Dim red returned for a moment before darkening once again. A catastrophic wale rang out across the sky as if some incredible creature had been wounded. Ransley grabbed Estelle's arm and pulled her forward with great haste.

"Mortesoon," he said with urgency. "We have to get inside! Now!"

A massive shape descended from the murky heavens. Orange lights burned through it. Gently falling toward the city, it rotated, the lights dimming now and then. It was only once it sat right above Web Obsidia that Estelle could see its form. It was a giant four-faced head. The orange lights were the eyes and mouth which screamed, blinked, and looked wildly around. Its call was reminiscent of a thousand tons of metal being dragged along a highway.

Ransley drew the woman into the lobby of a building supply shop. Its shelves had long been raided and its only wares were cobwebs and dust. Estelle's crow followed them inside and they observed the monstrosity through the window.

"What *is* that thing?!" Estelle shouted.

"That's not in my history book, unfortunately," Ransley said. "In Web Obsidia, we call it the Warden. We're safe now that we're inside."

"What do you mean?"

No sooner had the words left her mouth did a tidal wave of howling spirits spew forth from the Warden's mouths. They flew fast and swarmed like angry wasps. Estelle's heart skipped a beat as the specters flooded the streets they were just walking through. The Punished fled from the city's alleys and through the roads as the spirits swooped down and dismembered them with long bladed hands. Wraiths shot toward the shop where Estelle and Ransley took refuge. Instead of bursting through the glass, a faint blue light stopped where they made contact. Pale, skeletal faces with empty, black eyes gazed upon them with malice.

"They've never been able to get inside," Ransley said. "It's one blessing I never dared to question. Don't look at them too long. I've seen them hypnotize folk to draw them out."

Already a euphoric feeling spread through her mind as the spirits transformed into normal people with warming gifts for her. Cheerful men and women held plates of food and fresh clothes, including her loved ones. Marcel, his sister, Oscar, and even her father welcomed her with open arms. She closed her eyes and shook her head, feeling the shallow dread behind the illusion and turning away to enter an empty back room with Ransley.

The three hid themselves behind half a wooden door in what used to be a cash office for the business. A lone desk sat against the wall, which Ransley sat upon. Estelle peeked through a large hole in the wall at the wraiths whizzing by, not fifteen yards away.

"Now what?" the woman asked, pressing her back to the wall.

"Hard to say," Ransley said. "The Warden Storm can last anywhere from minutes to weeks."

"Ransley," the crow said. "What of the sky bridges? I

know they're patchy in some areas, but I could have sworn I saw one leading to the Catalina."

The old man stroked his beard.

"That could work," he said. "Providing the bridges haven't been compromised." Ransley nodded and approached the door. "Let me scout ahead. I'll search for the upper floors and see if they connect."

"What if something happens to you?" Estelle asked. "Maybe we should stay together."

"Don't worry, my friend," he replied. "I may be an old man, but I can take care of myself. There doesn't seem to be any Punished here, so I think we should be fine. Don't fret, lass. We'll get to safety before you know it."

After a hesitant nod from Estelle, Ransley left the room, closing the damaged door behind him. A few seconds later the Warden roared, trembling the ground. The Seeker sat amidst rubble and trash as her crow, perched on the desk, stared at her.

"Is this real?" Estelle asked. "The monsters? The red sky?"

"I wish I could say it wasn't," the crow said. "I wish I could say you wake up in your bed and go on living life. But you are here and so am I."

"What did you mean before? When you said I asked for this?"

"Is it not obvious?" a deep, familiar voice asked.

A knock came at the closed door and Estelle watched it with wide eyes. The second knock shook the door, and she jumped to her feet.

"Ransley?" she said.

"Open this door, young lady!" said the voice of her father.

Her mind twisted with the implications. How could her father be here? In a place she never knew with her home just as much of a mystery to others. Her body trembled, but she opened the door.

Indeed, Estelle's father met her in the doorway, but not him. Transparent and of a scarlet hue, Damian Grigori sauntered into the tiny office as his daughter watched him with large eyes.

"Estelle?" the crow asked. "What is it? What's wrong?"

"You don't see him?" Estelle asked, not taking her gaze away from the ghost. "My father?"

"I see no one."

"How has punishment suited you, daughter?" Damian asked. "Do you enjoy the death? The horror? This place was built for people like you. It's as wild and uncontrollable as you are."

"Please, Father," Estelle said. "Why am I here? What do I have to do to get home? I miss our house and Irina. I miss my piano and my friends. I just want to come home."

"You didn't seem to miss it before."

That was true, and Damian's words burned as she remembered her last conversations with Kamaria and Irina. She would have given anything to wake up in the house she hated.

"I just wanted a little freedom," Estelle said, her shoulders in a slump. "Just wanted to be my own person."

"You were free!" Damian's voice gained a pleading sound to it; gentler than the woman was used to. "We had power, influence, wealth- if you'd have focused yourself, you could have had anything you wanted."

"You never cared about what I wanted!" She screamed louder than she meant to. "You never asked what made me happy!"

"Estelle," the crow said. "Please calm yourself."

"After twenty-one years you couldn't see that you were making me miserable?! Every day of every year you had me followed or monitored. Your presence was suffocating!"

"What would have happened if I weren't there? You need discipline and wisdom! You'd have lost your mother's bracelet to that girl when you were ten; the last piece of her I have to hold on to. What about when you thought you'd try smoking, and the horse stables caught fire? And Easter when you were 17-"

"*Don't-* bring that up! You have no idea what that did to me, Father. You have no idea what *you* did to me."

The ruby eyes of her father bore into her and she thought he would scream or berate her. She clenched her jaw, waiting for a verbal assault.

"Very well then," said the ghost with a laugh. "If I'm such a nuisance, I'll leave you to your fate."

"Wait!"

"Just remember: you asked for this."

The vision of Damian faded before she could speak again. Estelle stared at the empty doorway as if he could reappear, but he never came. Ignoring the crow's pleas to speak with it, she went in search of Ransley. The crow tried to fly to her shoulder, but she brushed it away without a word.

## CHAPTER 6

# THE CATALINA HOTEL

Damian's voice echoed in Estelle's mind as she pushed through the storage room of the store. She held her stomach as she pushed passed tall stacks of boxes, and dusty, ragged sheets covering crates. She used them for support as she stumbled through the maze, finding a stairwell.

Cobwebs filled the passage upward, but there had been an obvious recent disturbance, clearing a path for her.

"Estelle?" the crow said, struggling to keep up with her. "What just happened?"

She rushed passed it, continuing to the third floor, then the fourth, where the remainder of the stairwell had collapsed. Estelle entered the floor to a large, open landing. Taking up the entire floor of the building, this room was designed as an observation deck.

Windows as high as the ceiling made up the walls with crippled telescopes mounted before them. Several benches would have allowed the citizens of the past to peer across to adjacent buildings; including the Catalina. A long, covered bridge connected the two, offering mandatory shelter from the storm. Estelle hesitated at the entrance of the bridge, searching for Ransley in the shadows ahead.

"Your face is flushed," the crow said, landing on a handrail. "Please, tell me what you saw. It isn't good to hold it in."

She turned and glared at the bird. She caught her words in her throat and sighed, running her fingers through her hair.

"I'm going mad," Estelle said. "I have to be."

"You saw your father. What did he say?"

"He came to remind me of all my shortcomings. To torment me even though I'm trapped in this nightmare- to remind me that I deserve it. Maybe I do."

"Listen to me." The crow waved its wings and shifted closer to her. "No one in Heaven or Hell deserves to be here. Least of all you."

"Then why?" her nostrils flared. "Why am I here?"

"You are destined for a greater life than you know. All of your dreams, once realized, will become tangible."

"I'm sensing a 'but.'"

"But you have work to do first."

"What do you mean by that? And what did you mean when you said I asked for this?"

The crow cocked its head and blinked.

"Come on, I'm not going to yell at you again."

"What do you want most?" it asked.

"My freedom."

"Your trials are the path to that end."

"By trials, you mean the magic keys?" She laughed. "Can you elaborate on that point?"

"As we go through experiences in life, the purity of our soul falls off. Like erosion on a mountain, each negative experience and choice carves a hunk of our spirit away. Certain events and choices rend our souls more than others. In order to earn your freedom, you must reassemble those pieces."

Estelle laughed again, kicking a small rock down the sky bridge as a wave of wraiths flew overhead.

"So I am here because my life finally caught up with me. All the fights, the attitudes toward teachers, the arguments with my dad, this-" she drew her violet sapphire and displayed it to the crow before stowing it again. "I'm being punished for my sins."

"It isn't that simple. I wish I could tell you everything, but even I don't understand it all. Your Guardian may know."

"So, why are you here? Just to keep me company?"

"I came from the realm of divine thought. I was given the chance to help someone who needs it. I offer wisdom, insight and compassion- as much as a bird can give."

"And what of the Guardian? What's his purpose?"

"To protect you during your trials."

"Well, they're doing a wonderful job so far."

Estelle stepped onto the bridge, keeping her sight fixed on the ground as wraiths pressed themselves against the tarnished glass. As she reached the other side, Ransley made his appearance accompanied by a towering dark skinned man standing around six and a half feet tall. He kept his head shaved and his face was carved with frown lines, though his dark brown eyes carried a gentle weight to them. His arms and neck were muscular and he held a pistol in his right hand as he walked slightly ahead of Ransley.

"Here she is, Reid," the old man said. "The woman I mentioned. Estelle, this is Reid. He lives a couple of doors down from me."

The man gave a shallow nod and half a smile before checking over his shoulder. Estelle and her crow followed them through the landing deck, up a few flights of stairs, and across a second sky bridge. The landing there separated into six doorways, the second from the right reading "*The Catalina.*"

They traveled down an empty, musty hallway and came to

a building with shining gray floor tiles, wallpaper of white, black and gray stripes and elaborate lamps that casted a yellow-green glow. At the window was a set of golden elevator doors, the car patiently waiting for them. Once inside, Reid pressed the button for floor 24.

"This thing still works?" Estelle asked.

Though it stuttered, the elevator slid into a smooth glide upward.

"The city is powered by nuclear reactors underground," Reid said. "Took me a couple years to learn how they work, but they do their job so well, they hardly need us. Just minor maintenance."

Being on the outer edge of the building allowed them an unobstructed view of the city. From so high up, more details of the Warden emerged. Massive bolts lined the sides of the faces and each displayed a different expression. Anger, despair, joy and indifference. It gently spiraled and occasionally released more spirits. A few latched on to the outside of the elevator, but the trio kept their eyes on their own reflections in the golden doors until they came to a stop.

The bustling sound of chatting people filled the corridor. People. Real human beings stood in their doorways and out in the hall talking with one another. Clotheslines held up laundry criss-crossing from one side to the other and chairs sat outside some doors. Reid continued on, vanishing behind a white sheet. Ransley removed his hat, and smiled at Estelle.

"This tower is something of a survivor hub," he said. "Lots of people pass though, or camp out on the other floors."

An elderly woman was met at the first door on the left. She wore a simple yellow dress with a floral pattern. A wooden cane held her up and her gray hair sat in tight curls. She smiled warmly at Ransley.

"Hello, Mauve," he said.

"Thank goodness you beat the storm," she said. "When

you hadn't come back yet, I panicked for you. We already lost Ron... we can't lose you too."

"I'm alright, truly. Look, I made a new friend today."

Ransley stepped aside and Estelle waved, nervously smoothing her dress.

"Found a stray?" she mused. "I'm only kidding, dear. Welcome to the Catalina!"

"Oh, thank you," Estelle replied. "I'm glad Ransley found me. I don't know what I would have done without his help. My name is Estelle."

"It's very nice to meet you, young lady. He truly is one of the good ones."

"She's a Seeker, Mauve," Ransley said.

"Oh, that's just a fairy tale! Don't get the girl's hopes up!"

"It's true!"

"Indeed," the crow said flatly. "Estelle my Seeker and I, her Familiar."

Mauve's face scrunched.

"Well, I'll be..." She trailed off, staring at the bird. "I thought I'd seen everything."

She and Ransley chuckled, and Estelle awkwardly followed suit.

"Please excuse us," he said. "We're beat from our walk."

"If you need anything, you know where to find me. Estelle, I make a wonderful apple pie. Come by and try it sometime."

With that, Estelle and Ransley continued down the hall. They passed several other occupants, including more elders, a young pregnant woman and a handful of children playing tag. They came to Ransley's door; fourth on the right, apartment 2406.

The old man reached inside of his coat pockets, rummaging around for the keys, and a grumble drew Estelle's attention down the hall. A seated figure with knees to the chest rested against the wall six doors down. Even from that distance, Estelle could make out wide, intense eyes fixed on her. She tried to ignore him, but her eyes kept wandering back to his. Thankfully, the lock clicked and she and her friend entered the apartment.

The strong scent of vinegar hit Estelle, as well as an underlying hint of something unpleasant she couldn't identify; something bitter and abrasive. Her nose twisted up for a few minutes before her mind became used to it, though her nostrils tingled.

"Please forgive the smell," Ransley said, hanging his coat on a hook near the door. "Not all who pass through the Catalina are peaceful. I've heard frightening things through the vents; screams and such- then the smells come up. There have been times when we posted guards at the elevator, but we've been lucky."

Ransley's apartment was spacious, with gray carpet and white walls. To the right of the entryway, a small kitchenette featured a tiny island used as counter space. A spacious armchair and two sofas, flanking a glass table, furnished the living room. A hallway off to the left went deeper into the home with small ceiling lanterns guiding the way. Estelle took a seat on a couch and sighed at the relief of weight off her back and legs. Her crow sat upon the island, observing. From the kitchen, Ransley entered, holding a glass of water and a small plate with more bread and some apple slices.

"I know it's not much," he said. "I'm still getting the hang of the cultivation center. Luckily, there's a man there who knows how it all works."

She gratefully took the food and tried not to eat too fast. Ransley had, for himself, a couple pieces of bread and a gray liquid he drank from a jar. It smelled faintly of blueberries, but looked tough to swallow. As well, he brought a plastic tray from the bathroom, topped with several white bottles that rattled when he set it down. As Estelle sipped her water, he divided his medication into assorted groups based on their dosage.

"What's that you're drinking?" Estelle asked.

"This?" he asked, tilting the jar toward her. "These pills are a mixture of supplements. A man my age unfortunately needs help for certain functions. I mix them with some fruit to make a convenient drink. Bananas, strawberries, apples. Blueberries are my favorite." He drank again. "How are you feeling?"

"Better than I hoped to," she said. "I'd be dead if it weren't for you."

"Thinking nothing of it," Ransley said.

"It's so dangerous out there. Why risk your life for me?"

For a moment, Ransley's wrinkled face drooped, falling into sadness. He capped his jar and rolled the bottle in his hands, deep in contemplation.

"It's what Ron would have wanted," he quietly said. "Besides, who would I be to deny aid to a wayward soul?"

"Mauve mentioned that name earlier. Is... was Ron a friend?"

"The great love in my life. I was looking for him in the outskirts when I heard the Punished chasing you. Ron was someone who believed in helping others, kindness and compassion. He's been gone for a month now. I'm fairly certain he's dead, but I still search for his remains to give him a proper funeral. Helping others is the best way to honor his memory."

"I'm so sorry, Ransley. May... may I ask what happened?"

"Ron and I met at a survivor camp years ago." His voice was low and grief hung on his every word. "Eventually that home was overrun by the Punished. We survived out in the city until we found this place. One day he went out for supplies and never returned."

After a small uncomfortable silence, Ransley spoke again.

"Do you think we could change the topic?"

"Yes, of course," Estelle said quickly, looking to her familiar. "Crow?"

The snowy bird flew to the glass table. It cocked its head and looked up at her.

"Yes?"

"What am I supposed to do with this?"

Estelle dug into the pocket of her dress and pulled forth the sterling silver key. For a few seconds, the angelic choir filled her mind, washing warmth over her aching body. She perceived a shimmer to the quartz as if a tiny star were trapped within it.

"Your keys unlock the Dimension Door. All I know is that it brings you to memories crucial to your fractured soul."

"That is a marvelous piece," Ransley said. "May I?"

Estelle shrugged, and handed the silver key to Ransley. He held it in his palm, then clasped it in his fingers, holding the quartz up to the light. A slight shake came over his hand and he released the key, letting it clatter on the glass.

"I swear I can feel the spirit in it! Hand's all tingly now."

Ransley laughed and he slid the key back to the Seeker. She twisted it between her thumb and index finger.

"How do I open this door?" she asked her crow.

"Honestly," it said. "I figured the door would manifest when you took your key. I'm still learning as you are. I think it's best to head north to find your Guardian."

"That's the Kern Museum, right?" Ransley asked.

Estelle drew her map and unfolded it, pressing it down on the table. Ransley examined it, drawing his finger over the city blocks.

"Kern is about 40 miles from here," he said. "It'll take all day. And this here-" He pointed to a thick line across the main road heading north. "That's a collapsed building. You'd have to go around, which would make the trip take even longer."

Estelle's shoulders slumped, and she gave Ransley a defeated look.

"You see my dilemma," Estelle said. "I don't know how I'm supposed to make it that far with monsters and God knows what else on my back."

Ransley pet his mustache, twirling the ends around his fingertips.

"I've been thinking," he said at length. "There's talk of a settlement in Serenus Acres- District 5. It's been growing in popularity and the myth is they have a secret device that can protect them from anything."

"I'd have to see that to believe it."

"My thoughts exactly. If it's true, this could be the first light of hope since the Blue Key Massacre. I wanted to see with my own eyes and after months of rumors, I figure it must have some credence. It's out of your way, but if you'd like, an old man could use the company."

Ransley pointed out District 5, labeled as *Serenus Acres.* The side notes on the map described it as a section of the city carved out for the elite, composed of mansions, modern homes and country clubs. It was about half the distance away than Kern was, but would add 20 miles to the museum journey.

"We should continue north," the crow said. "The quicker we find your Guardian, the better."

"We've done fine without the Super Stupid Swordsman. Besides, meeting more people can't be a bad thing. I could get supplies, food and water."

"We don't even know how valid this place is."

"You can say the same for the museum. Have you even been there?"

"No, but-"

"So you want me to travel twice the distance on the word of a letter. I don't even know where it came from. Do you?"

The crow was silent.

"It's more plausible that the District 5 settlement is safer, so that's where I'm going. Feel free to fly to the museum and wait for me there."

"Then it's settled," Ransley said. "Once the storm breaks, we shall depart."

Estelle nodded before finishing her water and walking over to the ceiling-high window. She gazed out as the ghosts slipped through the air like slithering wisps of clouds. The Warden grunted and groaned, coughing more wraiths out. At the moment, Despair looked in her general direction. She almost admired how something mechanical could be the size of a sports stadium. Its fiery eyes and mouth lit the sky a disgusting orange, like a false sun.

"Well," Ransley said with a yawn. "I think we've had enough excitement for one day. There's a spare bedroom in the hall. Second door on the left. My recommendation is that we get a good night's rest so we can think with fresh minds on the morrow."

CHAPTER 7

––––––––

# THE ROAD TO SERENUS ACRES

Chilling air raked her skin as Estelle awoke in darkness. Instead of the bed she had previously slept in, she lay on cold, hard ground. There was not light enough to see her hand in front of her face, yet she reached out as she explored.

"Hello?" she said, her voice echoing. "Crow? Ransley?"

The fading chorus of her own voice acknowledged her. A cold shiver crept up her spine and disembodied whispers came from every direction. The only thing she could make out were two hushed words.

"*Come back,*" it hissed.

Seductive like a serpent and malicious like a demon, it called twice more. Estelle's heart raced so fiercely, her pulse throbbed in her ears. As she peered into the darkness, a faint white light manifested some distance away. She tore after it.

The light grew brighter as she drew near, and she came to a small tree sapling. It grew from a snow covered patch of ground, its small branches trying to stretch with tiny green needles poking out.

*"Come back,"* the voice said again with more intent. *"We belong together!"*

Booming like an angry army and with the deafening volume of a church bell, the voice produced physical ripples. Estelle looked deep into the emptiness for the source. She took a couple of steps beyond the light, but kept her weight on her back foot. For a few anxious seconds, everything was still and quiet. The Seeker lost her breath. Out in the pitch black, a pair of dim orange eyes stared back at her.

The deafening rumble of thunder startled the woman out of her sleep. So powerful was the sound that the windows rattled. Estelle clamored out of bed and rushed to the window to see the Warden continuing its surveillance.

At that moment, a flash of light spread out in a wave from deep within the city. A marvelous bolt of white lightning sped across the sky and slammed into the Warden. The following thunder could have been mistaken for an earthquake. The Warden swung back and forth, producing a furious, scraping howl, and Estelle gasped as it ascended.

Tens of thousands of violent spirits retreated to their master and none lingered. The blackened sky faded to burgundy, then crimson. The origin of the bolt radiated in an enormous ring of glowing colors. Red faded to violet, then to blue and green.

"What just happened?" Estelle asked her crow, who perched on her nightstand.

"I cannot say," it said. "It must be something of extraordinary power to fend off the Warden."

Ransley burst through her door, breathing as if he'd sprinted up every staircase in the building.

"Did you see it?" he asked. "Hurry into the hallway! Everyone's talking!"

With that, he closed her door. Even in her room, the sound of the Catalina's survivors penetrated the walls. After a lukewarm shower, Estelle exited through the front door where chaos awaited. Twenty residents spoke over one another, pointing down the hall to the elevator or to the stairwells. She found Ransley near his door as he stood on the balls of his feet to peer over the crowd.

"We can't stay here!" a man said.

"We've ignored her for too long!" came Mauve's voice over the crowd.

"No one's ever attacked the Warden!"

"We should leave when the Matterhorn comes through!"

The crowd roared in approval.

"What's everyone talking about?" Estelle asked Ransley.

"They thinks it's the Pale Lady," he replied.

"The Pale Lady? Who's that?"

"What do you mean 'who's that?'" an old, thin man said. "You must live in the sewers or something."

"It had to be her!" another said. "We can't stay here any longer. It's only a matter of time before we're dragged into her bullshit. She's been expanding her territories with her god-awful Torchbearers. I've heard the stories. They show up in groups to force people from their homes and join them!"

The crowd erupted, and all words became indistinguishable. Estelle pushed her way through the packed corridor until she came to the elevator landing. Estelle's crow flew from beyond the hanging sheets, landing on the window's lip.

"I hate crowds," Estelle said. "With that thing out of the sky, we can get to District 5."

"Won't you heed my advice?" the crow asked.

"I get that you're trying to help, but it would be better to meet more people. Maybe we could even find help."

"Help wouldn't be a bad thing. But the streets are unpredictable. There's no telling what could happen to us on the way to 5."

"Look."

Estelle drew her map and spread it on the floor before the familiar. She pointed to District 7, labeled *Irontown*.

"There are no obstructions going east. There's nothing but obstacles going north. We can go around a couple if we go to the settlement. We get there, rest, grab supplies, and we'll be on our way. Nothing to it."

The crow clicked its beak, then bowed its head.

"A-apprentice," a quivering voice said. "T-the r-r-reaper's a-apprentice."

Estelle turned, but no one had come from the hallway, so she searched the landing. Hidden by the walls of the elevator car was a man huddled in the corner, leaning against the window. It was the man from the night before whose wide eyes frantically stared everywhere yet nowhere.

His haggard face was lengthy and thin. His long nose protruded, and drool hung from his crusted lips. Long, scraggly gray hair covered his mouth and hung down his face. Wrapped in a wool blanket, he twitched and rocked back and forth. When she approached, he buried his face between his knees.

"What's wrong with him?" Estelle asked her crow.

"From what I can tell," it said. "His mind is corrupted. I do not believe he was born this way."

"You'd be right about that," a woman said.

Emerging from the sheet that covered the corridor entrance was a slender woman with tan skin and a round, plump belly. Her smile took up most of her face, and her slanted eyes were an unusually bright shade of brown. She kept her curly black hair tied in a bun atop her head.

"I see you've met Cedric. I'm Amber, Reid's wife. He told me he helped Ransley with a new survivor."

"Nice to meet you," Estelle said. "I don't think I'd have made it here without Ransley's help. Especially during that storm."

Amber cast a sympathetic look at Cedric.

"I'm sure you've heard the stories about the wraiths; what happens when they catch you?"

"Yeah," she lied.

"Cedric is what it looks like when they get you, but they don't kill you."

"How did it happen?"

"Six or seven years ago, maybe- he was hypnotized by the storm wraiths. They willed him to the streets, where they grabbed hold of him. Sank their claws into his head. Just before they could kill him, the storm ended, and the ghosts left. Cedric survived the encounter, but was never the same again. He wasn't unlike Reid; strong, helpful and intelligent. True shame."

"I didn't know that could happen."

"Neither did I until that day. Between that and the night a burglar broke in, he's had it more than rough."

The makeshift veil moved, and the voices grew as the flustered crowd drew toward the elevator. Among them was Ransley, who stepped out of line to stand with Estelle. In small groups, they descended the Catalina until only she, Ransley, Cedric, Amber and the crow remained. The disturbed man tucked his head back between his knees and covered his greasy hair with his arms. Amber knelt next to him, stroking his back.

"It's the elevator bell," Amber said to Estelle. "The burglar incident was traumatic... made it an awful sound for him. That's why he stays down the other end of the hall. The crowd must have driven him this way. We shouldn't talk about it in front of him."

Estelle caught Ransley's eyes move toward the elevator and she turned to walk away, but Cedric caught her wrist with the speed of a frog catching a fly.

"Between the crosses, betwixt the veil," he said. "In endless skies and stormy gales. At the behest of the cosmic chime. And into the space of infinite time. Pondering secrets nobody knows. You'll find your answers between thunder and snow."

Estelle, her crow and Baron Ransley spent the first half of the day traveling east, into District 7. Ransley explained the streets were always quiet following a storm. They encountered the butchered corpses of the Punished caught in the Warden's assault along their route; the air reeked of metallic decay.

The colors of the strange flare that drove the Warden away lingered. The sky drank the hues as they expanded behind the clouds. Estelle grasped her sapphire in the confines of her pockets, letting her mind wander to her real life while dwelling on Cedric's lucid words.

On the sixth hour of their trek toward District 5 and the supposed established settlement, both Estelle and Ransley felt satisfied enough to rest, taking refuge on the patio of a smelting shop. They had long since passed into Irontown, where foundries, workshops and great metal mills surrounded them. Ransley divided a few slices of bread for the two and sipped his supplement.

"I'd have done anything for the one I loved," the old man said. "I understand why you'd want to elope with Marcel."

"I just wish I'd have had the chance," Estelle said. "One day we're planning our life together and the next, I'm here."

"Have hope," the crow said. "You may yet get what you desire."

"How? Even if I get out of this godforsaken place, how am I supposed to explain my absence? No one would believe me. Not even Marcel. He'll think the rumors about me are true. He'll think I abandoned him."

"What do they say?" Ransley asked. "I think you mentioned growing up in a mansion?"

She nodded. "I got tall the insults you'd expect. Snotty, spoiled, entitled. My father's reputation didn't help."

"What kind of man is he?" Ransley asked. "You haven't said much about him."

Estelle clenched her teeth.

"He's a man of power and control," the Seeker said. "I think he wants what's best for me, but we disagree on what that means. He's more devoted to his business empire than his daughter."

"That sound quite lonely. I'm sorry."

"Only a few people know how I feel. Because of my reputation, I'm forced to defend myself." She ran her hand over the slashed sleeve of her black shirt. "Sometimes physically. But I never wanted to hurt anyone."

"I hope this isn't a burden you bear alone."

"I could say the same for you- that came out wrong. I just mean this desolate, monster infested place... How can anyone live here?"

"We have little choice, I'm afraid." Ransley laughed. "This is all we've ever known. Sure, the monsters are a constant threat, but one I've known since I was a boy. We learn how to fight, how to stay safe and scavenge. Your world sounds confusing with so many rules, languages and your- what did you call them? Your overseers?"

"Politicians."

"A single group of people who control the entire country?"

"It's a bit more complicated than that. We need rules and

regulations to maintain order. Before I met you, three men attacked me. In my world, they would have faced justice or been too afraid of that justice to act. This place is so lawless."

"Not always. Let me see your map."

Estelle drew the paper and laid it flat on the ground. Ransley sat forward and placed a wrinkled finger on a block of purple at the Northeast corner labeled "Tamasha."

"The Blue Key Club is here," he said. "They're the most well-known group in Web Obsidia." He shifted to the green block below. "There was a big settlement here in Salvaura, about 20 years ago. So order has its place here." He then pointed to District 2, where they had been, though some ways north and in the center of Web Obsidia, crossed out with a red X. "This is the one place we can never go."

"The Kollektra Courthouse?"

Her companion nodded with a grim look in his tired eyes.

"That's where *she* has made her base. The Pale Lady."

"Is she really worth all that panic in the Catalina?"

Ransley nodded, and the chipper man melted away, and his blue eyes dimmed.

"There's a reason the Blue Key Club is famous," he said. "Two years ago, the demon we named the Pale Lady attacked them. All on her own, she killed half their army; two ore three hundred people."

"Why would she do that?"

"When does evil need an excuse to act?" the crow said.

"My thoughts, exactly," said Ransley. "Somehow they survived total annihilation. The demon has been quiet since then, but we know she's still out there. That the Blue Key still stands is a testament to their strength and organization."

Estelle scoffed. "But I'm not in Hell, right crow?"

An explosion several streets over drew their attention. Then there was an animalistic screech, and the wind carried indistinct yells, followed by the rapid popping of gunfire.

Keeping as far away as they could while maintaining their current trajectory, they continued on their path.

After another mile, they came to where northward would be the only option. Any further and they would need to backtrack. The commotion from earlier never ceased. Constant were the calls of men, the firing of rifles and the shriek of whatever beast they engaged with.

Another explosion rocked the buildings of Irontown, coming from the next street over. A terrible crash occurred and the brick and glass from the nearby smith shop shattered as a vehicle rolled through, missing Estelle by a few feet. She and Ransley fled away from the wreckage as it ignited and caught fire. The flaming bodies attempting to crawl from the twisted metal grasped the woman's eyes.

A long, slithering shadow rose from behind the building's rubble. It came up three or four stories and its width was at least that of a firetruck. Two glowing orange slits focused on the vehicle, then a mouth opened, baring fangs the length of elephant tusks. Glowing green liquid sprayed forward, covering the wreck and the face of a foundry. It spread the fire as if made of oil, then sizzled, melting away any surface it came in contact with.

# CHAPTER 8

## SHERMAN MANOR

Estelle, Ransley and her crow sped into an alley, covering their heads from a spray of acid. Coming to an intersection in the shadows, they tried to assess the situation. Estelle faced the impossible choice of turning back versus throwing herself into a brutal conflict to get to the District 5 settlement. Sunken low to a near crawl, the Seeker, her crow and Baron Ransley crept forward in the shade of the alley.

Three men stood guard at the end. Close enough to see, Estelle recognized them as soldiers; their uniforms were dark green and ash gray, and they carried long guns.

"Should we try to talk to them?" Estelle asked.

"They could be friendly," Ransley said. "They could also take us prisoner."

Another explosion sounded, and the giant snake screamed again. The guards at the end of the alley readied their weapons, aiming down the street. Orders shouted out as masked warriors ran to form ranks.

Estelle motioned for them to leave. As they made ready, Ransley bumped into a trashcan, sending the metal container clanking to its side. A light blinded them as a deep, harsh voice called out.

"Let me see your hands!" he yelled. Estelle and Ransley complied. "What're y'all doing out here?"

"We're just passing through," Ransley said. "Looking for the new settlement in 5."

Walking forward, the soldier revealed himself to be a grizzled, stern man in his late forties. He sported a short blond-gray mohawk and his gray-blue eyes were tired yet fierce. His dress was simple jeans, a black long-sleeved shirt, and a dark green tactical vest. A black radio clung to his right shoulder strap and a small ruby badge, wrapped in silver, was clipped to the left. He examined the two, then the bird.

"Name's Mike," he said in a rough, Southern accent. "Captain of the Sherman Manor Defense Force. We run the settlement you're looking for. If you need beds or food, we've got them. Head down the alley and get to a medical truck. They'll get you out of here."

"What's going on out here?" Estelle asked. "What is that thing?"

Before Mike could respond, a figure came swiftly from the shadows, tackling him and forcing him to drop his rifle. The assailant wore a dim red light on his chest that threw matted shadows around. They exchanged punches as they violently rolled on the cold ground. Several times, Ransley aimed his rifle, but could not get a clear shot. Estelle caught a flash of silver in the attacker's hand and Mike held his wrists as the blade came down toward his chest. Estelle took up of Mike's rifle, aiming at the attacker.

"G-get off of him!" she said. "Or I'll shoot!"

Her voice quivered, and she could hardly hold the gun steady. His red light shining on Mike's face, he looked over his shoulder at Estelle. A black sack tied at the neck covered his face with a horizontal slit for eyeholes. Just above it was a symbol; a red dot encircled by the flames of a star. His shoulders rose as he sniggered, turning to bear all his weight down on the knife. Estelle's finger grazed the trigger and the shot that rang out was not hers. The man's head jerked to the side, and he fell over. Ransley's rifle exhaled smoke at as Mike pushed the dead man away.

"Easy, girlie," Mike said, his hand gesturing in a lowering motion.

Estelle swallowed and handed the weapon back to its owner. Estelle's crow came to her.

"Steady yourself, my Seeker," it said. "We aren't safe yet."

As if predicting it, the serpent appeared, towering like an ancient black tree, beaming down at them with searchlight eyes.

"Get to the trucks!" Mike said, as the snake screeched.

They heard a splattering from behind, followed by the sound of sizzling and the stinging smell of burned rock. The crow was first to depart and fled into the streets, where a hundred green-clad soldiers engaged in a battle, shooting down the road at more hooded men. The snake cried out, coming over the buildings. As it did, several pickup trucks with mounted machine guns fired upon it, the bullets glowing hot like embers. The serpent turned away, disappearing into the next street over.

The garrison in Northern Irontown stretched about a mile and a half with the streets lit by tall flood lights. Many of their vehicles boasted heavy weaponry, including powerful guns, reinforced plating, spear launchers, and battering rams. Mike lead them to an old, white pickup with a red cross painted on the door before approaching a soldier.

"New arrivals," he said. "We're heading back to the manor." He grasped the radio on his chest. "Prepare to retreat. Lines three, four and five- cover lines one and two! I repeat, we're packing up!"

The soldier opened the door for them as Mike disappeared into the ranks, shouting orders. A tan skinned man sat in the drive's seat, looking back at them with a grin so wide his cheeks must have hurt. Catching the flood lights was a circular sapphire set inside a silver band on his vest. His short, curly hair formed a mop of dreadlocks that hung just below his ears. In the front passenger seat was a man clad in a heavy yellow hazmat suit. His helmet and respirator, which bore tubes connected to a breathing apparatus on his chest, obscured his face.

"Welcome!" said the driver. "I'm Theo, and the gentleman in the rubber suit is Knowledge 1."

The man in the hazmat suit turned as best he could and nodded to Estelle. Painted on his chest were two characters: K1.

"Surely that's not his true name?" Ransley asked.

"Ha! No, that's just the code we use in the field. He's Andrew."

Mike's voice came over the car radio, and Theo fell silent.

"Now's the time," Mike said. "Move out! Back to Sherman Manor!"

"Finally." Theo sighed, rolling his eyes. "SMDF is out!"

The truck's engine roared to life. The formation moved out one at a time with three groups of jeeps leaving before their turn came. Not five minutes into the trip, the sound of machine guns erupted. Everyone in the truck looked to see, but the night was setting in.

Theo drove faster, passing two cars in front of them. He had not gotten far before a great force flipped their truck, sending them rolling. The passengers tossed as they held on to anything sturdy, slamming into one another. They crashed into the side of a building with the truck coming to a rest on its side, its windows shattered. Estelle fell atop Ransley, and as fast as he could, Theo pushed his door open, and slipped away.

Andrew clamored up to the driver's side and drew a pistol from his belt. He stuck his head out, but the serpent's cry cut through the air, and he took cover again. Estelle grabbed the seats and heaved herself up to open her door. The metal plate made it heavy and took much of her strength, but she managed.

"Estelle, wait," Ransley said.

She poked her head out and was awestruck by what she beheld. Glowing orange eyes the size of beach balls glared down at her. A giant, forked tongue swept out, shaking the air, and shiny black scales lined the mammoth-sized snake. It opened its mouth, revealing bloody spears for fangs, and the woman froze.

"Here!" Theo shouted, raising his rifle. "You overgrown worm!"

He fired a hail of bullets at the snake, who seemed annoyed at best. It switched its gaze to Theo before coiling and striking. He expected it and rolled out of the way. The serpent missed by mere feet and upended an iron lamppost. Ransley fled the vehicle and drew his old rifle, firing as well. The snake could not decide who to attack and its dilemma worsened when multiple vehicles joined. With a threatening hiss, it turned its head and slithered down a side street. Theo rushed to the overturned vehicle and helped Estelle and Andrew out.

"We need to get to another truck," Theo said, looking up and down the lane.

His radio rang out with the horrific sounds of screaming, gunfire, and the snakes wailing. It appeared a ways down the road, striking high from a building, snapping at the back of the convoy.

A van screeched to a halt near them, and Theo lead Estelle to it, the crow flying down to follow. He slid the side door open and shoved her inside, where she landed in the laps of three soldiers. Theo screamed something, and they took off.

As they drove away, Ransley was being rushed into another truck with Andrew. The back seats in the van faced each other, with two soldiers sitting beside Estelle and one sitting across.

The Seeker clutched her bird to her chest like a stuffed animal as she tried to calm her herself. The soldier across removed their helmet, revealing a blonde woman in her late thirties.

With skin of vanilla, hair of wavy gold and eyes of blue-green, she offered a hand of reassurance to Estelle. A pair of golden bull skull earrings she wore fascinated the Seeker. Pinned to the right side of her vest was another jeweled badge. This one was a stunning emerald; circular, multi-faced and encased in a woven gold braid. Her eyes matched the glint of the emerald, both shining like stars of hope in the turmoil.

"It's alright, hon," she said. "You're safe now. We're gonna get a roof over your head and some food in your belly."

"Thank you," the Seeker replied.

"What's your name?"

"E-Estelle."

"I'm Sue. You know, you've got real pretty eyes."

She managed a weak smile.

"You're more beautiful than I am," Estelle confessed. "And you're a warrior. Where I'm from, they say ladies shouldn't fight."

"I'd love to hear them say that out here." Sue's pink lips curved into a smirk. "Anyone who says that should be knocked out. You can tell them I said so."

The soldiers laughed, and the other two removed their helmets. They were both men; one with short, black wavy hair and the other was bald with a thin mustache.

"She's not kidding," said the bald man, scratching his face. "Sue's one of the best we've got."

"The most reliable too," said the black-haired man. "Good ole Sue always comes through."

"Do you have to keep saying that?" Sue asked, blushing.

The three laughed, and even Estelle brought forth a small but genuine smile. The final sounds of the carnage had faded, and the van slowed. She poked her head up to find them approaching a pale blue light, so thin it was nearly invisible. She thought they'd run into it, but they passed through a hole just large enough to accommodate the convoy. A small gathering of Punished chased the vehicle, slamming into the light and being felled by exterior guards.

The convoy traveled on a stone driveway, down the middle of several plots of dirt. A four-by-four orientation of them made up the yard, each taking up an acre. Shaded figures of survivors attended tents, campfires, chairs, grills, and more. Many of them gathered to wave at the passing trucks, offering support and love. At the end of the road sat an enormous white house.

"Welcome to Sherman Manor," Sue said. "Home sweet home."

Awestruck by the grand house, it stood four stories with blue and gold trim that popped against the white wood. Many tall, rectangular windows were inset between white pillars and reflected the little light from the darkened sky. In the center of the facade, three sets of blue double doors rested at the top of a stone staircase. A series of white Greek-style pillars that held up a semicircular balcony, obscuring the doors. Above that was a majestic round window framed by swooping white and gold designs.

At the top of the manor, the gold trim extended around the edge of the roof with a white banister situated atop it. In the center was a golden statue in the cast of a golden eagle. Its outstretched wings spread above the rail like a protective spirit.

The convoy drove to the rear, which was just as spacious as the front. A crowd of survivors waited eagerly with grinning faces, bearing gifts of food and wine. They came to a stop and Sue opened the door.

Still holding her crow as the people piled out of the jeeps and trucks, comfort came from cheerful voices and boisterous laughter. Soldiers with white bands around their arms ushered her to a series of white tents about fifty yards from the rear of the manor. Bright lights shone over them as men and women in long white coats came and went through the flaps that acted as doors. A soldier directed to one, and she entered.

Estelle winced in pain as the woman across from her dabbed a stinging, bleeding spot on her arm. A droplet of the snake's venom touched her, blistering the skin. She sat upon a stool across from a gurney and beneath a bright white light, her sleeve rolled up. The mocha skinned woman had introduced herself as Mae Kenyon and was a newcomer to the manor with little more than six months under her belt. She kept her hair in a low afro and wore a white coat that she didn't bother to button. Beneath, she wore black jeans and a dark blue tank top. As the coat shifted, Estelle caught glints of a jewel; a topaz encircled in gold.

"How much longer is this going to take?" she asked Mae. "I already told you I'm fine."

"I know," Mae said, her voice flat. She applied an ointment to the burn. "You've said so three times in the last fifteen minutes."

"This little drop doesn't mean anything. Others had it worse than me."

Mae bandaged Estelle's arm and sighed, staring the Seeker down with tired, careless eyes.

"It's not just about your injuries. You could bring any number of pathogens in here. Something dark could have latched on to you. You could be a spy from Bleedstar. You don't get to just walk in from the street and make yourself at home. There are reasons we have these screenings. I have dozens more people to see, and I could do it faster without you questioning me every five minutes. May I work?"

Estelle bit her tongue as a rush of heat surged in her head. She nodded.

"I've never seen a snake that big in my life... And those people with the hoods. Who were they?"

"You met the Pale Lady's army. They call themselves Torchbearers. The snake is her pet."

"The old man I was traveling with mentioned her. Is she really as bad as people say?"

"Worse," Mae said, taping the bandages. "She could have given the SMDF the same amount of trouble on her own, if not more."

"One person?"

"One monster. I remember a time where her brazen attacks rocked Web Obsidia and no one would dare leave their homes."

"I find that hard to believe."

A scoff escaped Mae's lips as she pulled the bandage tighter around her arm. Estelle's wince caused the woman to chuckle.

"Please forgive her," the crow said, seated on a side table. "She is still new to this world."

Mae jumped and cursed.

"Oh right," she said. "I forgot about the talking bird." She drew Estelle's sleeve back down. "I don't know what your deal is or where you came from, but you need to get yourself together before you get killed."

"I'm doing my best," Estelle said sharply. "I didn't ask to come here. I fell into a hole and woke up in this crappy city. First, I get chased by crazy monsters. Then I get trapped by a flying metal head. The snake? What the hell else will I have to endure?"

"Don't stress yourself, Estelle," the crow said. "We'll get what rest we can here, then head for Kern. Once we find the swordsman, you will be on your way back home."

"Who's that?" Mae asked. "Friend of yours?"

"They're supposed to be the Guardian to my Seeker. The one meant to protect her during her trials. We are heading to Kern, where he hopefully is."

"I hear Seekers and Guardians are fairy tales."

"Why would we make this up?" Estelle asked, crossing her arms. "I'm supposed to graduate and start my life this year. One day I'm dealing with school and bullies and the next I'm dealing with the Punished and an acid spitting snake!" Estelle's voice sank to a whisper. "I'd take Nina and Clara over this any day."

"Well, what are you going to do about it?" Mae asked. "Moping around and being pissed off isn't going to get you closer to what you want."

"What should I do then? The one person who's *supposed* to be helping me isn't here, and I have no idea what to expect. I just want to go home."

Mae sighed. "Assuming you're telling the truth, you would need time to learn how to survive out there. It doesn't matter if you're traveling twenty miles or twenty yards- if you can't protect yourself or think on your feet, you'll die. I stay busy, but I'll help you where I can."

"You trust me all of a sudden?" Estelle raised an eyebrow.

"Most people who come here want to stay as long as possible. They make themselves extra useful to earn their keep. Then I meet you- a young woman, allegedly a stranger to Web Obsidia, who wants to get back to the streets as soon as she arrives. I don't know what to make of you, but I don't get the sense you'll cause trouble."

"That is the last thing we want," the crow said. "Hopefully, Estelle won't be in this city long enough to cause trouble."

"Well, be careful who you tell about all that. Most of us write it off as a fantasy, but others hate hearing it." Estelle's brows furrowed. "Assuming it's all true- you have to think of how it makes the rest of us feel. This is the only life we've ever known. Monsters, settlement wars, taking what we can where we can just to make it to the next day. You're allowed to get out, but the rest of us have to stay? What would any of us give to have your chance?"

A young nurse appeared at the door to request Mae's help. Medically cleared, the Seeker received instructions to make her way into the manor via the blue doors. She followed a spacious chain of soldiers with those white bands around their arms, though the majesty of the interior slowed her progression.

Down the long hallways of Sherman Manor stretched a magnificent carpet, a swirling blend of blue, gold, and green, patterned with intricate leaves and vines; it felt soft and luxurious underfoot. The walls were painted white and the moulding on the ceiling impersonated more vines that spread outward from glass chandeliers. Lights within gold circles and draping crystals projected flickering rainbows like the sun through a prism. The wide center corridor led to a wide circle with twin stairs on either side of Estelle.

A pair of soldiers with a tall green flag at the base of the staircase waved to her. They happily directed her up two flights of stairs and to the right. The banister was white marble with a gold-plated rail. Carvings of angels topped the posts where the stairs twisted for its ascent.

At the second floor landing she was directed to a tall, wide bedroom. Improvised cots stretched from one wall to the other, with over a dozen survivors already settled in. Glowing sconces on the wall gave the room a soft beige glow and glossy white curtains covered the ceiling high windows.

"Hey there, old timer," Estelle said, finding Ransley in the back corner.

"There you are!" He nearly dropped his jar.

Estelle sat on the cot across from him and the crow settled down on the pillow. Ransley handed her some bread and fruit the mansion staff had prepared and she ate quickly.

"This place was better than I could have hoped for," she said.

"It is marvelous, isn't it? Their shield technology is amazing. I've heard of stuff like this in Grace's Landing, but not here in Web Obsidia."

"Grace's Landing?"

"It's another part of the city. According to my book, it was where the first streets of Eve's Hollow were built. Everything started there. I wish I could see, but it's far across the abyss. Nothing survives out there."

"Well, I'm just glad these guys have it."

Silence fell between them as the inevitable question reared its head.

"What will we do tomorrow?" the crow asked.

"See if we can get a favor," Estelle said. "I'm not dumb enough to think I can make it to Kern on my own. Those trucks with machine guns would come in handy, but I'm sure they won't help for free."

"We did save a man's life," Ransley said. "Surely they'll take that into consideration."

# CHAPTER 9

## WE BELONG TOGETHER

Darkness surrounded Estelle, and her head buzzed with a faint, rhythmic humming. As her vision focused, vibrant fire light came into view. A ring of torches cast a dim, wavering light across the steel walls and the cold, rusty iron grate floor of the chamber, its rough texture palpable. Several figures stood in the room clad in dark red robes. They wore baggy pointed hoods over their heads with crude eyeholes cut out. They were the source of the humming. It sounded like a sad, dark song, yet made her feel unusually calm and chipper.

She walked to the middle of the room with confidence and authority. Standing on a large, red circular symbol, she stared straight ahead, chest out and shoulders back. The symbol resembled the ring of a red sun with a dot at its center; the same mark on Mike's assailant.

She ceased the humming with the wave of her hand. A heavy, iron door stood a few feet before her with its only defining feature a small barred window at eye level. Through the opening came sounds of grunting, yelling and laughing.

"Open it," Estelle said at length.

The closest Torchbearer rushed to unlock it. The rust of the door's frame screeched as it swung open. Orange fire light spread like a blinding sheet and the sounds grew louder.

Estelle entered a circular room with torches lining the curve. There were four men in hoods fighting a loner, obscured by the shadows. Standing just inside was a tall, muscular man clad in heavy black leather pants and a heavy leather trench coat. His double-bitted axe rested beneath his gloved hands as he leaned on it. The point of his hood was shorter than the others, with the lower section torn away, allowing a bushy beard to poke through like overgrown weeds.

Estelle watched the beating for several minutes before she realized the prisoner's ankle was shackled to the wall. He held his own against the hooded men, using calculated strikes and counterattacks to keep them away. However, they got in their fair share of punches to his face and stomach. In time, two of the men restrained his arms while the remaining duo took turns attacking.

"Stop," Estelle said. "Leave us."

Without question, the four men hurried from the room. The man with the axe looked at her with skepticism.

"He's no danger, Toraesis," she said, scoffing. "Leave. Now."

With a grunt, Toraesis departed and closed the door behind him. Estelle stepped forward, watching the stranger huddled on the ground. He coughed and wiped his mouth, spitting blood at her feet. He stood up straight as if unbothered by the bruises and lacerations, meeting her in the light.

Estelle beheld a tall, coffee skinned man with long black dreadlocks that hung to the small of his back. A black cloak shrouded the lower half of his face, leaving only amethyst colored eyes visible. He wore a black sleeveless robe with gray pants, black boots, and black sleeves that hugged his muscular arms. Strips of purple light accented his clothing; three around each arm and one that traveled down the front of his chest and to the hem of the robe.

"My answer is the same," the man said. "I will not help you. Not ever."

"You still refuse to see," Estelle said. "Refuse to see that these people are doomed, and only I can save them. What must I do to convince you that you can't win?"

"Demella, millions of people- billions have died throughout history fighting for unjust causes. Proprietors of genocide. Madmen who craved total domination. Warlords who rape, pillage and burn. Eventually, every last one of them wound up in the same place. Even if you take over this city and rule... someday someone will come along with more power than you."

"You and your master already taught me that. But he grows ever weaker while you belong to me now... Just like your lady love."

The man reached for her neck with writhing fingers, but she had positioned herself out of his reach. Estelle laughed and met the man's volcanic, irate eyes.

"How long has it been since I made her body my home? Two years? A little more? If you were going to save her, you would have by now. This dungeon is your home until you profess loyalty to the new queen of Eve's Hollow."

The man was stoically silent. Without thinking, Estelle felt her arm pull back, and she stepped in for a gut punch in a flash of speed. The man fell to his knees as he coughed up more blood.

"You will fail," he said, gasping, his dreadlocks covering his face. "I'll never join you. You'll have to kill me."

Estelle reached down and grabbed the man by the collar of

his robe. She pulled him in close with burning rage coursing through her blood. She resisted the urge to throw him into the wall.

"We belong together," she said through gritted teeth. "I've seen what you truly are. You terrify the people because they cannot see you as I can. I would allow you to be your true self."

"You're insane," the man said, laughing.

She sneered.

"You'll live your life in a cage and watch as I rule this wretched city. My congregation has seen my inevitable ascension."

"You mean your religious extremists? Yes, they scream sanity."

"Say what you will, but more and more join me every day. The only thing that matters in Eve's Hollow is power. As long as you have power, anything is possible."

She reached up to scratch his face with fingernails grown into sharp claws. She dug into his cheek and slowly raked him down to the chin. His protesting hands could not stop her. She dug in deeper and crimson trickled down her fingers. At the sight, she giggled like a child.

"Enough of your babble," Estelle said, licking her fingers. "I can sense deeper energy than you're showing... You're stalling. Another draining for you."

Estelle took hold of the man's shoulder with an armored hand. The other hand, bare, was set close to his chest. Heat rushed down her left arm and her claws extended three inches. The man's eyes widened, and he grabbed her wrist, but he was weaker than she. She pressed her claws into his flesh, scraping bone. He groaned and bent forward, but Estelle forced him to sit up.

Crackling red energy formed at her shoulder and bounced its way down her arm. Once it arrived at her hand, it engulfed the man. He gritted his teeth and grunted as Estelle drew his very life force from him. Warbling and the smell of burning flesh filled the room. After a minute, she let the man fall, panting and coughing. She peered down at him and felt a sickness in her stomach. Seeing him so feeble made her want to wretch. She turned her back on him and approached the door.

"Demella," the man called, gasping.

Estelle stopped, then looked over her shoulder.

"Yes, Supernova?"

"This isn't going to end the way you think it is. It never does for people like you and If you keep walking this path, you'll be buried right next to me. That is, if I don't get you first."

"My love. The day you defeat me is the day I crawl back to the Void."

Estelle exited the cell. She made her way through the crowd of hooded zealots and through a series of near pitch black halls. She came to a dark room empty of furnishings except a wall of bookshelves filled to the edges with tomes and a short, dark wood bureau sitting against the far wall. A large oval mirror adorned it, edges lined with pearl shards. It stood about as tall as herself and radiated a red miasma, filling the small chamber.

Estelle adjusted it and peered in, the reflection not her own. She was so pale she could be mistaken for dead. Long, wild black hair fell down her shoulders and across her forehead. She wore a silver tiara fitted with three stones: a ruby and onyx set in silver with a gold traced diamond between them, but in a large square. Jagged, black markings originated around her piercing orange eyes and fell down her cheeks, mouth and neck. Forming a figure eight around her throat and dipping between her breasts was the black outline of a snake eating its own tail.

She became trapped by her own gaze. Cold, glowing

orange slivers of humanity suffocating in a pool of misery and torment. Their sight was dedicated, sadistic, soulless and hateful. More than anything, the eyes were still and empty. They were like stillness before a predator strikes and they were hatred incarnate.

# CHAPTER 10

## 4-1

Estelle's emerald eyes sagged with fatigue as she stared at her reflection in the bathroom mirror. At four-thirty-eight in the morning, she found herself restless and unable to sleep. The tiles were a mixture of blue, green and teal with the counter and sink made of azure alabaster. Estelle winced as she ran her fingers through her dry, tangled hair.

As she studied herself, she noticed something peculiar. A thin scar wrapped itself in a ring around her neck and she had no recollection of how she received it. She touched a finger to it and swift visions of a snowy forest flashed in her mind. There was red splatter in the snow and a headless body. Then, just for an instant, the face in the mirror turned haggard and wrinkled; gone in the blink of an eye.

"What is wrong with me?" she asked her reflection.

"What's bothering you?" her crow asked, hopping forward on the counter. "You've barely slept."

"I had a terrible dream. It felt as real as my words right now." The crow titled its head. "I think... I think I saw my Guardian. I called him Supernova. He was in this prison cell being beaten."

"I'm not sure what to make of that."

"Welcome to my world."

Dark mist filled the glass and Estelle jolted upright, backing away. It turned deep maroon and took the shape of a man standing behind her. She whirled around, yet no one was there.

"Estelle?" her crow said, waddling closer. "What's the matter?"

"He's back."

Cast in dark red was the shade of Damian Grigori, alongside Estelle's reflection.

"So you live," he said. "Are you enjoying your stay?"

"Leave me alone," Estelle said, leaning over the sink. "Just go away."

"Why? Have you found all the answers? Do you need no more wisdom to make it home?"

The beginning of a shout rose in her throat, but the guards that patrolled Sherman Manor came to mind. She dwelled on the lonely city streets, the Punished, the serpent and her choking nightmare.

"Fine," she said. "What do you have to tell me?"

"That you aren't doing as bad as I expected. But you could do better."

"I am doing better." Her angry voice echoed harshly off the tile. "I'm going to earn a favor to get me where I need to go. Find the key. Find the Guardian. Get home."

Damian cackled.

"What good is finding your next key when you don't know what to do with it? You haven't even opened the door for your first key."

"Pray tell, Father. How would I open the door?"

"You must be willing to face what's behind it."

"What does that mean?"

"Learn not to fear the past you hate so much. Learn discipline and wisdom as I've been trying to teach you your whole life. Do that and you'll find your way home."

"You're as vague as always. You never could just tell me what you want. It was always a riddle; always a lesson."

"Do you think you're above learning something new?"

"What could you teach me? How to control the world with money? How to neglect my kids?"

"Careful." Damian's voice dropped, and it reverberated between her ears. "What would you have if not for me? The only reason you have options is because of my blessings. Other families have to send their daughters to be nurses or waitresses. My wealth provided you with the luxuries to be a dancer or musician. You think Nina has that option?"

"I-"

"That girl works in a cotton mill to help her parents. Every day after school and for ten hours on the weekends. The idea of working was repulsive to you; securing a job was never even a consideration. You were always content to criticize my methods, but quick to enjoy the benefits. Is that what you're going to do with these people? Use them for their resources and abandon them- as you would do to me?"

Estelle ground her teeth as she beamed at the man in the mirror. Her breathing quickened, but before she could speak, Damian's scarlet image melted away, leaving whining silence in her ears. She sighed as her head hung low.

"What did he say this time?" her crow asked.

"The same thing he always says. That I'm not good enough."

Estelle ran a finger across her scar, anticipating more flashes, but nothing came. She left the bathroom and, heading right, wandered the second floor halls. The detail on marble statues standing between the windows was impressive. Each one depicted a different magnificent being. Some wore crowns of spikes, some had angelic wings and others held objects of importance, according to their plaques.

The sky beyond the window had gained an orange glow on the horizon, forcing the wine colored night to flee. White lines of static appeared on the shield and blipped away if one focused enough to see them. Guards patrolled the borders both inside and out and their silhouettes glided back and forth.

Continuing down another corridor, Estelle checked the different rooms. To the left, the first door, painted red and adorned with silver cherub designs, led to a theater. Multiple rows of seats stretched from the back to the front, where a large wooden stage obscured the wall. Long, lush red curtains draped the sides, framing a gold backdrop.

The second door on the left was dark green with designs of simple gold leaves. This room had many round tables with stools surrounding them. In the far right corner, a bar took up half the front and right walls. The wood was a beautiful dark red, and dusty glasses hung above the serving area. Bottles lined the mirrored walls behind the bar. As Estelle moved on, a sweet aroma filled her nose.

She made her way to the rear of the corridor, where the windows ceased and more rooms replaced them. The scent of honey and lemons drew her to a royal blue door adorned with gold musical notes. She entered a large white room full of instruments. Cellos and violins, trumpets and trombones lay strewn across scattered chairs. Near one window was a large, flat shape covered by a tan sheet.

Flying through the door, the crow landed on the windowsill. Estelle pulled the sheet back, revealing a polished white grand piano. Her eyes grew wide, and a smile formed. She ran her hand across the reflective surface. Some sort of hard coating made the keys iridescent blue. She drew the bench and toyed with the notes. Before she knew it, her hands had dedicated themselves to *Beethoven's Für Elise.* She only stopped once she realized the hour; a few minutes after five. She sighed and replaced the lid.

"You're quite talented," the crow said.

"It's one of my dreams," Estelle replied, tracing the shining keys. "To play around the world."

"I'm glad they're still alive. It's easy to lose hope in these circumstances."

"My dreams are the only thing I have to hold on to. Playing music, dancing, being with Marcel... He must wonder where I am. And my father must be furious. It'd be too much to hope for him to worry."

"Yet you see him here in the Hollow."

"My head hasn't been right since I woke up here."

"Don't be so sure. Hauntings are common in Eve's Hollow for most everyone. The spiritual nature of the Seeker's journey means you will face your hauntings or be trapped in this realm forever. I'm sure your true father would worry if he knew where you were."

"*Forever?*" The words came out as if she had been slapped. "When I said I wanted to get away from him, this isn't what I meant."

"Maybe it isn't him you're trying to escape?"

Estelle rolled her eyes and returned to the hallway, retracing her steps to the bedroom. She was just in time to hear the voices of several people standing at the top of the stairs. Among them were Ransley and Mike.

"There she is!" said Mike.

"We were wondering where you'd gone," Ransley said. "We're just about to head down to breakfast."

After a filling meal of danishes, fruit crisps, pancakes and chopped potatoes, Estelle, her crow and Ransley explored the manor grounds. A surprisingly pleasant demeanor awaited them. The survivors were in high spirits despite the battle taking place the night before and they socialized as the blood orange sky turned scarlet.

They ventured to the Northern yard, behind the manor. Two acres of land served as a training ground with an obstacle course, firing range, and a wide patch of dirt where they studied hand-to-hand combat. No one was practicing, though.

A tight circle of civilians and soldiers shouted and laughed, calling cheers like *"Go, Raphael!"* and *"You can't be beat!"* Once Estelle and Ransley arrived at the back of the huddle, curiosity pushed them into the crowd.

The crow took to Ransley's shoulder as they slipped in sideways. They came to the edge of an opening of where the soldiers left a circle fifteen feet wide. Sue paced within, watching two young men sparring hand to hand. The dominant one, a husky boy of eighteen or nineteen, had the leaner freckle-faced boy in a headlock, though not fully clenched.

"Don't get sloppy on me guys," Sue said. "You're starting to look like wrestling puppies out there! You've almost got him, DJ! I thought you knew how to get out of the headlock, Raphael!"

Keeping his hand on the bend of DJ's arm, Raphael slipped his head of red hair out. He rolled away, and both jumped up, raising their fists. DJ threw several punches that Raphael blocked before tackling his legs. He hooked them, forcing DJ to fall back. While his arms flailed to catch him, Raphael pounced, stepping on his arm and pulling his fist back.

"Match!" Sue said. "That's another win for Raphael."

"Four in a row, baby!" he said, flexing his biceps to the roaring crowd as Sue helped his opponent up.

"Don't forget about sportsmanship," she said to Raphael. "Ages ago, when the cities competed against each other, they strove to maintain a competitive yet *friendly* conduct."

"You're right, I'm sorry." Raphael offered a handshake, only to pull his hand away from DJ at the last moment. "But like you said, teacher, that was ages ago."

Raphael laughed along with a small section of the crowd while his opponent glared. Like a bull, DJ attacked him from behind with reaching arms. Dust kicked up as Raphael turned to catch him. The two tussled in the dirt and Sue observed with a furrowed brow. While DJ took an early advantage with his wide arms, Raphael was more nimble, able to wriggle free. He wrapped the larger boy's arm behind his back and pinned him to the ground.

"You give up yet?" he asked, panting and grinning.

"That's enough," Sue said, waving him away.

Raphael applied pressure to the hold, and another soldier stepped forward to break it up and help DJ away. Raphael pranced around the circle, flexing, jumping and boasting. After coming to Estelle, he stopped so fast he nearly tumbled over. His grin widened as his eyes traced her hourglass figure. She crossed her arms and raised an eyebrow.

His face held the softness of youth even if it was thin enough to see his cheekbones. His nose was short and round and his face came to a defined cleft where the prickly beginnings of a beard formed. His wavy, burnt orange hair fell to the top of his shoulders and his bright blue eyes were wide and confident.

"I've got a new fan, I see," Raphael said, introducing himself. "I haven't seen you around. You are-"

"Not impressed," Estelle said to the young man's amusement.

"That's because you didn't see the last three matches. There's a reason all these people are cheering for me."

"Because you treat your friends like dirt? I might be new here, but I know that isn't how you treat people who fight beside you."

"You can't be weak on those streets, babe. If I had been anyone outside the manor, that would have meant death. We're the Sherman Manor Defense Force- are we not?!" The gathered soldiers cheered. "There aren't a lot of big settlements anymore and if we want to survive, we have to be tougher than anyone else."

"That doesn't give you the right to pick on someone weaker than you."

Raphael shook his head at her, then scratched his chin.

"I get it," he said. "You're a woman-"

"Excuse me?" Sue said, humanity receding from her eyes.

"Women are best at nurturing. Not saying they can't fight. We have many fine women serving with us. But sometimes we have to put love and caring aside for survival."

"I understand plenty," Estelle said, inches from his face. "You're an asshole."

"Too bad you're a girl, or I'd show you like I showed DJ." He scoffed and reached for her cheek. "I'd hate to dirty that pretty face, though."

Estelle slapped his hand away. "Don't let that stop you."

"Stand down, Raphael," Sue said.

"I can handle him," Estelle said fiercely.

Estelle removed her blue dress, shoving it in Ransley's hands and leaving her clad in black leggings, boots and a long-sleeved black shirt. Despite everyone's protests, she headed toward the center of the circle. A group of boys, similar in age to him, hyped him up while questioning if he would need help to defeat her. Estelle turned her body sideways and put her open palms up, her left slightly ahead of her right. Raphael took a wrestling stance, smiling at her with a lock of his hair hanging down the left side of his face.

"It's not too late to quit." He smirked.

"I'll quit after you do."

The jovial young man threw a couple of playful punches her way, short enough that they would not connect. A rush of adrenaline spiked in Estelle and she caught his third punch, twisting under his arm, dropping and pulling his weight so he would tumble over. The audience gasped as Raphael swept her leg, leaving her sprawled on her back. Both combatants regained their footing and squared off again.

Raphael, covered in dirt, took on a more serious disposition. They exchanged punches and blocks with Raphael grazing her cheek. He smirked again and heat rose in the woman's face. She cast a rage filled punch, but he anticipated it. He caught her arm the same way she did to him and spun her, pinning the limb behind her back. The more she pulled away, the tighter he held, wrapping his other arm across her abdomen and gripping her free wrist. The crowd murmured and looked at Sue to intervene, but she watched in silence.

"What did I tell you?" he said with a snicker. "You're just not strong enough."

Estelle hooked her foot around his heel and, with a grunt, pushed herself backward. They fell, and she used her body weight to knock the wind from his lungs. His grip relaxed, but she kept hold of his hand. With the flexibility of a vine, she clenched Raphael's arm between her legs and extended them across his chest. With all her strength, she bent the limb back, causing Raphael to scream out. He rolled and thrashed, but she held like tempered steel.

"Say it!" Estelle said through gritted teeth. "Say it or I'll break your arm!"

"Stop!" he said with glossy eyes. "Let me go!"

With one last bend as a warning, she released him. Raphael

clamored to his feet and watched her with wide, curious eyes as he held his elbow. For several seconds, the silence resonated like a bell, then like a bomb, the crowd erupted in cheers and applause. Estelle expected Raphael to attack again, but he slipped away through the gathering as Sue hugged her. The people closed in as well, asking her so many questions, she could answer none.

"Give her some space!" Sue said in a boom of a command.

Many of them laughed, but gave her a few feet of room.

"That was quite the display," Ransley said, handing over her dress. "Where'd you learn to fight like that?"

"Madame Katherine's martial arts electives," she said with a smile.

"Whatever that was," Sue said. "You've got to teach us some. Raphael has been at the top of his class for three months. I didn't think anyone could best him. Just between us, he needed to be checked."

"It was my genuine pleasure."

With pats on her shoulders and back, the crowd dispersed. Lingering behind was a lone woman. The warm ivory of her skin was unblemished, a perfect canvas. Her cheekbones sat high on her face and red lips smiled above a sharp jawline. Her eyes shone like dark gems beneath the moonlight and she wore a long green dress that hugged her slim figure, accompanied by a black jacket. She walked so elegantly, her steps could have been mistaken for a glide.

"Hey there, miss Nona," Sue said. "Estelle, Ransley, this is our fearless leader. Nona, these are the two that saved Mike's backside."

"I'm happy to meet you both," Nona said, bowing her head. "Why don't you come up to my office so we can talk more comfortably?"

# CHAPTER 11

# THE TALE OF THE BLUE KEY MASSACRE

In Nona's third-floor office, the medium green walls seemed to absorb the light, contrasting with the heavy gold curtains that draped the tall window behind her desk, creating an air of quiet authority. There were bookshelves against the walls and two marble reliefs of eagles flanking the door. In place of the chandelier hung a gaudy lantern. Panes of stained glass decorated the spacing of its iron bars. Two red leather chairs sat before the desk, which Estelle and Ransley occupied, the crow beside its Seeker.

"The Pale Lady has been a constant threat," Nona said from her brown leather armchair. "Thankfully, she hasn't found this location, but last night was the third engagement we've had with her. It'll only be a matter of time. So if you're looking for a new home, be aware of that fact."

"I wish I could stay," Estelle said. "But..."

"We need something else," the crow said.

Nona's eyebrows rose.

Estelle shifted in her seat, picking at her fingernails.

"We hoped to acquire an escort," Ransley said. "We're en

route to Kern Museum in Northern Kollektra. One of those trucks and a couple of soldiers would be more than enough."

"Understand our position. The SMDF might seem imposing, but we need every single member. There are patrols, training exercises, and keeping the nasties at bay. I am curious, though. What's so important about some ancient museum?"

Mae's words rang out in Estelle's mind. *Be careful who you tell all of that.*

"There's a friend waiting for me," Estelle said.

"They must be quite special. There's nothing up that way except for E.A.Es."

"E.A.Es?"

"That's what we call all the stronger monsters. Eve's Advanced Entities; Ogres, Dreamers, Praeformae."

"They all sound horrid," Ransley said. "Fortunately, the Punished are what I have most experience with. I've seen one or two Praeformae."

"I'll never get used to seeing those man beasts. Have you encountered them, Estelle?"

"I haven't," the Seeker said.

"They're creatures that feed on whatever they can find. They take on the traits of whatever they eat as a form of camouflage. Rats, birds- humans. The results aren't pretty. They're cowardly, but if they're hungry enough, they'll attack anything. Could you imagine? A thing trying to mimic your face?"

Estelle watched Nona for a time. The leader's eyes were bold and daring as she leaned forward.

"Definitely not," Estelle said. "But whatever's out there, I need to get to that museum. It's my only chance to get home."

"Home? Meaning?"

"All I can say is I have someone waiting there who is going to help me get where I need to go. You asked when we sat down if there was anything you could do to repay us for saving Mike. One car with one driver."

"Are you suggesting saving one life is worth risking another?"

Nona's stare made Estelle cast hers toward the carpet. Though she needed help, the woman was correct: would it be worth saving one life if it meant sacrificing another? Any number of things could happen in the depths of the city without the slightest hint that Nona's soldier would return. She would be responsible.

"She's not saying that," the crow said. "Estelle does not belong in Web Obsidia, and the one person meant to help her is forty miles away. We must proceed on foot without your assistance. What good is an army if a single soldier would not help a woman in distress?"

Nona eyed the crow, then looked Estelle up and down.

"She seems to know how to handle herself," Nona said. "Poor Raphael ran away without a word."

"He had it coming," Estelle said. "I watched him beat on his teammate then laugh about it. Is that who your soldiers are? Bullies?"

"I'll admit our younger recruits get too eager. But Sue will train that out of them. And perhaps you should show a little more gratitude for the force that saved you from the Torch-bearers."

"It is not gratitude she lacks," the crow said with a chirp that sounded like a laugh. "Just patience."

Nona played with a gold pen, twirling it between her fingers. She sat back and crossed her legs.

"I sense there's something you aren't telling me," she said. "I'm responsible for the safety of these people. If you bring danger to us, you will be subject to our laws. I'll ask you just once: Is there anything I need to know?"

The milk white crow landed on Nona's desk and hopped

toward her, watching with black eyes more human than animal.

"Estelle is my Seeker," it said. "She has come here on a spiritual journey. My purpose is to guide her through it. She received a letter leading us to the museum, so once we unite, we can proceed with her trials. We seek the Supernova Swordsman."

"You know the swordsman?" Nona asked.

"We haven't met yet," Estelle said.

Images flashed in her mind of the nightmare. Supernova's bleeding wounds, the smell of smoke and blood, the humming that made its nest in the back of her mind.

"Do you know him?" Ransley asked.

"I know of him," Nona said. "Have you heard of the Blue Key massacre, Estelle?"

"Ransley mentioned it to me," she said. "That pale woman killed half a settlement."

"She did that and more. She leveled city blocks. Civilians died. The Blue Key's leader fought, but it was his apprentice in the swordsman who waged true war against the Pale Lady. It's referred to as the Three-Day Storm."

"You never said the swordsman was involved, Ransley."

The old man shrugged. "We all know of that event, but I did not know it was your Guardian who battled her."

"The man is a mystery, to be sure," Nona said. "But therein lies the issue. If this person is supposed to be your companion, how could the Pale Lady not be involved? How can I send my people with you? How could you guarantee their safety?"

Every option she thought of was met by the snake, the Punished or the storm wraiths.

"Maybe we can split the difference." Estelle said. "Give us one vehicle; the oldest, least useful one. As long as it runs, I'll figure the rest out. That way, no one else gets dragged in."

Nona contemplated her words. Estelle's eyes were wide and sincere, with a group of wrinkles on her forehead.

"Keep out of trouble. Show you can contribute, and I think I can part ways with an old truck."

A soft knock came from the door. When it opened, a depressed Raphael waited in the entry, his eyes fixed on the floor. They grew wide when he and Estelle saw each other. His long burnt orange hair hung in his face, obscuring his sullen expression, a petty glare peeking through.

"Ah, Raphael," Nona said pleasantly.

"Mae is ready for the demonstration," he said.

A group of two dozen SMDF soldiers socialized before a long folding table at the edge of the training yard, Raphael mingling among them. Each man and woman had been selected to view a secret project that occupied what little free time Mae had. Upon the table was an assortment of weapons; firearms, bullets, grenades, and melee weapons such as knives, crowbars and metal bats. A small metal box sat at the center of the table. Four glass tubes were arranged on top of each corner, with copper plates fastened to the sides. Cables ran from the front to a small black platform about the size of a serving tray.

Each of the ranking soldiers attended, with Sue, Theo and Mike standing beside the table while Mae fiddled with a duffle bag beside the box. Estelle, her crow, Ransley and Nona observed a perplexed crowd.

"Everyone ready?" Mae asked.

The woman turned to the table and picked up the metal bat. She placed the hitting end on the plate and flipped a switch atop the box. The unit hummed, the tubes gaining a blue glow with sparks arcing between them. The glow extended to the copper plates, then ran down the cable. To everyone's astonishment, the bat absorbed the energy.

After a minute, Mae turned the box off and picked up the weapon. It left faint radiation trails as she waved it. She picked up a small pipe, tossed it up and swung at it. When the bat made contact, it let off a small pop and the light of a tiny reaction. The pipe went flying and came to rest about twenty yards away. It glowed red hot and smoke rose from it.

"What the hell was that?!" Estelle asked.

The crowd murmured and questioned the demonstration with mixed emotions.

"So," Nona said. "This is your secret project?"

"I'm pretty proud of it," Mae said, smirking. "I found a way to channel the shield's power into our weapons. It gives metal objects their own unstable electromagnetic field. Upon impact, it produces a small reaction that super heats the target."

The interested soldiers drew closer, staring at the glowing box.

"Are you sure that's safe?" Sue asked.

"As long as you're not on the receiving end."

"How does it work?" Ransley asked.

"It's complicated."

Theo nudged Mae's side, and she shot him an aggressive look.

"I'm sure you can dumb it down," he said. "At least for those of us who aren't technologically inclined?"

She acquiesced with a sigh.

"The shield surrounding us is a magnetic barrier," Mae said. "A generator in the basement produces a nuclear grid's worth of power. It's channeled through wires to the four corners of the property and a device on the roof gives it structure. All I've done is use the same energy to charge our weapons."

"If that's what it can do for a bat," Mike said. "Imagine what it'll do for our bullets and grenades."

"Slow down, wild man," Mae said, raising an eyebrow. "We're starting slow. Just handguns today- if Nona approves."

The leader watched Mae for a time with hands on her hips.

"As long as it's safe to use," Nona said, nodding. "I haven't doubted your skills in the time I've known you, Mae. I won't start now. Have you done any field testing?"

"I was thinking Theo and Mike could bring them on patrol this afternoon."

"Patrols are fine, but hunting the Punished for an experiment? Is that such a good idea when the Pale Lady attacked yesterday?"

"Maybe Mae's invention will finally best her," Theo said, chuckling.

"I want to go with them!" Raphael exclaimed.

Several soldiers looked at the young man, as did Nona, a skeptical expression on her face.

"Absolutely not!" a voice said from the ranks.

A man stepped forward. Standing over the other soldiers, he was imposing with burly shoulders. A thicket of a beard colored rust and silver partially hid his face. A prominent brow cast shadows over his deep brown eyes and a black beanie covered his head.

"Come on dad," Raphael said, his shoulders drooping. "I'm ready!"

"I'm afraid I must agree with your father, Raphael," Nona said. "You only started training three months ago."

"You're not ready," the boy's father said. "And your mother would never forgive me."

"I *am* ready!" The young man glared at his father, trying to match the stoic demeanor. "I swear I'll be careful and stay near the truck."

"Maybe it'll do the boy some good, Ralph," Mike said, though he sounded unsure.

"He's only twenty, Mike. What's out there will change him. I just want my son to keep his innocence a little longer. I just can't allow it."

Everyone fell silent. Nona and Sue both looked compassionately toward the father. Mike, Theo and several of the other soldiers seemed disappointed, though none more than Raphael. His head was bent down, and he clenched his fists so tight they could have bled.

"Hey," Ralph said, approaching his son. "Later on, we'll do some target practice. Just you and me. Would that be okay?"

Defeated, Raphael nodded.

"Alright, everyone," Nona said. "We've got to get back to it. You're all doing an excellent job. Theo and Mike are the only ones leaving the compound, along with other *scheduled* patrols. The casualties from last night weren't as bad as they could have been, but we still lost thirty people to the Torchbearers. Your safety means more to me than anything. We're taking a step back until things cool down."

"*If* they do," Mike said. "I share the sentiment about our safety, but that's why we need to keep pushing. The witch won't let up. It ain't like we're gonna be friendly neighbors. Eventually she goes or we do."

"I'm aware of that." Nona was stern and unshakable. "There's no profit in rushing in before we've found a definitive way to win. It would cost more lives. We will beat her. Not today, but we will."

Mike opened his mouth to debate, but he met Sue's glance.

"I have to go check on the cultivation situation," she continued. "So, if there's nothing else, leaders?"

Mike, Sue, Theo and Mae shook their heads, and with a

quick nod, Nona departed. Sue cleared her throat and addressed the crowd.

"Alright guys," she said, projecting. "We're heading to range two! Let's move!"

The group walked in unison, following their current commanding officer. They gathered at the firing range, some fifty yards away. Mae was kneeling down by the side of the table to a lump of cloth Estelle had not noticed before. Beneath was another duffle back that she dragged atop the table.

"What's in there?" asked Ransley.

"Mae made us some new toys," Theo said.

"Didn't want to make the others jealous," Mae said, unzipping the bag. "I went to a lot of trouble to make these for our top two."

First, from the bag were matching handguns. They were slim and made of a dark silver alloy with identical pearl grips. Mike's gun bore red highlighted areas, whereas Theo's displayed blue. They came with six eight-round magazines, and she repeated the charging process with them.

"Those are the kids. And these...," she said, hunching back down and reemerging with two long assault rifles. "Are the fathers."

Ransley whistled as she laid them on the table for Theo and Mike. The men took them up like children on Christmas morning. It was the first time Estelle had seen Mike appear genuinely happy. His old face curved into a smirk and he scoffed to himself. The rifles were black with traces of red and blue accents, respectively. The magazines Mae presented already produced the glow of the charge.

"These are great, Mae," Theo said. "You've really outdone yourself."

"I gotta agree," Mike said. "This might be the game changer we need."

"Be careful before we know that," Mae replied. "The testing I've done is minimal. I basically made sure the bullets wouldn't explode in the barrel. This will be their first taste of action, so treat it like you would any other day in the Web."

"Don't worry, Mae," Theo said. "We're reckless, but we don't have a death wish. I swear we'll be careful."

"I expect to see everyone at dinner and in once piece."

Theo and Mike agreed, then made way toward the parked vehicles lined beside the obstacle course. Mae returned to the manor's workshops, her work never finished.

Ransley caught sight of something and nodded his head toward it. Raphael returned, his hands dug in the pockets of his navy blue pants, and holding his head high. Estelle smirked at him, placing her hands on her hips.

"Can we talk alone?" Raphael asked.

"I don't see why," the crow said. "Whatever is good enough for her to hear is good enough for me."

"I'll manage," Estelle said to her familiar. "Go with Ransley. I'll catch up in a few minutes."

"Oh, I don't doubt it," Ransley said. "Behave, you two."

The crow perched on the old man's arm, and they left.

"What do you want?" Estelle asked.

"I hear you're looking for some favor around here," Raphael said.

Estelle's eyes narrowed. "What business is that of yours?"

"You're not one to sit around and wait for approval. I can tell. What if I showed you a way to earn everyone's respect?"

"Even if I believed you- and I don't- why would you help me?"

"I can admit you surprised me during our fight. If I'd have been serious from the beginning, it would have turned out different. But we want the same thing. We both want to prove ourselves to the leaders."

"What makes you think I need your help? I made it this far on my own."

"You don't have to accept my offer. I just figured you weren't the type to work in the kitchen or do yard duty. Those are jobs they give to anyone they don't know what to do with. You'll earn their trust, eventually. But what if there's a way to make a bigger impact?"

## CHAPTER 12

———

## THE DREAMER

Theo reached into the back seat of the truck, pulling a satchel into his lap. He unzipped it and rummaged though as Mike drove down the road. Their rifles from Mae rested on the back seat, the magazines glowing. Theo inspected his pearl-handled pistol, a medical pack, as well as a small velvet bag that he caressed with two fingers. He peered through the window, counting the Punished that followed them in vain.

"Think she'll be out there?" Theo asked.

"What's your gut tell you?" Mike said.

"She's busy with bigger things. The small fry are out, so the predators aren't around."

"If she's distracted, it could be a good chance to finish the job."

"I know you want her head on a plate, but we don't have the intel for that yet."

"Don't act like you don't want her dead, too."

"I don't wish death on anyone, man. I'll admit that might be the only way to stop her, but if there were another option, I'd take it."

"Like what?" Mike laughed. "What are you going to do? Put her in jail? Send her to therapy? Put her on chore rotation?"

"I've heard stories and rumors. Seen all kinds of things. You never know how it'll play out."

"There's only one way when it comes to the witch."

Theo said nothing, and Mike's brows raised.

"Almost seems like you feel bad for her, Theo."

"I do," Theo said, blunt as a butter knife. "Plenty of things in the Hollow are born messed up. They're monsters from the start. I've also seen people turned and twisted into things. Like the Punished. They were all once human. We kill them because we have to, but once upon a time they had hopes and dreams, families and friends. Jobs, for God's sake! We do what we have to, but that doesn't mean we have to be monsters like them."

There was another moment of silence between the two as Mike turned down a long main road.

"You're not wrong," Mike said. "But that attitude can get you killed out here. There's men out there who'd kill you for your shoes. I don't want to see something happen to you, friend."

"Likewise," Theo said, smiling. "Speaking of- we play it safe, yeah?"

Theo's friend nodded. "We can't take too long, anyway. They'll figure out we're not on patrol and assume the worst. We're just looking for anyone who survived that fight."

"Providing they didn't get eaten."

Theo and Mike drove well beyond the boundaries of their patrol area in District 5 and into District 7, where they battled the serpent. Mike slowed the truck, and the two searched for Punished, but only heard distant groans through the cracked windows. Mike pulled over.

The street was fifty yards across, with a concrete median

dividing it. Street-level fog enveloped the monumental mills and forges, obscuring vision beyond thirty feet.

Theo hopped out and opened the rear door. He took up his new rifle, ensuring the safety was off, and Mike did the same. To ensure silent attacks, both weapons included suppressors. Theo kept the satchel at his side and checked it once more before the two set off.

A shrieking creature in the distance gave them pause as they left the vehicle behind. They listened intently to the wind. The red fog dimmed and evening would be upon them sooner than later.

Mike and Theo walked faster as they eagerly made their way toward the battle site. Not eager to be there, but eager to find an ally in need or a survivor looking for safety; anything to make the trip worth it.

Mike held his fist up with his arm at a right angle. They both stopped and held their guns close. Shuffling could be heard and the rantings of several Punished.

"I hate it here," one said loudly. "I love... Love hating it here!"

"To serve is to die," another Punished said. "To die is to serve. To live is to suffer! To die! To die!"

The men looked through the murk and made out several human shapes. Four Punished paced in a small circle, hardly aware of their surroundings at all. Two more laid on the ground, their hands reaching up toward the gloomy garnet sky.

"Three for you, three for me," Theo said quietly.

"Not if I get them all first," Mike said with a smirk.

Theo shot first, killing a grounded Punished. Mike shot one just as it looked over at him. Its skin was sickly gray and green and its stomach hung bloated to the thighs. Mike shot through its face, but didn't finish it. Another round to the brain fixed that.

The remaining four Punished turned their hate-filled eyes to the duo and charged. They howled with rage, rotting hands grasping, but it was over quickly. The rifles sputtered, ending the skirmish with the sound of empty shells ringing against the pavement.

Theo turned to face the opposite direction of Mike, and the two held their positions for about a minute. They aimed their guns down the streets and the alleys, waiting to be attacked by more. When none came, they relaxed. Mike kept his gun up, and Theo hurried to the closest of the slain. The man laying in the street was bald with a tuft of hair on his chin. His hands were worn to the bone, being held together by tendons. His eyes were dark, and he remained motionless as Theo examined the bullet holes.

Skin around the entry wounds was seared and the passage of the bullet left a faint blue smoke that wafted like incense. Theo ran his fingers across the wound and studiously inspected the damage. He took a combat knife from his belt and cut a chunk of flesh out, placing it in a small plastic bag and shoving it in his satchel.

"Mae will be grateful for this sample," Theo said, standing.

They neared an intersection. The fog was thinning, but still left a rose-colored tint. Mike and Theo approached a cafe with broken windows to their right and a public park diagonal from that. A couple blocks further was where the worst of the battle happened and slumped, bloated shadows came into view.

"Hear that?" Theo asked. "People talking."

"They don't sound injured," said Mike. "Maybe scavenging the trucks."

Proceeding with caution, they crept forward until the glow of torches was visible through the fog. Half a dozen shadowy figures stood in a circle, humming a low, melancholy tune. They inched closer, sticking to the alleys and walls as much as they could.

"There are only two options," a deep voice said. It was husky, domineering and rumbled as if it were painful to speak. "You either join the Lady and the ranks of Bleedstar- or you join the slave pit."

Theo raised his gun to shoot, but Mike rested his hand atop the barrel. Glinting outlines of weapons- guns, hatchets and machetes were in the enemy's hands. The speaker was very tall, standing around seven feet and built like a castle. His torch hovered higher than all the others and he held in his other hand a heavy battle axe with wide, jagged blades. Theo tapped Mike on the shoulder and pointed. Just beyond the man were three shades, kneeling. The glow of the torches gave just enough light to see the dark green uniforms.

"You needn't worry," the man continued. "If you serve and you obey, you will be rewarded. If you don't, you'll be damned to labor until you die. If you rebel- well, you've already had a taste of Nagira's venom... What say you?"

"I'd never help you," said one of the kneeling men.

The Torchbearers cackled.

"If you all feel the same, we'll see if a few weeks in the pit make you change your mind. Bring them."

The torches moved as the kneeling soldiers were forced to their feet. Theo looked urgently to Mike.

"It's now or never," he whispered.

The two raised their rifles. Theo aimed at the large man and rested his finger on the trigger.

"Help me!" a voice shouted from behind.

"Raphael!" Estelle yelled, followed by the sound of a Punished.

"Death!" it said. "Death to the Blamed!"

Theo and Mike spun around to see the young pair less than twenty yards away. Mike raised his gun and fired at the creature, knocking it away from Raphael. Theo turned back to his original target to see four torches heading toward them.

"Who's there?" one Torchbearer called. "Show yourselves!"

Theo nodded toward the youngsters. Mike moved away, keeping as low to the ground as a lizard. Theo put his gun down, raised his arms, and stepped forward. By the time the bearers arrived, Mike had already hurried Estelle and Raphael into a nearby alley. Three hooded figures approached, two guns aimed at Theo's chest. The middle figure spoke.

"You look well fed," a woman said in a tired, spiteful voice. "Same colors as the prisoners, so I assume you're from the same group. Where are the others you came with?"

"What others?" Theo asked with a chuckle. "I came looking for survivors, but you're the first people I've seen. I just want to get those folks back to their families."

"Presumptuous of you. The Lady has claimed them as prisoners of war. You weren't captured, but you're more than welcome to join them."

"No!" the man with the axe shouted. "We take all that we will. He comes with us!"

The Torchbearers stiffened, gripping their rifles and hatchets. Theo took a step back, but a bearer shot the ground near his feet. The crack of the shot rang out, getting softer as it bounced between the buildings and he froze. Every instinct in his body told him to feign compliance, then draw his gun as fast as he could. He knew Mike would back him up.

"Three more!" said a man from behind. "Hiding in the alley! Move!"

Theo turned to see Mike, Estelle and Raphael forced from their hiding spot at gunpoint. At first, Theo did not know who caught them. Then the faint red glow of flashlights emerged behind them. Two figures in dark brown and black clothes kept his friends in check. Under threat of gunfire, they were backed toward Theo so that all four of them formed a tight cluster.

"We have them, Toraesis," said the older woman with pride.

"Bind them," the axe wielder said. "All together, they make ten prisoners in a day. A fine haul."

A wild wind lurched through the streets, bringing with it heavy black smoke. Darkness enveloped the road, and all sound was sucked away. Pressure drew down on them and its pull was so great it nearly dragged the people from where they stood. Small patches on the ground bled sticky gray sludge. A slip in the gravity passed, one word slipped through.

"DREAMER!"

Panic swept across the intersection as black tentacles from the smoke appeared and latched onto anything not fastened to the ground. Two of the torchbearers were dragged away, their flames dying out with their screams. The bubble around them popped, and the sound rushed back. Screams and gunfire erupted, drowning the streets in auditory torture. Estelle and Raphael knelt with their hands over their heads as Mike and Theo shot at the ground, keeping the slimy tendrils at bay.

Toraesis violently cut them away, his axe taking on a scarlet glow. He swung his weapon with ferocity and great strength, but suddenly stopped as something drew his gaze upward.

Dark smog congealed before them, stretching up fifty feet. It made itself thin with most of the tentacles wriggling at the bottom. A round set of long, sharp teeth bore themselves at the top. Above them was a single luminous orange eye, a black slit looking wilding below. Its tentacles smashed into the ground and the surrounding alley walls before screeching loud enough to loose bricks from their foundations. Everyone clapped their hands over their ears and fell to their knees.

At the Dreamer's base, entwined in its smoking limbs, were the decaying cadavers of humans and the Punished. They stuck in the creature as if it were quicksand. The various stages of decomposition ranged from skeletons to the fresh men it had just taken. One of the Torchbearers struggled fruitlessly to escape his fate. His mouth moved, but no sound left.

Everyone with weapons, regardless of loyalty, attacked the Dreamer, sending a barrage of bullets at its eye. It screeched again as its tentacles lashed out in their direction. One of the red light bearers was struck and thrown into a brick wall, his bones producing a noticeable crack. He fell to the ground, crumpled and twitching.

Theo reached into his satchel and pulled out the small black velvet bag. He opened it as a lash swept as his legs. He rolled out of the way as solidified smoke crashed through the wall behind him. In the process of his dodge, the item flew from his hand and landed at Estelle's feet.

"Throw it here!" Theo yelled to her, pointing to it.

As Estelle took the bag up, a flailing tendril sent her flying into a metal mailbox. Though not with enough force to maim, the impact knocked the wind out of her. She curled up in a ball as she gasped to catch her breath, the bag clutched in her hand. Mike looked over to her and made as if he would rush to her, but another black whip attacked Raphael and Mike defended him.

Theo scrambled to his feet and stumbled to Estelle. He helped her to the alley, where they both collapsed. The woman sat against the rigid bricks, on the verge of hyperventilating. Theo forced himself up and rested his hands on her shoulders.

"Are you okay?" he asked, winded. "Estelle?"

She nodded, her face slick with sweat. She held the bag out for Theo and he grinned. He opened it and drew out a shrunken, mummified monkey's head. Estelle's nose twisted up with a grimace.

"Don't worry," Theo said, seeing her discomfort. "He's a friend. El Diablillo."

The small head glowed. At first, it took on a blue shimmer like the shield of Sherman Manor, but became more vibrant. A spark of light materialized and leaped from the small ornament, forming itself into a hyper realistic monkey. It was small and black fur covered his whole body with white fluff on its face. Its arms and legs were long, with a slender tail acting as a fifth limb. Around its neck was a thinly woven hemp necklace with a silver sun pendant. It happily jumped toward Theo.

"Guerrero!" Theo said. "I missed you, amigo. We need you guys. Bring some of the family."

Guerrero nodded, and scurried out to the street to observe the Dreamer. He let off a screech, challenging the monster. Theo's monkey head glowed once again and a small hoard of identical animals sprung forth. Ten, twenty, then fifty flooded out and followed Guerrero's charge against the Dreamer. The chittering mass raced across the street, leaping on to the tentacles and biting feverishly. They swarmed upon their enemy as it cried out in rage. Its tentacles retracted from their attack as it tried to free itself.

"Can you walk?" Theo asked Estelle.

She managed a nod.

"We gotta get Mike and Raphael, then our people out there. You stay here until it's time to leave."

Theo darted into the street, rushing to Mike and Raphael. The red-haired man seemed more a boy, panting and moaning, with Mike knelt beside him.

"His leg's broke, Theo," Mike said. He struggled to keep him still enough to render aid.

"I'm gonna go get the other three," Theo said. "Get him to that alley and wait for my signal to run."

"You're crazy," Mike said over Raphael's wales. "You'll get yourself killed!"

"I've got him," Estelle said.

Without waiting for their protest, the exhausted woman helped Raphael sit up. He put his arm around her shoulder.

"You've got to help me," she said. "I know it hurts, but we have to get out of the way."

With a cry of pain, Raphael shifted all his weight to his good leg. He was barely on his feet when a mighty roar came at them. Mike fired his gun full force at Toraesis, who rushed them with murderous intent in his black eyes. The man held his weapon before him and it created a red field that blocked the bullets. Theo joined his friend, and the combined force of the two guns was enough to push the enemy back. The remaining two torch bearers whisked the hostages away from the fight.

With shocking agility for a man so large, Toraesis dove away from the gunfire and hurled his axe. The blade behaved as if it had a mind of its own and spun toward Mike. Theo pulled him to the ground, and it flew over their heads. As it curved its way back, Mike and Theo turned to shoot, hoping to slow it. As soon as they turned their backs, Toraesis charged, drawing a pistol. He fired, hitting Mike in the middle of his back twice. He fell to the ground with a grunt and was still.

"Mike!" Theo screamed.

Theo dodged the returning axe as it spun to its owner and he fired once again upon the dark stranger. His red shield reconstructed, and he walked forward. He raised his pistol at Theo's head and smiled through the shadow of his beard. Just as he pulled the trigger, the ground shook, diverting the shot.

The Dreamer pulsed, gurgled and moaned. The same gravitational pull from its initial arrival returned and everything went silent again.

The screech from the beast was so loud this time, it pierced the hands over their ears. The monster produced a shockwave that shattered the monkeys and sent everything tumbling away; debris, vehicles and people.

~

Estelle did not know how much time had passed when she awoke on the floor of the cafe. Her back and legs ached and her throat was dry and sore. She lay on her back, trying to focus her eyes, making out the remains of a destroyed light fixture on the ceiling. She moved her hand, then her arm, feeling her head. Dots of blood wet her fingertips.

It took her several minutes to get to her feet, and she supported herself with a dilapidated counter. She limped toward the door, gritting her teeth with each step.

The streets were quiet, and the Dreamer was gone as far as she could tell. Stepping through the threshold, Estelle froze and held her breath, listening for any threats. She only exhaled when she saw her friend lying on the ground.

"Mike!" she said, her voice cracking.

She knelt beside him, remembering the two bullets he took. Estelle thought the worst and cold dread filled her body. Theo was nowhere to be found, and neither was Raphael. She left her crow back at the manor, fearing it would give her away as she snuck out on Raphael's dare. She knew she would not make it back, even with her map. She would surely die.

The woman's soul nearly fled her body when a breath escaped Mike's mouth. He coughed and groaned.

"Mike! How are you still alive?!" she asked.

"Vest," he said, clearing his lungs and spitting. "Still hurts like a bitch. What happened? Were those- monkeys?"

"You'd have to ask Theo. Everything was so chaotic. That thing screamed again, and I got thrown across the street. That's the last I remember."

"So Theo? Raphael?"

The woman shrugged, with lines of worry like trenches on her face. The Sherman Manor warrior rose and dusted himself off. He took up his rifle and checked it.

"We've got to go after them," Mike said.

"No," Estelle said. "We have to go back to the manor. We need soldiers and weapons. You saw that madman with the axe! What do you think you're going to do on your own?"

"I don't know, but I can't just let them get away. The longer we wait, the greater the chance that we never see our friends again. So I'm going."

"That's idiotic! You're going to die before you reach them."

Mike started down the street toward the truck, ignoring Estelle.

"You can't just leave me out here!" she said, glaring. "What am I supposed to do?"

"Do whatever you want, girl. I have bigger problems than you."

The Seeker blocked his path, and bared her teeth.

"I don't even know how to get back!"

"Who's fault is that?!" Mike rose, his blue eyes wide. "No one told you to hitch a ride in our truck! The point of saving you in Irontown was so you could be behind the shield- *safely*. What are you even doing out here?"

"That's my business." Estelle's lips clenched and Mike laughed.

"That's how you want to play it? Fine. I'm going back for the truck. When we get to Bleedstar, you can wait for me to get back."

"Bleedstar?" Estelle's face twisted. "You mean where that pale woman lives? Are you crazy?!"

He turned his back on her and began walking. She

watched him take a few steps, hoping he was bluffing. But he continued until his figure almost melted into the fog.

"I was trying to prove myself!" she said.

Mike looked over his shoulder as she rushed toward him. He turned to her and clasped his hands at his waist, studying the woman.

"I need a favor from your leader," Estelle said. "I need to make it to the Kern Museum and Nona said if I prove myself useful, she'd consider giving me a vehicle."

"If you wanted to be useful, you could have helped with the new recruits. You could have worked in the kitchen. What possessed you to come out here when you know you aren't ready? Is some dusty museum really worth risking your life?"

"I wish it weren't."

"And you won't tell me why?"

"I am sorry, Mike... I can't."

He inspected Estelle, wrinkles prominent in his quizzical face.

"I get it," he said. "There are things from my past I can't tell anyone. I want to trust you, but you're making it hard. I don't like to have to think about who's around me; not knowing what their real motives are."

"My only motive is to get to that museum. I don't want to hurt anyone, and I don't want to cause trouble. I've done enough of that." Images flashed in her mind of Clara's bloody, swollen face after using it to break a mirror. "Raphael said I could impress Nona by coming with you and Theo. We knew you wouldn't agree, so we stowed away in the truck. I didn't know this was going to happen."

"And your first instinct is to abandon Raphael? You both made a mistake and it might cost him his life."

"I didn't expect-"

"Let that be a lesson," Mike said with a scoff. "The unexpected can always happen. Neither you nor Raphael are ready for this- him less than you, but still. Regardless of what we want, I have to assume Theo was captured and he may not be able to wait. We go to Bleedstar and you hold down the vehicle until I get everyone out."

"That's the dumbest idea I've ever heard." Estelle laughed cynically. "You're going to walk into enemy territory and what- ask for our friends back? You'll die."

"Do you have a better plan?"

"Get. Help. I don't understand why we can't go back. More guns and more soldiers would-"

"Nona wouldn't do it!" Mike snapped. "She was already skeptical about us coming out here. If she knows we met the Torchbearers, she'll lock the manor down and cut her losses."

Estelle frowned. "She wouldn't do that."

"You don't think so? What do you think she'll do with you when she finds out you were a part of it? Think you'll get that vehicle?"

Estelle looked away and pursed her lips. *You will be subject to our laws,* Nona said. The Seeker imagined returning to Sherman Manor and having to explain to the leader that two members were lost because of her. What would they do with her? Lock her away? Banish her to the streets? Would Ransley abandon her? Mike's face softened, as if he could see the images in her mind. He motioned for her to follow.

The street was stained black from the Dreamer's tracks. Rotting body parts stuck to small piles of solid smoke left in its wake. Estelle scanned the alleys and roads, wondering what threat would emerge next. The woman felt a tug at the bottom of her dress.

Estelle jumped with a shout. Mike wheeled around, grasping his rifle, but confusion came over his face. The Seeker looked down to see a glowing blue monkey holding on to the end of her dress with a sad expression upon its face. A glimmer of light shone on Guerrero's silver sun pendant.

"What the..." Mike said.

"Guerrero!" Estelle said. "You survived!"

The monkey began chittering and waving his little arms about. Mike stared in disbelief, and Estelle tried to understand what he meant to convey. At the end of his babbling, Guerrero flopped to a sit with a frightened whimper.

"I've seen dogs and rats," Mike asked. "A few birds now and then, but never monkeys."

"Guerrero and his friends saved us from the Dreamer."

"Apparently, they didn't save Theo or the boy."

Guerrero began his chirping again and hurried to the street. He sniffed the ground, crossed the road and came back. The small animal touched the ground and before their eyes, a blue wisp of smoke materialized. It stretched away from them in a straight line, traveling down the block and around the corner. Guerrero tugged at Estelle's dress.

"What's that?" Mike asked.

Estelle allowed herself to hope. "I think that's how we find the others."

# CHAPTER 13

## BLEEDSTAR

The blue wisp brought Estelle and Mike West, out of District 7 of Irontown and into Kollektra. The further they drove into District 2, the darker the streets became until they took on firelight. They parked the truck, Mike leaving his rifle behind, and proceeded on foot down a torch-lit road. With Guerrero leading them, they followed the wisp.

Red-robed figures continuously fed great braziers on every other corner. About two hundred yards ahead was a group of people standing before a large, dark wall. As their eyes adjusted, they discerned tires, windows and doors. Smashed, mangled cars made up a structure that cut off a portion of the city.

Hung along the length of the wall, breathing with the Hollow's breeze, were deep gray banners. Each one bore the symbol of a hollow crimson sun with a dot at its center like a bullseye. Dozens of people mingled beneath, traversing the area without hoods or torches. Of course, the Torchbearers were present, but the amount of civilians was not unlike Sherman Manor's population. The starkest difference was that these people seemed far less cheerful and infinitely more cautious. They looked over their shoulders and went out of their way to avoid each other, keeping companions close.

"This is such a stupid idea," Estelle said, walking beside the man. "This will never work."

"You can still wait in the truck," Mike said.

"And if you don't come back? What am I supposed to do?"

Mike did not respond. His focus remained glued to two guards at the wall's entrance; two Torchbearers, both tall and strong, both armed. The blue trail faded a block before the gate, at which point Guerrero vanished.

The gate was a large chain-link fence on wheels that rolled to open and close. Banners flanked either side of it, the bottoms shredded by the weather. The wall was gruesome at a closer proximity. Large black spikes protruded from the cars, melted, and fused together.

Bodies decorated most of the poles. As well as humans and the Punished were beasts Estelle had never seen. Among the monstrosities were a man with the horrifying features of a rat; sharp bucked teeth protruded from his mouth and a long, fleshy tail hung lifelessly behind him. There was also a tall, thin ghoul draped in a ragged black cloak and a woman with sickly yellow flesh who's tangled hair covered her face. Estelle nearly mistook her for human, then realized instead of arms, she bore great leathery wings. Most of the Punished were haggard and weak and several still lived.

The guards took notice of them about thirty feet away. Their faces shrouded by hoods, they stood relaxed with their hands lightly grasping shotguns. Scraps of sewn burlap made up their hoods, and makeshift armor covered their clothing. Estelle and Mike weaved through the wandering people and one of the guards stepped forward to meet them.

"What do you want in Bleedstar?" he asked in an angry, intimating voice. "Answer."

"Me and the girl are looking for shelter," Mike said calmly. "Don't want any trouble; just some scraps and a bed for the night."

"What kind of pervert are you?" asked the shorter guard, raising his firearm.

"He's not like that!" Estelle shouted, holding her hands up. "We came from the Catalina. My parents died a year ago, and he's been looking out for me ever since."

The guards were silent momentarily, though the man with his gun on Mike hesitated to lower it. The outburst drew the attention of several other survivors. Mike remained calm, like trees on a windless day. His eyes were quiet with a loud fury behind them like a war veteran's. Estelle could not help but notice it. She wondered what it took to survive and what it must do to the people of Web Obsidia. The short standoff ended as the guard relaxed his weapon.

"No one comes in who doesn't pledge themselves to the Pale Lady," the first guard said.

"What's that mean?" Estelle asked, cocking her head.

"It means if the Lady arrives and needs you for something, you obey or get sent to the pits!"

"She's not here?" Mike asked.

"The Lady has important business of her own," the second guard said, shifting in place. "That's not your concern. Can you handle the demand or not?"

Estelle and Mike knew they would not be in Bleedstar long. Just long enough to get Theo, Raphael and the others.

"Sounds weird to me," Estelle mumbled.

"What was that?" the first guard asked, gripping his weapon tightly.

"We can handle that," Mike said sternly, putting his hands up. "We have no problems. Right, Estelle?"

She nodded.

"Two rules," the second guard said. "No stealing and don't make trouble for the other survivors. You're responsible for where you sleep. Any violation will be met with extreme retaliation. Do you understand?"

"We understand," Estelle and Mike said simultaneously.

"Swear beneath the Sanguistella: 'Lady, I am yours.'"

Both repeated the phrase, tasting like bile in Estelle's mouth. Though the guards stared them down still, the first eventually turned and waved his hand to a person they could not see. The fence squeaked, and rolled open. They breathed a sigh of relief once it closed behind them.

~

Estelle and Mike found themselves on a forked street, creating two aisles of two-story buildings. These places were broken stores, homes, workshops, delis, pet shops and more. The lamps were black iron poles, tops stuffed with lit kindling and wood, while others produced an incandescent glow from bulbs.

Night fell over Web Obsidia and it brought with it an icy wind. The survivors huddled together on stoops of apartments and shops, the pungent scent of kerosine on the breeze. Many of the people looked miserable, frightened or paranoid. Few walked the sidewalks, leaving mostly the grim-hooded Torchbearers, and each one surveyed Estelle and Mike as they passed.

"Where do you think they'd be?" the Seeker asked.

"Not sure yet," said Mike. "Ain't seen a police station or anything."

"We need Guerrero."

"So what? you just call his name?"

"I think so. We should find somewhere secluded."

They soon arrived at the empty husk of a store on their right side. Looking through its broken windows revealed tall, empty shelves, perfect for concealment. They stepped carefully on the warped wooden floor as they approached a worn counter with an empty cash register on top. The two hid themselves near the back, beside a pile of debris and unwanted items.

Torchlight from a nearby post gave some visibility toward the front while casting shadows toward the back. Two armed guards passed on patrol, ignorant of their hiding spot.

"Guerrero," Estelle whispered. "Are you here?"

Nothing happened.

"Guerrero," she called again. This time, he appeared in a pop of blue light.

He jumped around, making low, whooping and chirping sounds. His human friends struggled to make sense as Guerrero tugged on Estelle's dress and pointed out the window. He hopped over to Mike and tapped his boots, repeating the same gesture.

"Looks like he found Theo," Mike said. "Is that right?" Guerrero responded with a sad coo.

"Is he okay?" Estelle asked, kneeling down. "What about Raphael? The others from the manor?"

Guerrero chittered, running off to the pile of discarded junk. He slipped into a bent chicken cage and looked to them, holding the bars.

"They got them locked up," Mike said with a sigh.

"Can you show us where they are?" asked Estelle.

More chittering. Surely, the tiny primate could lead them to Theo and the others, but he was trying to tell them more. He continued to point toward the street, pulling at their clothing. Estelle looked at Mike, who shrugged. The girl pursed her lips in frustration, crossing her arms and bowing her head to think.

"I wish I knew what he was saying."

The sudden fluttering of wings caught both Estelle and Mike off guard. To Estelle's astonishment, her faithful crow came flying through the storefront. It landed atop the counter and faced its Seeker.

"The prisoners were interrogated by Toraesis," the crow said. "They are hurt, but alive."

"Son of a bitch with the axe," Mike said, scowling.

"How did you find me?" Estelle asked her familiar. "We're miles away from the manor."

"I can sense you to a degree. I won't pretend I'm not hurt that you abandoned me, but I came to help and brought friends."

"Aw hell," Mike said, scoffing. "You're gonna get them killed!"

"Who came?"

"Sue, Mae, Ralph, Jabari, Tessa, and Bron."

"Wow, Sue and Mae?" Mike sounded amazed. "Don't know if I ever seen Mae leave the shield."

"Worry not," the crow continued. "I will scout ahead first and report to them before they move."

Mike breathed in relief before looking down at Guerrero. Their small friend pointed outside once more. The crow tilted its head to the side.

"What's he saying now?" Mike asked.

"Continue down the street to the courthouse. Prisoners are being held on the basement level. Few guards. No blue trail to avoid attention."

"Didn't Ransley say we shouldn't go to the courthouse?"

"We're already in the shit, little miss," Mike said. "I know the place. I passed by it before this wall came up some years ago. It'd be a good place to keep people; real big building. Alright, crow. Can you take a message to Sue? Tell them to get the truck down the road from the South gate. We'll head that way for exfiltration. If we're not out in an hour, we might not be coming back."

"We're definitely coming back," said Estelle. "I'll be damned if I die out here like some stray."

The crow bowed its head and took flight once more as Guerrero vanished. By the time they stepped back on the road, the people had gone inside. The torches still burned with the regular patrols, but they too, were few. They paid no mind to the Estelle or Mike as they kept a quick pace down the street.

At its end, they found themselves in a massive square that once served as a park. Several groups of people loitered there. Many were Torchbearers but most were survivors. There were twenty to thirty tents dotted around the large space, small pyres and belongings spread around. A gray walkway cut through the dirt, dividing it in two halves. Looming at the end was a monumental, gray building, towering like a cruel king. Directly in the middle of the park was a tall rusted iron statue of a woman with wings. In her right hand she held a long broadsword and her left, a pair of scales. The woman was blindfolded, yet her demeanor suggested ease and confidence.

"Lady Justice," Mike said quietly. "That'd be nice after all this."

Far to the right, another block away, a single street flourished with torches, disappearing between the buildings. Mike observed this area for several moments, noting three vehicles coming in and out.

"There might be another gate down there," Mike said, Estelle following his eyes. "Don't seem like too many people, so maybe we head that direction when we're out?"

"Let's just hurry," she said.

The courthouse was slate gray, standing five stories tall, and each of its four corners rose higher than the main building. The colonnade at its facade stretched up four stories, covering the entire entry. A wide marble staircase sat at its center. The pillars were cracked with chunks of it missing and some had deteriorated completely. A large golden cupola rested tt the center and at its apex. Steel beams bent from the base to its top where a golden spire pointed to the sky.

"Oh my God," Estelle gasped as she froze in place.

"What is it?"

Mike fell silent when his eyes found what hers had. A small crowd gathered at the front of the courthouse. A short way before the steps was a large wooden platform with a beam structured to run across the top. Ropes hung from the beam and bodies hung from the ropes. The nooses lynched tight around their necks, the stiff forms of the victims swayed with the blowing wind.

"Here," he said, resting his hand on her shoulder. "Walk on the other side. Don't look."

"This wouldn't be my first time seeing a body." She moved his hand away. "My father deals in corruption and death. I was nine when I saw one for the first time."

"Yeah," he said, as if disappointed. "I might have been around that age. I was living in a settlement in District 4 at the time. Saw a woman walk out of our safety zone and right into a hoard of Punished. My dad told me she was 'sick.' No one your age should have to see those things."

"My father always says that one should never squander power. And if something bad happens to you, it's because you were wrong. You got caught unaware. You failed. Maybe if those people had been more careful, they'd still be alive."

The bystanders at the gallows dispersed, and the pair approached, keeping their eyes on the three Torchbearers who remained. One remained on the ground in front of the hanged and two more stood watch atop the courthouse steps. As they approached, the details of the noose's victims became clear.

Two of the departed were dressed in a simple white jump-suit, while the final and most recent addition wore familiar dark green fatigues. Each one had a cardboard sign attached to them. The person on the left was a man with shaggy salt and pepper hair and a thick mustache and beard. His sign read "water thief." The person in the middle was a woman around Sue's age. Long, straight brown hair fell to her belly. The sign pinned to her jumpsuit read "peace disturbance." Finally, the Sherman Manor soldier was a young man a few years older than Raphael. Wavy brown hair hung over his face and his sign read "P.O.W."

"Shit," Mike muttered. "That's Jake. The night we got attacked was his third mission…"

A boom of thunder sounded in the distance, and multiple heads in the area snapped to the sky. The temperature spontaneously dropped and heavy white fog blotted out any glimpse of red. It rolled over the walls, through the camp and across the rest of Bleedstar. Estelle would not have been able to see Mike had he not been standing directly beside her.

"Never been grateful for shitty weather before," Mike said.

Estelle kept close as he slowly paced through the dense fog, nearing the white-orange mattes of the torches.

"This fog's freezing," a man said at the top of the stairs.

"It's never been this cold before," said a woman. "Should we go grab some jackets?"

"Are you crazy? You saw what happened to the last guards! They'll label us deserters and we'll be strung up next."

"Then you stay here. I'll be right back."

"Wait! Heather!"

"You think the prisoners are going somewhere? Nothing's getting passed the dogs!"

One torch moved away, descending the steps. Then, lightning struck the spire of the building. The bolt was so intense, Estelle felt its heat from the ground. The succeeding thunder boom was so strong the windows rattled and the lone guard on the steps was shaken enough that he dropped his torch.

It was in that moment that Mike put his hand on Estelle's back and nudged her forward. She hurriedly moved with him and as they climbed the stairs, the soldier scrambled for his torch. After rolling into the dirt, its flame weakened enough that he could not find it. His worried moans gave Estelle a sense of comfort as they breached the courthouse. Standing in a grand corridor, Estelle and Mike found themselves alone in near darkness.

"Look there," said the woman, pointing to a door on their left.

Slivers of light escaped, and Estelle remained three paces behind Mike as he approached. He pulled the knob and a flood of light blinded them. They found the landing for a flight of stairs and a sign on the wall directed them down to the basement. They waited at the landing, listening for voices, but there were none.

A path of blinking wall lights guided them down two flights. At the bottom was a steel door with a tall glass rectangle for a window. Mike kept to the side, using one eye to get a peek in.

"Someone's sleeping on the job," he said. "I bet we could sneak right-"

"WAKE UP!" the voice of Toraesis bellowed.

Mike ducked down as a loud bang shook the door. He grabbed Estelle's arm and rushed her beneath the stairwell. They curled up in the deepest corner and in the shadows, Mike drew his pistol. The calamity in the next room was immense as the bearded man hollered and berated the guard for his accidental slumber.

"YOU ARE NOT WORTHY!" Toraesis said, his voice sharp and heavy like his axe. "I'LL SEE YOU STRIPPED OF YOUR POST AND YOUR RANK! YOU'LL BE LUCKY IF YOU'RE NOT HANGED!"

The door burst open as the man barreled through in a

fury. His heavy footsteps climbed the stairs, with the pitiful guard following in a rush.

"Give me another chance!" He begged and sobbed. "I was up all last night with my newborn son. I'm sorry! PLEASE!"

The steps continued upward until there was only the sound of buzzing lamps. They carefully entered the guard post, and the walls were a dull off-white with two desks framing the doors in and out. One desk had been broken in half with a metal folding chair crumpled nearby. The second table was covered with items such as hoods, handcuffs, zip ties, ropes, batons and burlap bags. A black duffel bag and Theo's weapons laid at its edge. Among the items was a ring with several keys on it, and Mike smiled as he picked them up.

"Guerrero," Estelle whispered.

The monkey appeared, and phased through the opposite door. The pair were met with suffocating darkness on the other side. Mike doubled back to the table and took a flashlight from Theo's bag.

The two followed Guerrero down a long, dilapidated section. Doors lined each side, and the monkey brought them to the fourth on the left.

Heavy, thick steel made up the door, and it bore a large red "X". Mike flipped through the keys, trying each one on the lock. There were so many, and he cursed to himself in frustration. Estelle stood beside him, looking to see anything she could in the dark. It was nearly impossible. The bath of white light faded to an end about five feet away, leaving reflective glints in the distance.

"Yes!" Mike said.

The lock clicked and Guerrero scurried inside as soon as the door cracked. Estelle pulled it open as Mike shone his light inside. The miserable forms of eleven people sat huddled together in a small room. There was only enough space to walk between them if one turned to the side. Most of them were strangers, but seated in the middle, sporting a black eye and bruises, was Theo. His hand raised, shielding his eyes from the flashlight. He looked up with contempt and spite before Guerrero jumped into his lap.

"You alright, brother?" Mike asked, looking around the room.

"Mike?" asked Theo. "What? How?"

"You oughta know I wouldn't leave without you. We followed your little friend here. The girl's crow showed up and told us Sue and Mae are waiting outside the walls."

"Man, you guys really came through." Theo pulled Guerrero to his face for a hug. "But Mike, they took Jake..."

"Yeah," Mike said after a pause. "We saw him..."

"I tried to hold him back, but he was always so headstrong. He wanted to protect us and they took him."

"It ain't your fault. Right now, we have to focus on getting everyone to safety."

Mike handed the flashlight to Estelle and drew a small knife from his pocket. Looking around for Raphael, she found him propped up against the wall in the corner, his broken leg haphazardly bandaged. Estelle counted two more survivors in Sherman Manor clothes and seven new faces. Mike knelt down and cut Theo's bonds. He sighed and chuckled while rubbing his wrists.

"They worked you over good, huh?" Mike said.

"It's nothing. I'd have taken it all for our friends if I could have."

Theo's left eye was swollen to the size of a golf ball. Blood dripped from beneath it and at the corners of his mouth. He tried to use his dreadlocks to cover some of the injury, but they were not long enough.

Estelle helped a nearly catatonic Raphael. His hands bound before him, he whimpered and the Seeker found the fear of a lost child in his eyes. She got to work untying his restraints as he stared in disbelief.

"H-how did you find us?" he asked, voice quivering.

"A magic monkey," she said, remembering the dancing buffoon in the fight circle. "I guess this is what we get for trying to be bigger than we are."

"I just wanted to show Dad I was ready."

By the time Estelle freed him, Theo and Mike had released everyone else.

"Let's get a move on," Mike said. "We don't know how long we've got."

"Guerrero," Theo said. "You've been incredible, but I need you to deliver a message to Mae. Let her know we're coming out soon and we need a safe exit."

"Tell them there may be another entrance to the East," Mike said.

Guerrero happily chittered, showing his tiny sharp teeth in a smile before fading away. Mike and Theo gave each other a nod, and they all left the room. Mike lead them to the guard post. He checked the doorway before signaling for everyone to follow. Theo was first, and Mike took his light back from Estelle. Raphael went through the door, helped by one of the manor soldiers, and Estelle waited with Mike at the rear, watching the corridor.

A pair of moving glints in the darkness caught her eye and a low rumbling came from the unseen. They froze. The two glints sunk low to the ground and a monstrous bark echoed through the hall. Estelle and Mike turned to flee, but felt a rush as something flew past them and threw itself against the door, slamming it shut. Mike jumped back, pushing Estelle behind him. He aimed the flashlight and revealed a creature.

It seemed human at first, but it hunched forward, and its face looked painfully elongated. Fur sprouted from its back and arms, and its skin was slick blue-black. Its hands had been mutated into claws and bones tore through its flesh along the arms and back. Its breath smelled of rotting meat and its eyes were reflective green. It drooled hungrily and fixed on Estelle.

"Mike!" Theo screamed. The door burst open and Theo flew upon the monster's back, his rifle caught in its jaws. "Run!"

Mike shoved his flashlight into Estelle's shaking hands and drew his pistol, holding his knife in his left hand. Mike attacked the monster's midsection, yelling with each stab and slice. Estelle stumbled back as the battle continued. The squeak of another opening door drew her gaze. Estelle pressed her back against the opposite wall. Her breath quickened, and she heard her heartbeat in her ears.

The low grumbling of a second dog-man came from the room as it poked its ugly head through the doorway. Estelle rushed forward and slammed it in the frame. With all the might in her body, she tried to shut the door but failed. The beast threw it open, knocking her to the ground. She scrambled up and backed down the hall, away from Mike and Theo as they fought the first. The monster walked toward her, locking with her eyes and crouching. Estelle scrambled to her feet and fled.

Heavy grunting and panting meant the creature was right behind her. She ran with all her stamina, using the flashlight to guide her. She slid under a table as the dog-man lunged and barely missed her. It crashed into the wall and stumbled, sliding as it regained its footing. Estelle did not stop, turning a corner and rushing forward.

She jumped over bones and debris, fooling herself into thinking she was making headway. The thought didn't bring her as much comfort as she hoped. The monster rushed around the corner, spotting her immediately. It released a deafening, gurgling howl that came from a human throat. The call summoned two more wolves who emerged from rooms Estelle had already passed. All three screamed in unison as they tore after her.

The trio of hybrids snarled and fell over each other, hunting their prey. Estelle's heart slammed against her chest, sweat poured from her face and she felt herself tiring her out. She knew the monsters could have lunged and attacked her, but they had not. They were tiring her out. Once she was exhausted and had nothing left, she would be an easy meal.

Just as she gave up hope, she saw a glow at the end of the hallway. Just maybe she could get through and close the door. It might not stop them, but it would hold them off. Hopefully.

Just as she made it to the entry, one dog leaped forward and slashed her back. She cried out in pain and was thrown through the doorway. Hot, searing pain spread down her back and warm blood wet her dress. She crawled forward, turning to sit toward the entrance.

Torches lined the walls here, with two doors leading to other hallways, and a heavy iron door standing between them. Heavy red paint depicted the Bleedstar banner's symbol on the iron floor grate.

One by one, each wolf entered the room, as if letting Estelle's fear marinate. She scooted back, tears welling in her eyes. What should she do? What could she do? Shaking to the bone, the woman closed her eyes and resigned herself to her fate. Failure was her feeling with a dim, yet desperate hope that Mike and Theo made it out alive.

The wolves were within feet of her, opening their mouths, baring their fangs. The click of the door behind Estelle made them pause as they prepared to pounce. She held her breath and turned her head. The presence in the room brought an intense gravity that made Estelle feel dragged to the ground. She noticed the wolves were struggling to stand, shaking with their legs nearly buckling.

A tall man dressed in black robes with long dreadlocks emerged. The purple bands on his arms shone like strips of violet sunlight. The last time she saw this man, a covering of clouds hid his face. This time be bore no cloak. The almond shape of his eyes was familiar to her. So was his short, round nose, and she would recognize his full lips if he were not scowling.

"M-Marcel?" she asked, her voice shaking.

The man's furious amethyst eyes beamed down at her. "Who the fuck is Marcel?"

# CHAPTER 14

## THE PALE LADY

The stationary dog-men snarled and growled at Estelle, fangs as long as her fingers snapping at the air. The Seeker's attention snapped to the man beside her, and an invisible force dragged the dogs to the ground, forced into a prone position. Estelle locked eyes with the familiar stranger.

"Marcel," she said. "How is this possible? How are you here?"

"I don't know who that is," the man said.

He held his fingertips to the center of his chest and a thin white outline appeared as his cloak. Clouds and tiny flashes appeared within its borders; a storm in the fabric. His smooth, coffee-colored skin seemed to glow. Black dreadlocks hung down his shoulders and the sides of this face, falling to his navel. His eyes shone with an otherworldly presence.

A spark of light appeared at the center of Supernova's chest and it grew to the size of a tennis ball. It shone so brightly it overtook the torches, bathing the room in harsh white. There was a buzzing around the room, and Estelle's hair lifted a small way off her shoulders. The sphere of light spat out three jolts of lightning, each one striking a different dog-man. In an instant, they fell to the ground, dead.

Estelle's eyes bulged. The ravenous demons that threatened to kill and devour her now lay silent, like sleeping pets. It took him hardly any effort. The pressure in the room lifted, giving her the feeling she could jump and touch the ceiling.

"I saw you in a dream," she said, studying the figure. "You're the Supernova Swordsman?"

"I love when people know my name before I've met them," Supernova said, scanning the room. "Who are you? Why are you here?"

"My name is Estelle. I've been looking for you."

"That's comforting. What are you, some kind of assassin? Or a spy?"

The glow in his eyes intensified, and the pressure returned to her body.

"So much for gratitude! I'm the one who let you out of that cell!"

"To gain my trust or complacency. Only to drive a knife in my back when I'm not looking. How do know I can trust you?"

"I came here to rescue people from my settlement." Her mind told her to insult and berate the man, but so far within Bleedstar, she thought it best to stay her temper. "We were looking for survivors from a battle and they were brought here. I wouldn't have found you if those things hadn't chased me here. All I want is to get as far away from this place as possible. Don't you?"

Supernova watched her, his eyes still. She winced as the slashes in her back seared. The man's gaze softened, and he approached. He examined her back, placing a sturdy grip on her shoulders. He pressed his hand to the wound, and Estelle groaned.

"What are you doing?!" she said, clenching her teeth.

"Just wait," he said.

A warm rush spread across her back and she gasped as the pain receded. She physically felt the lacerations close.

"What did you just do?" Estelle asked.

"I healed you. Let's go."

Supernova left the room without waiting for a reply. The two retraced Estelle's path to the stairwell. In the pitch black, Supernova held a violet light in his hand to illuminate the way. Visible were a macabre assortment of human parts stashed in corners, and bones with gnaw marks scattered around the floor.

"We need to hurry," Estelle said. "We have to find the people I came here with."

"They're fine," Supernova said. "You're in more danger than they are."

"What's that supposed to mean?"

"You freed Demella's favorite prisoner. You'd better pray she never sees your face."

Estelle and Supernova came around a corner to the main hallway. Supernova's body tensed and he clenched his fists as a bright light shone on them.

"Nova?!" a man said, lowering his gun and flashlight.

"Theo?"

"Is this where you've been the last six months?"

"Unfortunately," the swordsman said as the two embraced. "I hoped I'd never see you here, brother."

"You two know each other?" Estelle asked, looking from one man to the other.

"Me and Nova go back," Theo said. "But that's a story for another time. We have to get back to Mike and the others, then beat feet away from this place."

The three made their way toward the stairwell. Slumped near the wall was a dark figure. The protruding bones, fur and glossy skin made Estelle's heart skip. Closer observation revealed several wounds. Broken teeth, lacerations and bullet holes put the creature down, the circular wounds emanating blue smoke.

"What *are* those things?" Estelle asked.

"Praeformae," Supernova said, stepping over the beast.

They moved through the guard post and ascended the stairs. The dark entrance hall was silent. Just outside the front doors, through the windows, was the unmistakable dance of two torches. Theo guided the two to a conference room near the entrance, knocking four times.

Shuffling came from within and hushed voices, but eventually the knob turned and the door cracked, with Mike sticking his pistol out. He breathed in relief when he saw Theo.

"I was getting ready to come find you," Mike said, letting them in.

The dark wood conference table took up most of the room, with the survivors spread out around it, comforting each other as best they could. Raphael did his damndest to relax in the corner near a tall boarded window. Mike stood near the center of the table, examining the swordsman, who remained locked in conversation with Theo.

"You didn't think to drop us a line?" Theo asked Supernova. "We've been worried for months, man."

"I was trying to keep her away," Supernova said. "I hoped if she focused on me, she wouldn't hurt anyone else." He eyed his friend's wounds. "I was wrong about that. I thought I could find a way to exorcise her, but I have nothing to show for my absence."

"Don't start that blame game with yourself."

"How do you know each other?" Estelle said, interrupting.

"That's something we should talk about when we're safe."

"I'm the one who found him in the jail cell. I want to know."

"I'm curious myself," Mike said. "Who's the man in the dress, Theo?"

Supernova's eyes narrowed toward Mike.

"Don't be cocky," Supernova said to him. "I could leave you here to rot if I wanted to. You'll never get out without my help. Not with a dozen people."

"Big words coming from a man who was just in a cell."

"Who are you, exactly?" Supernova asked, facing him.

"I'm the man who came to save these people, asshole." Mike's hand rested on the grip of his pistol.

"You mean you're the madman who waltzed into a demon's fortress?"

"To rescue our people. You telling me you'd have left them? What kind of man are you?"

"I'm the one who takes the pain so others don't."

"Tell that to my dead squad mates."

The two glared at each other, the tension like an ocean's weight atop the room.

"We don't have time for this," Theo snapped in a hushed voice, stepping between them. "Once they find out prisoners are missing, it'll be a lot harder to escape."

Both Mike and Supernova pushed their pride and egos down as the room fell silent.

"We have backup on the outside," Theo continued. "Mae and a few others from the new settlement."

"I'll cause the distraction, then you guys make a run for it," Supernova said.

"You say that like it's easy," Mike said.

"I'm doing the hard part. Unless you want everyone chasing you on your way out?"

"A distraction is hard for you?" Estelle asked Supernova,

raising an eyebrow. "I just saw you kill three of those wolf things."

"It will attract the Pale Lady because she knows my power. It's crucial you're all gone before that happens."

Estelle scoffed. "What if she captures you again?"

"She won't."

"Not going to lie," said Theo. "I'm thinking the same. We just got you back and I can tell you're not at full strength. What are you going to do when she shows?"

"I'll figure that out when the time comes."

The swordsman placed his hand on the knob, but hesitated when Estelle pulled his arm. In movements and in voice, this storm-clad warrior reminded her of Marcel.

"Be careful," she said.

Supernova looked down with squinted eyes. She saw in him the same reckless spirit that others had condemned in her. His eyes were warm like the sun and just as distant, his personality abrasive and untouchable; except for when it came to Theo.

Supernova hesitated at the door, and she thought he would speak again.

~

In a flash, the conference room detonated, igniting, shredding, blazing. The walls ripped apart, and the ceiling crumbled as the space filled with destructive, glowing red energy. Estelle braced for boiling pain, but to her surprise, she was untouched. Standing tall as a cliff and strong as iron, Supernova held his left fist held up in a defensive stance.

Emanating from it was a golden blue light that took the shape of a clock face. Its outer rings glowed brightest with the zodiac symbols pulsing between them. One circle sat in the center with a larger ring rotating around it, illuminating the numbers as it passed over them. As its light fought to ward away the red energy, the quiet ticking of a clock echoed around Estelle.

The energy died, and the ticking silenced. A charred hole in the side of the courthouse replaced the conference room with only the floor intact. The survivors remained unharmed as they cowered. Intense heat singed the air and as the smoke cleared, a shadow stood just a few feet away.

A heavy weight came down around them. It felt like the darkness that filled the voids tucked between buildings. Sound became muffled, yet whispers of death hung in the air like a fog on a cold morning. The very air itself seemed to take on an electric charge as the shadow shifted forward.

Her aura was petrifying. Sickly, radiating orange eyes glared through the smoke. Her hair fell in wild curls down her shoulders and the gems of her tiara glinted among the embers. Canines extended into fangs gave her the appearance of some wild animal.

The woman wore in a simple gray tunic with a royal blue skirt, a slit up the left side, and her legs were clad in knee-high boots. A dull steel gauntlet of armor encased her right arm; thick shoulder plates attached to a guard on the upper arm. A smaller guard protected her forearm and hand. The black outline of a striped snake coiled its way around her neck and chest, and the Pale Lady's black lips curved into an unnatural grin.

"I was hoping you wouldn't let my fun end," she said in a sadistic way. Her voice echoed as she spoke, layers of whispers and hints of anguish entwined with her words.

The survivors behind Supernova hunched in terror near the story-high breach, with Theo and Mike already aiming their guns at their enemy. The Pale Lady leaned to the side to glimpse Estelle. The Seeker's blood ran cold.

"That one is interesting," the Pale Lady said. "Her scent makes me drool."

"Your business is with me," Supernova said.

"My love. It isn't your place to tell me what my business is."

The Pale Lady raised her armored hand, and a bright red sphere of energy formed.

"*Tempus,*" Supernova said.

He waved his hand, and the clock reappeared. Starting from an open palm, he clenched his fist, stopping as if squeezing an imaginary ball. The clock pulsed and the Pale Lady's form slowed drastically. The energy of her attack continued to swell, but at a snail's pace. Supernova looked over his shoulder to Theo.

"Get everyone out!" he said, grunting under the pressure. "*Now!*"

Theo rushed to the hole in the wall, peered over to the table, then to Mike. He gestured for help with the elongated furniture and Mike rushed to the opposite side.

Most of the survivors moved aside, but a few joined in lifting the table. With a great heave, they stumbled with it to the edge and let the tip drop to the ground. There would be a four or five-foot drop, but they could slide down afterward.

Supernova's stance weakened, his body shaking and the clock faltering. Lady's face flexed with her twisted smile and her sphere grew in size. Ripples spread through the circles of Supernova's ward and a deep buzzing reverberated in the air. Estelle turned her back to flee, Theo reaching his hand out to her with panic on his face.

The explosion roared like a hundred lions, the survivors narrowly making it to the ground with one straggler: Estelle.

A jet of crimson shot forth, shattering the clock. At the last moment, Supernova turned and wrapped his arms around the Seeker. The blast shot them both out of the building. It was all Estelle could do to keep her eyes closed and brace for the impact. Seconds later, Supernova slammed down in the giant square at the feet of Lady Justice. He rolled, making his arms a cage to minimize the damage to the woman.

"On your feet, girl," he said once they came to a stop.

"I'm fine," she replied, scrambling up.

She rose as fast as she could, scanning the area for her friends. Mike and the group were already making their way toward the lit street to the East. In the turmoil, they seemed like the other survivors, fleeing the conflict. They stayed close to a dark alley as guards, alerted by Lady's attack, aimed their guns at the square from several directions.

Estelle and Supernova found themselves surrounded. The hooded guards formed a captive circle, shrinking ever smaller. They only held their positions when a red lightning bolt crashed down a stone's throw from the duo. The Pale Lady appeared there, grinning like a hungry dragon.

"Listen!" said Supernova, addressing the guards. "This conflict is larger than any of you. When you die, you'll be able to pass on in peace. However, if you die by my hand, know your souls don't belong to you anymore. They belong to whom I serve."

"Puppet of the Gods," the Pale Lady cooed. "Nothing more than a meaningless servant destined to die for a worthless cause. A weapon. A tool."

"Serving you would be better?" Estelle said with a laugh. "All your soldiers are bullies and degenerates! Not a drop of class among the bunch."

The Pale Lady's untamed gazed moved to the Seeker.

"Sweet child," the she-beast said in a condescending tone. "Those who know nothing should say nothing. But I love your arrogance and that fire in your eyes. You should work for us."

"What if I do?" asked Estelle.

"You'll be part of the greatest kingdom to exist since Father Torment's. I'll make you a soldier in my ranks. I can tell you're smarter than most of the cattle. It would be a shame to waste your potential."

"Don't talk to her!" Supernova said, shaking Estelle. "Her words are poison wine! You won't have her or anyone else today, Demella!"

"I'd love to see you try to stop me," Lady said, her red aura swirling around her.

"*Locus*!" Supernova shouted. "*Shu Nut Ra*!"

A circle of shining purple light opened beneath the swordsman. The light rose around him, creating a shimmering pillar. Centered at his chest was a point of light connected to the purple power by a dazzling arc of white electricity. His eyes, ablaze with amethyst ferocity, stared angrily ahead at his enemy. Estelle expected to feel the boiling heat from his power, but it felt soft and warm like the days at summer's peak.

"Estelle," he said quietly. "I'll create an opening for you. When you can, get to safety. Get ready."

Supernova pushed his power out, and the pillar extended in diameter. Demella's red slashes grew wider in response. The two forces met and sparks sprayed outward. The storm cloaked warrior assumed a battle stance and extended his arms to the side.

The bands on his clothing shone, and a burst of force emanated from Supernova, rapidly expanding. The Pale Lady stood her ground, her hair and skirt blowing back, while her soldiers fell on their backs, rendered unconscious.

"Go," Supernova said.

Estelle fled for the fire-lit street, thunder cracking behind her. The Pale Lady roared and Estelle swore she felt fingers grasping at the back of her neck. She heard Supernova yell and Lady grunt. Whatever was happening behind her was a powerful struggle that she knew she had no place in.

Lady appeared in front of Estelle, cackling and brimming with crimson flares. She lunged for the Seeker. In an instant, Supernova was there, exchanging chains of punches and kicks, too fast for Estelle to track. Lady fired what appeared to be another beam of energy. Supernova dodged it and threw a wave of violet lightning at the demon, throwing her back.

Estelle was a hundred yards from the mouth of the brazier-lit street. The battle raged on behind her, sending quakes beneath her feet. The guards stirred, and knowing they could not aid their lady against Supernova, they would prove their loyalty by recapturing at least one prisoner. Toward her desti-nation as well, a small platoon of guards spotted her. She skidded to a stop, whirling around and seeking a way out. Then, like a shooting star, Estelle's crow soared into Bleedstar. Shining white, it dove for the Seeker and perched on her shoulder.

"You're not alone," it said.

A mighty metal crash drew the attention of the guards. A powerful engine revved as an armored SUV tore down the Eastern street. A man in the truck sat on the door with his upper body through the window. He fired an assault rifle, killing two Torchbearers. It screeched to a halt with several green clad soldiers emerging and at its lead was good old Sue. Wielding a black and yellow automatic rifle, she fired at the men to Estelle's right, felling three.

The Seeker ducked as bullets whizzed overhead and the crow guided her toward the Sherman Manor group. Fighting through paralyzing fear and the urge to curl into a fetal posi-tion, Estelle made her way toward the vehicle. Clear as day, Raphael's father stood next to Sue, providing cover fire for Estelle. On the other side of the car, shooting like machines, were Mike and Theo.

Estelle was nearly there but found herself pulled backward

with incredible strength. Sue's reaching hand and fading voice were all she was left with.

Demella turned the Seeker and clutched her by the front of her dress, staring into her eyes with naught but malice. The foul figure smelled of smoke, burning meat and brimstone. Red and black aura concentrated in Lady's armored arm then encroached on Estelle.

"Look at you," Lady said, hissing like a snake. "You're so full of raw power... What could I do with a soul like yours?" The demon closed her eyes and when she opened them, they were wholly black. "Estelle? Such a pretty name for such a wicked girl. The things you've done! Who is Nina? What did you do to make her hate you so much? Who's Marcel?"

The crimson power tangled like vines around Lady's fingers, and Estelle felt her very life draining from her. It became more difficult to resist, barely mustering enough will to kick at her assailant. On the brink of surrender, the swordsman saved the woman. Speeding in from the side, he slashed the Pale Lady's arm off.

Estelle fell back and summoned the strength to scoot away. Supernova held in his right hand a long curved katana, fresh blood dripping from the blade. Purple cloth wrapped the black handle, and the guard was a golden circle decorated with birds engraved in it. The Seeker looked over her shoulder at her friends. They stood by, helpless to intervene in the conflict. To Estelle's dismay, the Pale Lady regrew her severed arm.

"Watch out!" Supernova called, grabbing the Seeker in a bear hug.

The feeling of electricity being forced to circuit her body was excruciating. Even though the swordsman tried to protect Estelle, they were both enveloped in a wave of red lightning. The pain was so intense she could not scream. Lady's boisterous laughter clawed passed the violent buzzing. When she relented, the pain felt as if a thousand needles had pierced her flesh. Quivering and gritting his teeth, Supernova shakily held himself up while Estelle fell to her knees.

"How stupid do you feel?" Demella asked Supernova. "I bet you never thought you'd regret teaching her how to wield the lightning. Never thought it would be mine."

"Enjoy it while you have it," Supernova said. "I'm going to kill you!"

"Not without killing *her*. And that's no way to speak to your future queen. I'll show you your place."

The Pale Lady smiled so hard her cheeks could have torn to her ears. Electricity surged through her hand and another wave shot forth. More than a dozen dancing fingers of power ripped across Supernova's body. The coffee-skinned fighter held his ground, holding his arms in a defensive stance to reduce the effects. The bands on his wrists shone brilliantly as violet electricity of his own pushed back. He managed just enough to cancel out Lady's attack. After the pop of the bolts, silence followed. She raised her hand once more, charging a greater amount of energy.

"Stop!" Estelle cried out. "This is madness! Why can't you just leave us alone? What did any of us ever do to you? We're just people trying to live our lives in peace! Haven't we suffered enough?"

Demella's eyes widened.

"*You know nothing of suffering!*" the demon screeched.

The pitch of the scream brought Estelle back to her first day in Eve's Hollow. The scream she heard in Garnet Grove was the same one directed at her.

"Spend ages in the infinite darkness! Have your very essence ripped to shreds over and over! Have the devils use and twist you! Feel the burn of hellfire and the torture of the Void-*then*- tell me of suffering... You both need to learn the true meaning of pain."

Estelle was taken aback, her heart beating so hard her

vision blurred. Demella raised both of her hands to prepare for another attack. The Seeker decided if she'd die, she would do so with courage and stood her ground as she would against any tyrant. The blast fired as Supernova tried to push Estelle away. The electric force was faster, enveloping them at once.

Neither could help but holler out in pain, falling to their knees. Even though the flashing and violent buzzing kept them in place, Supernova forced his hands up, pressing back. Ruby and amethyst danced around them. To stable herself, Estelle tried to use Supernova to stand.

The raw power went from tangled purple and red to pure white. The warriors lost what control of it they had. The surge encircled the Pale Lady, forcing a scream of rage from her black lips. The bolts grew in number and intensity, capturing and eventually swallowing them in a blinding white sphere.

Estelle shut her eyes and prayed for the pain to end. Every cell in her body screamed when all at once she went numb.

A furious surge in her chest expanded to her torso and filled her limbs. Though the pressure kept its boot on her back, she got to a single knee.

She could not believe what was happening to her. To her astonishment, the power flowed with her blood, tingling her whole body. Her mind expanded to understand the current, and she could will it. The white light cycled through every shade of every color. The magnificent rainbow felt cool and smelled of fresh rain. Turquoise blue surrounded her.

Welling the power in her belly, she shot to her feet and released a massive roar. Every photon of the turquoise aura drew into her body, then released in an incredible burst. It produced an eye burning flare, kicking up dust and dirt. Then silence.

Supernova looked at her, awestruck. The Pale Lady, eyes narrow slits of fury, bit on her own teeth so hard they could break. The she-monster raised her hand to attack again, but

Estelle reacted faster. She took up Supernova's katana and sped forward faster than she thought she could, impaling the Pale Lady through the stomach. Eyes of rage and shock stared down at the new woman as Lady freed herself from the blade and stepped back. In this moment of hesitation, Estelle raised a hand and unfiltered, icy blue lightning shot forth, sending the demon flying.

Sparks flew from her fingers and she held more and more power as she fixated on it. She aimed her palms in the direction she sent Demella.

"Do not!" Supernova yelled.

"Why?!" she shouted back. "After all she's done? This might be our only chance to stop her!"

"This is still beyond you."

"I can do it. I know I can."

"No. You cannot. She's been toying with us. If she gets serious, she could level this entire district and kill us all."

"What makes you think I can't, too? Do you have any idea what it's been like for me? Every single day has been a gamble on life. I was so weak that I couldn't do anything. All that has changed today, and no one is taking that away from me!"

Lightning struck a nearby building at the crescendo of Estelle's voice, eyes ablaze with frost colored anger. She expected Supernova to challenge her. Deep down, she wanted him to. Instead, he looked upon her with gentle eyes that possessed an underlying layer of sadness.

"That's the power talking," he said. "I get. You felt helpless before. I did before I could use the storm."

"You don't get it!" Thunder rumbled above. "I've done nothing but rely on strangers for help. I've seen *terrible* things happen to people and I've been powerless to help any of them. Now I can repay the people who risked their lives for me. Theo, Ransley, Mike and Sue! Everyone! It's my turn to protect them. Now I have power- and I can't waste it!"

Estelle looked at her hands and smiled, almost laughing at the sight of her fingers arcing electricity.

"You are untrained, unfocused and too emotional. This power is unstable and takes years to control. In your current state, I have no idea what could happen. You could blow off your arms or detonate like an atomic bomb."

"Better to take her with me..."

"You'd sacrifice all these people? They're not just Torchbearers. They're also survivors- the people you just lobbied for. Women and children. You want to kill them too?"

Estelle clenched her teeth. "So, what? We run?"

"We live to make wiser decisions."

The Sherman Manor Defense Force backed toward their SUV as the torchbearers emerged from shadows and alleys. Sue was being pulled back by Ralph, and a second later, the vehicle pulled away, with a rain of bullets falling on them. They attempted to pursue, but Supernova pulled Estelle away from a slash of energy that would have rended her in two. The Pale Lady appeared and threw a punch at him so hard he fell to the ground, clutching his gut.

"You," Lady said to Estelle. "Who are you? What are you?"

Estelle willed her power into her hands, but before she could act, Demella was upon her. With frigid hands, she grasped Estelle's shoulders, digging her nails into the woman's flesh. She cried out and fell to kneel.

"How did you take my power?" Lady asked. "Give it back!"

"I- I didn't do anything," Estelle said.

"I've seen your cruelty, thief. I've seen your sins! Return my power!"

"I thought I was dead!"

"Oh, you will be, you little dog!"

An armored fist rose above Estelle, threatening to crush her skull.

"Demella!" Supernova said.

The swordsman held his arms outstretched and the light at his chest balled itself between his hands. Estelle met his eyes. They motioned to a manhole cover beneath her feet. Somehow she "felt" what he was thinking.

Raising the sword in her hand, she cut the fist shooting toward her head. Lady's arm split in half, spraying blood all over Estelle's face. The Seeker delivered a blast to her enemy and rolled out of the way.

"*Mortestella!*" Supernova said.

The star in his hands detonated in a massive ring of burning colors. They began white, fading into yellow, green, blue and violet. The explosion focused into a bolt of silver lightning that ripped across the ground and hit Lady in her chest. It burned a trail in the dirt and launched the demon a block over.

As the soldiers recovered from the radical light of the attack, Estelle was snatched up and brought down into the under-city, leaving the manhole rattling above.

# CHAPTER 15

# CALDONIA'S RIDDLE

For an hour, Estelle and Supernova followed a maze of underground tunnels. Miles of wet, rusted catwalks stretched in all directions beneath the city. The air smelled of heavy metal and dampness and the sound of rushing water was ceaseless. According to the many maps in glass cases, a path labeled the "green run" would bring them north in Kollektra, then east into Serenus Acres. It was during the northward portion that they discovered an enormous section missing, carved out in a wide circle, twenty or more feet across. The brick and tile came to a sudden end, dropping at ninety degrees.

Smoke and fire of red, gold and orange churned at the bottom of the black hole, at least six hundred feet down. Faint echos of whispers and moans periodically came up. Strong, gray roots crawled up the edges and four stone pillars sat fixed at equal distances around its circumference. Estelle's memory reignited at the sight of grasping hands at the edges of the hole.

"Can you explain the Void again?" Estelle asked. "I'm still not sure I understand."

"They say God created the universe," Supernova said.

"The Void would've been the canvas he painted on. What was before."

"And why is there a hole to that place in Web Obsidia?"

Supernova stretched his hand over the pit and inhaled through his nose, as if savoring the scent of sulfur.

"Maybe because Demella is herself a Void spirit," he said, fixating on the light at the bottom. "Only she knows why she's been digging holes like these for the past year."

Estelle sighed. "I hope our friends made it."

"Of course they did."

"How do you know?"

"Because I do. But right now, I'm more interested in you."

Estelle swallowed. She felt his eyes boring into the side of her head, but she kept her attention trained on the pit.

"You show up out of nowhere. You steal half of Demella's power. Somehow, you know my name. Start explaining."

"You ought to be happy I found you. How long were you in that cell, exactly?"

"Long enough to know no one would open it. Not without risking Demella's wrath. You survived an encounter with her when I could not help. Someone on her side could pull that off."

"I was being chased by monsters! I didn't want to be there, you asshole! I went to rescue Theo and Raphael- not you. In fact, if I could have survived that encounter without you, I would have."

"No one survives the Praeformae... unless Demella wants them to."

"Let me ask you this, smart-ass: if I were working for the Pale Lady, why did she try to rip my arms off?!" Estelle pointed to the red puncture mark above her collarbone. "If you hadn't saved me, she wasn't going to let me go. She screamed for her powers back."

Supernova kicked a rock into the hole. As it clattered off the edges, long, dusty arms reached out to grasp it.

"Speaking of," he said. "You need to give those powers up."

Her face scrunched.

"What?" Estelle said. "Why the hell would I do that?"

The cloaked man grumbled.

"Being a Storm Caster is a privilege and an honor. You didn't earn it and you don't know how to control it. You don't deserve it."

"I'd be dead without them! How would I even give them up?"

"Just say 'I, Estelle, release the storm to the heavens.'"

The woman smirked. "Now that I know what to say, I never will."

"Yes, you will."

"Are you going to make me?"

"If I have to."

Supernova's eyes were lazy, as if he could fall asleep where he stood, but so too were they deep and encapsulating. Without his power active, they were deep, dark brown. Just like Marcel's. The love of her life would never speak to her in that manner. Supernova exuded a condescending air, and he was so self assured she ground her teeth. Without thinking, Estelle ran.

A rush of excitement filled her lungs as she ran faster than she ever had before. She lost count of how many corners she turned and challenged herself to be quicker. She had been on skiing trips with her friends before and her current foot speed reminded her of jetting down the powdered mountains.

She ran so fast that she could not stop herself from crashing into a row of chain-link cages housing a system of water tanks. They appeared before she could register them and she tumbled as she dug her heels in. Clanking metal bounced off the concrete walls as a tank the size of a car fell atop her, pinning her legs. She felt no pain. Her legs must have been crushed. She frowned when Supernova came around the tank as if he had been right behind her the whole time.

"I have a job to get to," Supernova said. "You're taking up a lot of my precious time and I don't appreciate it."

"I can't feel my legs," Estelle said, wincing. "I think they're broken."

Supernova sat down beside the woman.

"Give up your powers and I'll help you."

Estelle panted. "No."

"You'll risk destroying yourself and everyone around you?"

"Teach me then."

"Even if I wanted to," Supernova said with a laugh. "I don't have time. Other people need me more than you do."

"We're stuck down here together." She tried to shift under the weight and sighed. "You can't give me a little advise? Or a history lesson? Or- get this damn thing off me?!"

"Stop being so dramatic. Move it yourself."

A shout of frustration left Estelle's lips and when she glared at Supernova, he shot his chin up toward the tank and waited. Although sheepish, she placed her palms on the rusted steel. She pressed, and to her amazement, it rolled. With a heavy push, she freed herself. Not only could she stand, but her legs were relatively unharmed, baring a few scratches through her torn leggings.

"Why didn't you tell me I could do that?" she asked.

"You'd already convinced yourself you couldn't."

She sighed, brushing dirt and rust from the fabric.

"This is my favorite outfit," she said with a huff.

"Then why are you wearing it out here?"

"I didn't exactly plan on winding up in a sewer."

He chuckled and Estelle faced away, her black hair hiding

her face. She hated being laughed at, let alone by Marcel's doppelgänger. She considered running again.

"Physical strength," Supernova said. "Mental discipline. Spiritual balance. Those are the three pillars of storm casting. It's difficult for anyone to master all three. If you do, though, you get abilities like this."

The man placed his hand on Estelle's shoulder, and instant warmth spread through her body. It brought the comfort of soaking in a hot spring. His purple aura extended to her, and she felt the pain in her wounds leaving. The punctures left by the Pale Lady's claws healed, then her clothing repaired itself as if she had just bought them.

"How did you do that?" she asked, feeling her hair. Soft like it was just washed.

"Storm casting isn't just about destruction. It had many applications that the warriors of old stopped using. The first of the Elementis Populus were mystic terraformers, able to communicate and be one with nature."

"What about that white bolt? Could they do that too?"

"No," he said. "The man who taught my master created the Nova Bolt."

Estelle squinted, crossing her arms.

"Then it was you who attacked the Warden?" she said, remembering the metallic head fleeing to the red sky.

"I was in Demella's dungeon at the time."

"Then who could have?"

"The man who taught me. Master Eze is the only other person alive who knows the technique."

"Maybe I'll get him to teach me, since you won't."

"Don't flatter yourself. You're too undisciplined to even understand the power you're *borrowing*."

"Well," Estelle said, walking passed Supernova. "It's not like we're trapped underground with nothing but time."

"You're serious about learning?" Supernova's brows rose, yet his eyes remained sleepy.

"Try me."

~

The Supernova Swordsman spoke at length about the origin of his powers. On a distant, parallel version of Earth, the people could harness the powers of the elements. Fire, lightning, water, ice, vegetation and more. Along with control came a higher state of mental awareness, physical strength and spiritual potential. These people once lived in harmony alongside nature; made homes in thousand year old trees or high atop frozen peaks. They created division by keeping to their "kind." As Supernova put it, "When it comes to men, division is always the beginning of war." And war is what wiped out the Elementis Populus.

The pair traveled down a long, dark tunnel that leaked noisily on the steel grate at their feet. Supernova used the light at his chest to illuminate the way. The white star was called *Life Lightning*, the physical manifestation of the individual's literal spark of life. Using this light, they located a ladder to the surface.

"Ladies first," Supernova said.

"Are we at the manor?" Estelle asked.

"How should I know?"

"What if the Pale Lady is up there?"

"It'll be faster getting there once we can see *above* the ground. I doubt Demella knows where we are. We don't even know where we are."

"We're following the red tunnel to the Southeast, then we take the blue tunnel north in Irontown."

"You really don't want to see her again, do you?"

Estelle looked away and rubbed her arm.

"On we go, then," he said, rounding her.

"They say you fought her two years ago," Estelle said in stride with the swordsman. "The three-day storm?"

He nodded.

"How did you beat her?"

"We fought until we were both exhausted. Neither of us had the strength to kill the other. I am haunted by that day. I lost everything to that c-"

He grunted and bit his tongue.

"I'm sorry, Supernova," Estelle said. "I can't imagine what that's like. That's why I'm trying so hard to get home. My school, my friends, my boyfriend."

"Where did you say you were from?"

"Let's just say very far away."

The tunnel narrowed as they continued without a branching path or another ladder in sight. The floor opened beneath the grate and the sound of sloshing, roaring water accompanied them. The scent of wet rust hung in the air and the humidity weighed on the woman's lungs. She heaved a forlorn sigh when they came to a steel bulkhead, tightly locked with a green "X" painted on its surface. Estelle looked to her companion.

"What?" he said.

"Can't you- I don't know- blow the door open or something?"

"I guess they don't teach physics in 'very far away.' We'll double back and go up the ladder. I don't care what's up there."

As he turned to head back, a rattling occurred above them. A second bulkhead slammed down, trapping them in a ten foot long box. Supernova grappled the heavy door and tried to lift it. The gears squeaked, but they remained stationary.

"Fantastic," Supernova said.

"Now what-"

Without warning, the floor dropped. The two plunged into the frigid, gray water and the current tore them away. The freezing water tossed her about like a wet rag, and whenever Estelle's head breached the surface, she took as big a gulp of air as she could. Time became lost as her body thrashed in the tunnels. At last, it came to a stop when the stream fell into a tall, dark, cylindrical room. Estelle's body hit a slick metal surface with a loud clatter. Coughing, groaning and sopping wet, she pushed herself up.

The grate she stood on stretched to the concrete walls of the room where the mist of many waterfalls dispersed. More bulkheads surrounded her, and Supernova was nowhere to be seen.

Putrid yellow smoke rose from below, congealing and taking the form of a squat elderly woman draped in the leathered pelt of a hog. She stood only three feet tall and gave off a low, dry laugh as she paced around Estelle.

"Who- what are you?" Estelle asked, backing up.

"Caldonia, the Deep Witch!" she said, jumping up. "I wonder who this one will choose?"

"What are you talking about?"

"You, my dear, are here to see- the gruesome, hanging coffins three."

Heavy chains rattled above. As the woman said, three caskets bound to them fell from the black ceiling, stopping to a sway about a foot from the grate. A revolting yellow-green glow came from below and the scent of chemicals and rot came with it.

The leftmost coffin was simple, glossy and black. The one on the right was made of dark redwood and its details were sleek gold. The casket in the center was gold-painted wood and bore the image of an Egyptian pharaoh.

Caldonia danced in circles, vocalizing a song. Estelle clenched her fists and felt for the surge of power, but it did not come. Her legs shook and haze filled her mind, making concentration difficult. The small woman shuffled closer to her.

"Are you ready for my riddle?" the Deep Witch asked.

"A riddle?" Estelle asked. "What happens if my answer is wrong?"

"My sweet, delicate winter iris. Choose correct and you avoid my virus. Should your answer fail and be shoddy? I'll poison you and eat your body."

The woman smiled, her brown teeth caked with grime. Nausea overcame Estelle as she inhaled abrasive fumes. Her vision became blurry, and she staggered.

Before she lost the rest of her energy, she lunged at the woman, falling to the ground an inch or two before her stubby, hairy toes.

"The only way out is to play," said Caldonia.

Estelle pushed herself up, growling.

"What-" she coughed, covering her mouth. "What do I have to do?"

The tunnel goblin clapped, and the coffins opened. At the first glance, Estelle turned her back, fell to her knees and retched. The decaying bodies of her loved ones faced her when she looked again. The right coffin held her father, Damian Grigori. A yellow pallor touched his shriveled face, framed by brittle, gray hair. The body to the left belonged to her dearest friend, Irina. A snapped neck left her corpse grotesquely twisted, its hollow, white eyes fixed upon her. Burned flesh and exposed bones made up the center body. She recognized the purple button-down shirt and the remnants of a goatee. Marcel. She could not bear to see them and the Deep Witch met her, pulling her hands away from her face. She had not the strength to protest.

"Here is my riddle, Estelle," she said. "Who will you save? Who will save you? And who will grant you your freedom?"

Estelle coughed again, and the witch inhaled through her nose as if smelling a bouquet of roses. She snorted, embodying the hog she wore.

"Will it be your trusted confidant? Your gentle lover? Or the overbearing father? You tell me! Or I'll have your flesh! I'm oh, so hungry!"

As Caldonia moved closer, Estelle pushed her away, falling once more. Tears welled in her eyes as she fixated on Marcel's burned body. She swallowed her anguish.

"We have to get you home, little sister," Irina said, her head leaning against the side of her casket. "We've all been so worried since you disappeared!"

"I- I've been trying to get home," Estelle said. "I swear I'm doing everything I can."

"We just want to know you're safe," Marcel said, his charred skin flaking around his mouth.

"We must *ensure* you are safe," said Damian's body. "Our legacy lives on in you. You are the future, daughter."

Estelle could only look at them a few seconds at a time before the lump in her throat would betray her bravery.

"'You're more trouble than you're worth,'" Estelle said. "My father said those words to me... Irina may want to help, but she would never cross him. Marcel would do anything for me... I know he'd save me."

"I would do anything for you, snow crystal," Marcel's remains said.

Estelle's voice wedged itself at the base of her throat. She tried to remind herself of where she was and what she needed. Sherman Manor; she had to get back. She reached into her pocket and grasped the violet sapphire. She could not believe she had not lost it.

"What about you, Father?" Estelle asked Damian. "Would you save me?"

"I could never allow harm to come to you," he said. "You

are my offspring; my image. There is a reason your record is clean."

"Nothing to tarnish the family name. You'd hide your disappointment of a daughter, but would *you* come to save me? Not your men, not mercenaries- you?"

Damian's pale lips kept tight.

"Marcel is who would save me."

Marcel's gold coffin closed, and the chain hoisted it up passed the waterfalls. The Deep Witch clapped and danced, tumbling forward and springing up like a gymnast.

"Very good!" the hog pelt bounced as she pranced. "Now, two more. Go ahead! I'm hungry, girl!"

"Back off!" Estelle felt a tiny spark in her gut. "Give me some space... Who would I save and who would give me freedom? There's only one of them I'd save, but..."

The more Estelle contemplated the riddle, the more unsettled she became. Irina would undoubtedly give the woman her freedom, but she'd be saving her father out of obligation, the same way he would save her.

"I know my father would never give me freedom," she whispered. "Even if he says he will."

The toxic fumes made it most difficult to think, and a wheeze accompanied her cough. She had the notion that even if she stalled to answer the riddle, the fumes would make her pass out. Then Caldonia would have her.

"If you would only earn that freedom," Damian said. "All I'm looking for is one good sign that you can handle yourself."

"Estelle," Irina said. "You know I'd do anything for you. You're my little sister, and all I've ever wanted is to see you happy."

"I would save Irina," the Seeker said sharply, turning away and massaging her temples.

The witch grumbled as Irina disappeared into the waterfall.

"Does that mean Daddy dearest would grant you freedom?" the witch asked, grinding her teeth and drooling.

Estelle hesitated to answer, her mind swimming, her vision doubled. She wondered where Supernova must have been. Was he being tormented by his own goblin? Would he even try to find her? Estelle shook her head and focused on her father's withered cadaver. His frown lines cut deeply through his face, stopping at his bushy gray mustache. She had not realized how slumped her head was until the Deep Witch lifted her chin.

"Answer," she said, orange eyes shaking in their sockets.

The choice was obvious; too obvious. And she understood.

"I would free myself," Estelle said through burning tears.

Caldonia broke into a tantrum, screaming, spitting and slamming her feet on the grate. Damian's coffin shut and the noisy chains drew it away. Though the yellow clouds permeated the area, Estelle heard buzzing in her ears and her strength returned. Power surged through her veins and she grabbed the witch by her pelt, holding her several feet off the ground. She squealed and thrashed, but Estelle took hold of her arms and squeezed her.

"How do I get out of here?!" the Seeker shouted through a cough. "I played your game. Tell me or- or I'll burn you to a crisp!"

"Now, now," the Deep Witch said with a forced laugh. "These fumes are flammable. One spark could turn this whole chamber into a firetrap. Let's not be too hasty."

"You were hasty enough to eat me! I can still rip your arms off!"

Icy light flared in the Seeker's eyes, and the deep witch held her breath. The small woman rattled like a frightened pup and a twinge of sympathy arose in Estelle that she did not want. Others made her feel helpless before. Ms Volkova. Nina. Her father. In that spirit, she set the witch down and stepped back.

"If you help me," Estelle said. "I promise to spare your life."

Caldonia knelt, bowing her head. "Thank you. Yes. Thank you, pretty lady."

"Can you take me to the surface?"

The witch fiddled with her hog pelt, pulling at it and rubbing the leather through her hands.

"Well," she said. "The wolf won't want me to."

"Wolf?"

"He rules these waterways. We are all beholden to him."

"There's more of you?"

"Oh yes, mistress. Dozens of Deep Witches. But Wolf is first and strongest. Angriest."

"Well, if we run into him, he'll have to deal with me."

## CHAPTER 16

## DEEP WOLF

Caldonia brought Estelle through a maze of tunnels and runoff rooms, each separated by bulkheads. The small creature knew of a safety release switch hidden in the frames, taking seconds to open. The Seeker remained several paces behind the Deep Witch, attempting to avoid the tingling scent of rotten eggs wafting from her. The humidity of the sewers gave the woman's hair wide waves that she stroked to straighten in order to pass the time.

"A friend was with me before I fell down here," Estelle said. "Do you know where he is?"

"I know not, my lady," Caldonia said. "He could be lost in the tunnels or at the mercy of my siblings."

Estelle scoffed. "You don't know him if you think he'd be at anyone's mercy."

"I saw inside your mind. That man has two faces."

"That was pretty messed up, don't you think?"

Caldonia made an uncomfortable groan.

"It is... our way. Taught to us by Deep Wolf. Long ago, he showed our grandfather's grandfathers how to haunt."

"Like a ghost?"

"Indeed. It takes great energy and effort to manipulate reality and cause hallucinations. All waterways here are haunted by Him. Caldonia is best among tribe though."

Through a leaky tunnel, across another runoff room and up more stairs than the Seeker bothered to count, brought them to a large treatment center with a grid of twelve open vats. Green, yellow and orange liquids swirled in them, creating a thick cloud in the rafters.

The Deep Witches made their home here, using sheet metal, chain-link fences, dismantled catwalks and water tanks to build a subterranean village. Estelle counted no less than thirty stunted forms, all draped in the leather hide of one animal or another. Sheep, cows, feral canines, and more hogs turned toward them as they entered.

"Outsider!" one cried from the group.

"Interloper!" said another.

"Caldonia has betrayed us!"

Their voices erupted in frustration and worry. Some referenced the wrath of Wolf, declaring Caldonia would be "dipped" for her treason. Estelle's reluctant companion looked up at her and shrugged.

"Everyone, please," Estelle said, raising her hands. "Just a moment- QUIET!"

Sparks cracked, and her voice boomed like thunder. The Deep Witches fell silent and shrank back.

"I don't want any trouble," Estelle said. "I just want to find my friend and get to the surface."

"We should dip them both! Wolf will reward us!"

The crowd murmured and nodded in agreement.

"What does that mean?" Estelle asked.

"It is our deadliest punishment," Caldonia said. "You are suspended by chains in the death vat until your body is eaten away. Please have mercy, mistress. We fear His wrath."

"I'm really starting to want to meet this wolf."

There was the sound of a sharp, metallic screech. It came as if something was clawing through the unseen pipes. The Deep Witches scattered, vanishing into small huts or vent openings. Caldonia grasped Estelle's boot and dropped to her knees, trembling.

From the nearest vat came a slender hand with pointed fingers twelve inches long. Lanky arms came up, dripping with green chemical waste. The patched face of a wolf emerged, and a tall, gaunt figure crawled out like a monstrous spider. A pelt of sewn animal hides covered most of its body. Beneath the cloak, Estelle glimpsed pale yellow flesh covered in puss-leaking blisters. Orange eyes glowed in the holes of the wolf mask as it drew itself up, standing eight feet tall.

"You called, Little Blue?" His voice gurgled. "I am the Deep Wolf. It's so rare that my food comes to me. You'll make a fine meal, yes?"

"I'm just passing through," Estelle said, stepping back. "I'm looking for a friend. Tall man? Long hair? Super discourteous?"

The wolf laughed and happily scratched the concrete floor, digging flakes up.

"Ah! The mighty Supernova Swordsman. I never thought I'd get to devour him. He is already in the clutches of my spell. If he is your friend, then your bond will make you both taste just delectable." The wolf cast his eyes to Caldonia. "That one will be for dessert. After she marinates in the vat for a day."

Caldonia gasped in fear and tore away into a nearby hole in the wall.

"Now, girl, I hunger."

He reached for Estelle.

"Don't touch me!" she demanded with a grimace and casting a bolt of blue lightning at him.

Deep Wolf skidded back, but shook it off, producing a

scream that sounded more like a retch. He encroached and Estelle stepped forward, throwing a punch at his midsection. The lanky devil grasped her, his fingers covering her entire forearm. He held her up to his face and screamed, belching smog in her face.

"Wait!" Estelle said, her eyes burning. "Can't- can't I at least see my friend before you kill me?"

The deep wolf laughed, waving a clawed hand in the air.

"I think not, Little Blue."

"B-but wouldn't we taste better if we saw each other right at the end?"

Deep Wolf tilted his head, scratching a bulbous nose beneath the pelt.

"I cannot decide! Let's say you answer a riddle. If you answer wrong, I take you to him bleeding and screaming, yes?"

She had no choice but to agree.

"Fine! Fine, yes! Now... What's invisible that kills and never stands still? Too much, and it has no worth, to some a gift and to others a curse. What is it?"

Estelle searched the holes in the wolf's face, the orange pinpoints rattling. She forced herself to think. Deep Wolf's claw came up to her face for a playful scrape.

"Hold on!" she said. "Let me think! It's... it's time?"

Deep Wolf howled. "This one is smart! Yes! Come now, Little Blue. Suffering! More suffering!"

A dark opening to a tunnel lay at the opposite end of the room and the wolf pointed to it, relinquishing Estelle and pushing her forward with such force she fell to the ground. She briefly considered trying to fight him again. Perhaps if she channeled more power, she could overtake him. Her gut told her to refrain and with a low growl, she proceeded to the tunnel with the toxic menace literally breathing down her neck.

Supernova was trapped in the den; Deep Wolf's personal section of the tunnels that he alone dwelled in. It was dark and cold, with most of the wall lights destroyed and corners packed with filthy yellow barrels that leaked foamy sludge. Every time Estelle passed one, she gagged at the scent of decaying chemicals. Deep Wolf inhaled them as if he were breathing for the first time.

Estelle's captor brought her to a chamber comprised of a long metal walkway with several rooms off of it, each one visible via a pane of glass. Most of the rooms were vacant, but when they stopped at the third window, Estelle sighed. Supernova stood in the center of the empty chamber with his back to the glass, shrouded by his storm cloak.

"You see him," Wolf said. "Now you are ready to be eaten!"

Estelle took a deep breath and looked into the lifeless mask.

"I want to talk to him," she said. "Think of how delicious we'll be if we get to speak before we die... Yes?"

The wolf shivered, reared up and threw his head back.

"This one is *very* clever! Yes! Trap you both in the spell. The flavor! The flavor!"

Wolf opened the door and shoved Estelle inside. She stepped on broken tiles and the gray walls made it feel like a prison cell. The light above flickered on and off, and each time the room went dark, Supernova disappeared. Even without the light, she could make out the outlines of the corners, the window, the broken tiles; but not him. It was like he didn't exist when the lights were off. She reached her hand out, touching his shoulder.

When the lights flickered again, they bathed the room in a deep red light. Instead of an empty chamber, three metal tables sat in the center, covered in human-shaped sheets.

Supernova looked down at the center table, the face of the body exposed. It was the Pale Lady, but not as Estelle knew her. Deep, vibrant blue colored her lips with matching shades of eyeshadow and absent were the jagged black marking that crawled down her face.

"Supernova?" Estelle said. "You have to wake up. We need to leave."

The Storm Caster kept his eyes focused downward, still as a statue.

"Wake up!"

That metallic scratching came from above. Estelle looked up to see the Deep Wolf emerging from the shadows. He clung to the ceiling like an insect and twisted his masked head to gaze down.

"Well?" he asked. "Have you had your fill of misery and heartbreak?"

She shook Supernova harder this time.

"I need you!"

"What is your problem?!" the swordsman snapped, glaring at her with scarlet eyes.

"We're about to be eaten, you asshole! Would it kill you to be present?!"

"You think this thing is a threat to me?!"

Deep Wolf dropped and stood over them, his claws stretching.

"Enough talk!" the monster said. "I'm *starving!*"

As the creature lunged, Supernova took hold of the pelt, throwing him against the window.

"*Locus,*" he said, his eyes turning purple.

Violet lighting surged around his right hand and he drew it back as Deep Wolf recovered. Supernova waited for the thing to attack before delivering a powerful blow to his face, sending him flying through the glass. As he crawled away, the lights flickered, bringing them to the original version of the room. Estelle made to chase after Deep Wolf, but something grabbed her arm and jerked her back.

"You couldn't handle that thing?" Supernova asked, huffing and narrowing his eyes.

"I came to save you!" Estelle shouted. "He told me you were under his spell!"

"*You save me?* He who defeated the Pale Lady? Who can shatter mountains and bring moons crashing down? You came to save yourself!"

"How was I supposed to know you enjoy this shit?! I didn't think-"

"That's your problem! You don't think."

Supernova exited the room, walking so fast she only glimpsed his cloak. His words stunned her and left a tight feeling in her chest. She had not the time to dwell on them.

Estelle pursued Supernova, who pursued the wolf back to the Deep Witch village. She came through the tunnel entrance just as the Storm Caster took hold of Deep Wolf's foot. Supernova stopped him from escaping into the pipes by dragging him away from a vat. The swordsman then whipped the lanky creature into one of the small houses as though he were a rag doll.

Deep wolf scrambled up. Forced into a corner, he slashed at the swordsman with his putrid claws. Dodging each attack, Supernova drew his katana. He leaped back and assumed a stance, holding the sword at a horizontal angle nearly hidden behind him. In a flash of purple lightning, he appeared behind Deep Wolf in the same stance, leaving behind a glimpse of a flaming ball whose tail arced through the monster. As Deep Wolf turned to attack again, his arms detached, spraying blue blood all over the ground. Before he could scream vengeful threats, his head fell from his neck and rolled away. His body dropped and convulsed.

As Estelle approached, the Deep Witches cautiously

filtered from their hiding spots, with Caldonia returning to the Seeker. The small people kept their distance from the Supernova Swordsman as he eyed each one, his pupils so small they ceased to be.

"A whole den of them," Supernova said. "I'll clear them out."

Supernova's first slash came to Caldonia. Had her perception not been blessed by the storm, Estelle would not have been able to save her. She caught her companion's wrists as they came down. He broke free and attempted to round her, bringing a stab at Caldonia. Again Estelle saved her, pulling her weight against his and forcing him to flip over her. He landed as gracefully as a cat.

"So you reveal your true self," Supernova said, brimming with violet sparks. "I knew it was only a matter of time. Why else would Demella give you that power?"

"That's ridiculous!" Estelle yelled at the top of her lungs. "You need to listen to me. I'm-"

"You're a serpent, just like her. Already making allies of the enemies bolster her numbers. I won't be fooled! Not again!"

"You're not thinking right," Estelle said, pushing Caldonia back with her foot. "These fumes have you all messed up."

He stepped toward her, his power flaring. He exerted a heavy pressure, and mentally Estelle tried to press against it with her own energies. It felt like trying to shove a train. He walked her backward until her back pressed against Deep Wolf's escape vat. The lightning in his cloak struck violently as external arcs licked the surrounding metal.

He watched her unblinking, as if waiting for her to attack. Estelle's father did something similar when she got in trouble. He'd give her the chance to explain herself, only to tear apart any reason or logic she put forth. Supernova was the same; any answer was the wrong one.

Estelle slid her hand in her pocket, slowly while keep the other in clear view. She offered her letter to the wrathful man. Suspiciously, he took it and read it, his eyes shooting from the paper to her.

"You?" he asked, clenching his jaw. "You're the Seeker? Why didn't you say that?!"

"I can't say two words to you without it becoming a fight!"

She braced herself for the shockwave of his voice, but it never came. The glow of his eyes quieted, leaving them so deep a brown they appeared black. Caldonia shyly approached Estelle.

"Take you to freedom now?" she asked.

The Deep Witch guided them, vocalizing her song, through various tunnels until finally they came to a tall iron ladder. As far as District 5 was concerned, this would be the closest exit. After bidding the Caldonia farewell, they ascended.

The sky faded from wine above to burnt orange on the horizon. Supernova reached forth a hand to help Estelle from the manhole, and she swatted it away.

They came out at a water station nestled in hills packed with elaborate houses. Their shapes were strange, with some being constructed as stacked spheres or patterns of triangular designs. High iron fences with withered remains of shrubs surrounded each home. At the crest of the hill, the plots of mansions and manors became visible several miles to the east.

They arrived at Sherman manor around noon, spending the hours in silence. The giant houses kept the distance of five or six acres between them, decrepit stone walls lining the battered streets. Barricades and checkpoints increased in number as they drew closer, though they were unmanned. After the third checkpoint, a half dozen soldiers clad in green patrolled the final hundred yards to the manor.

"Hold it!" a masked man said. "What's your business here?"

"That's *her!*" a younger soldier said. "The girl who rescued our people! Blue dress, black hair!"

For the first time in hours, Estelle's cheeks burned with the beginning of a smile.

"You mean the girl who brought the war with Bleedstar here?"

What hope fluttered in her heart died like the moth to the flame. The first guard looked them over but let them pass with a scoff.

"I'll get the car," the second soldier said.

"No. They traveled this far. They can walk down the damn street."

He chuckled as they passed, the others silent as the grave. The next round of guards they came to were at the manor's shield. Two small booths sat on either side, with a pair of operators in each. To Estelle's surprised the two out front emerged as friends.

"Thank god," Sue said, throwing her arms around Estelle and squeezing.

"Thought we lost you guys," Theo said, grinning.

"She needs to rest," Supernova said. "She's going to pass out."

"I feel fine," she said.

"You need to rest."

"What are you, my father? Don't tell me what to do! Especially with the way you acted!"

"Says the girl snuggling up to the Deep Witches. They'd

have picked your bones clean as soon as you turned your back."

"You saw that thing that ruled them! They were scared! They were-"

Estelle's vision darkened and her speech slurred as she stumbled.

"Somebody catch her!"

CHAPTER 17

SHOTS FIRED IN THE THEATER

Though her last memories were on the streets before Sherman Manor, Estelle awoke in the dark place again with only a tree for company. Previously, the gleaming sapling sprouted a couple inches from a layer of snow, but it had grown to twenty feet tall. Its branches reached outward, fuzzy with fir needles. Its light expanded in a circle, the snow ending at the edge where darkness began.

A sweet and spicy scent caught her attention, and a warm pulse expanded along the ground. A pool of light formed just beyond the end of the snow and cautiously, Estelle wandered closer to it.

In the center of the pool, a twig pushed itself up. It grew tall and thick in seconds, making Estelle fall back a few paces. As the new tree rose, it sprouted thick branches covered in bright green leaves and bell-shaped flowers of royal blue, indigo and violet, each one glowing like a tiny lamp. Before long, a grand rosewood tree loomed over Estelle's adolescent fir.

A small space opened near the rosewood's trunk. White threads, long and thin, formed within. One connected to another, expanding and taking the form of a human skeleton. Aging with the tree, organs, muscles, tissue, skin and hair formed. Flowers grew between her ebony locks and vines wound around her arms and legs, encased in the trunk.

A blue skirt peeked through heavy roots, the armored arm fastened to her side by unwavering bark, and the three-jeweled diadem held slivers of highlights given by the flowers. This version of the Pale Lady was of ivory skin and she lacked the black facial markings of her evil counterpart. Her lips were a deep, vibrant blue with shadow on her eyelids to match.

The Pale Lady slept in peace. Estelle stepped closer and reached up to feel her hair. The wavy lock was softer than silk and thick with spirals at the ends. The Seeker furrowed her brow as the woman in the tree slowly opened her eyes; hazel flecked with green.

"Why is the Pale Lady in my mind?" Estelle asked.

"My name is Vileena," the woman said. "Lady of the Pale Headlands. You are the woman who fought alongside Nova. You're quite brave to have attacked Demella... or quite foolish. Who are you?"

"I'm Estelle. I guess I wasn't thinking about it at the time. But I have to ask: why are you in my head?"

"This isn't your head. It's the core of your spirit, called the Sem Tso or the Mind Lake."

Estelle frowned and shook her head.

"That tree behind you," Vileena continued. "We all have one. It signifies our growth as people. The larger it is, the greater your spirit."

"That still doesn't explain why you're here. I feel like I should be worried about seeing the Pale Lady in my spirit."

"This is who I truly am. That thing you did battle with has control of my body- my lightning. I tried to stop her from attacking you, but-"

"But what?"

"I don't really remember what happened."

"I don't understand," the Seeker said. "What do you mean, you tried to stop her?"

Vileena's hazel eyes looked into the blue-black beyond the light of the trees as she shifted beneath the roots.

"I am possessed," the Pale Queen said. "Forced to watch Demella carry out atrocities from the back of my own mind. During the fight, I wrestled with her for control of my body and failed. You're actually the first person I've spoken to in two years."

Estelle turned away and massaged her temples. Though she was unwillingly becoming used to the hauntings, she found Vileena to be the least horrific to look upon. She felt that if she were trapped in a tree, she'd lose her mind like a rabid animal. But the woman before her was as calm as a sleeping jaguar, watching Estelle with curious eyes.

"How did this happen to you?" Estelle asked.

"I traveled to Eve's Hollow with Nova," Vileena said. "I was helping with him complete his labor- to vanquish a brood of evil spirits here in the city. We succeeded, but when we returned some years later, one of the spirits had as well, unbeknownst to us. I remember that night so clearly. It was the last time I was truly happy."

Vileena's eyes gained a gloss and her blue lips frowned. Estelle did not want to ask her next question.

"What happened?"

"The last thing I remember is Nova and Theo's smiling faces. We were having a grand party at the Blue Key Club. I blinked- then fire. Screaming. Death." Vileena's mouth tightened. "I saw glimpses. Standing over the fallen. Dismembered civilians. Nova's terrified face..."

A soft whimper escaped the queen's lips.

"The Blue Key Massacre," Estelle said, eyes growing wide.

"Is that what they call it?" Vileena's head hung low. "The city must despise me now."

The Seeker had not the heart to confirm that truth.

"Tell me how I can get you out of this tree," Estelle said, pulling at a root.

"I wish I could," Vileena said, heartbroken. "That's what Nova has been working on. I've seen him through her eyes. He dwells on how to save me."

"Is that why he's such a dick?"

Estelle had not meant to insult him so and only realized it when Vileena's eyes widened and she pursed her lips.

"Tell me, Estelle. What is your relationship with the Supernova Swordsman?"

Vileena's voice deepened and despite her physical prison, she exuded an aura of dominance with fixed eyes and steady, controlled breathing.

"I'm not supposed to be in this city," Estelle said. "I woke up with a note, a key and a crow, and I've been trying to survive ever since. Supernova is apparently my Guardian."

Vileena raised an eyebrow.

"You are his eighth labor?" the queen asked. "The Seeker he is supposed to guide?"

"His lack of manners, superiority complex and nonchalance make it difficult."

The queen laughed, nodding in amusement.

"That sounds like him. I know he can be abrasive. But deep down, his intentions are good."

"Then why is he so cruel to me? It's like he hates me."

"It isn't you. When I met him, he had nothing to hold on to. I was the same. We found each other to support. My predicament brings out certain obsessions in him that I thought were managed."

"What do you mean?"

Vileena looked passed Estelle rather than at her and a sneer came across her face.

"Vileena?"

"I want you to promise something," the queen said.

"It depends on what you're asking..."

"If Nova should fail to... I want you to kill me."

Taken aback, Estelle shook her head. This gentle woman in the tree seemed so kind, so tranquil. Yet she asked to be destroyed so casually without a drop of hesitance.

"There must be a way to save you," Estelle said. "I mean, there're exorcisms and all that?"

"Do you think he hasn't tried? Nova spent two years trying to figure out how to save me. Even with all the resources at his disposal, I remain trapped. I am certain that death would take both the demon and myself... Estelle, if you don't, she could destroy everyone and everything."

"Why me?"

"You possess the storm now. You siphoned a portion of my soul during the fight; that's why I'm here. That's why you can storm cast. I couldn't have known it was possible, but here you stand with all the potential in the world."

"Still-"

"Master Eze is too old and Nova may not have the heart. I can sense your passion and your drive. In the right circumstance, you may be the only one who can prevail."

Estelle's teeth clenched, and she dug at the skin under her fingernails.

"I can't," she said. "I can't face her again."

"I understand her power is great-"

"She's the devil! She knows things about me... she knew my name. I just can't."

Estelle stared into Vileena's hazel eyes and the queen nodded, her eyebrows falling.

"There must be a way to help," Estelle said. "A way that doesn't involve either of us dying."

"You remind me of him. Always trying to find the compromise. I know you don't see it, but he has a heart of gold under all his frustrating qualities. He just has the weight of the universe on his shoulders."

Estelle rolled her eyes.

"I wish I didn't take it personally. How can I not- especially when he's so nasty to me? I only want to go home. I don't want to be a burden, but that's how he treats me. I try to be a nice person, but he brings this... rage out of me."

Vileena laughed again.

"Take my advice, Seeker. If you want to earn his respect, ask for his insight."

"He likes to hear himself talk?"

"He sees things deeper than we do. Some answers we struggle for he can see, like the rising sun. When he becomes unreasonable, walk away and say nothing."

"But-"

"Say *nothing*."

Vileena's face was stern and unblinking. Estelle agreed.

"Now," the Pale Queen said. "You're going to wake up soon. Be warned, Seeker." Her face bunched as if waging a mental war with herself. "Estelle, do not tell Nova you spoke to me."

"I don't understand-"

"Promise me!"

She spoke with the commanding voice of the royalty she claimed to be. Estelle's heart skipped a beat and again she nodded. As the woman in the tree spoke, her words became slurred as if an audible river washed them away. The Sem Tso around her melted.

～

It had been two days since Estelle and the Supernova Swordsman arrived at Sherman Manor and she awoke in the first floor infirmary. Beeping machines stood beside her and she traced their wires to her arms, chest and temples. In place of her blue dress, she wore an old white t-shirt and sweatpants. The pink room was lit with warm yellow lamps on nightstands between the beds and sheer white curtains covered the windows. Estelle's bed was one of six, arranged in two rows of three, and she was alone. That was all she could make out before sleeping again.

She awoke again an hour later as Mae leaned over her, pressing a cold stethoscope to her chest. She explained to Estelle that after securing a blood sample from her, she found it tainted due to the toxic fumes from the tunnels. She had not expected Estelle to wake for at least a week. In forty-eight hours, her health returned to normal.

After checking her vitals, Mae allowed her to change back into her clothes. As Estelle reached for the door, Mae grabbed the knob and shot her a glance.

"We need to talk before you go," she said.

Once the door opened, Theo, Estelle's white crow and Supernova entered. The bird flew to the bed nearest to her and Theo flopped down next to it. Supernova leaned against the closed door, wearing a deadpan expression.

"What's wrong?" Estelle asked.

"Two years ago," Mae said. "Supernova and his girlfriend returned to Eve's Hollow. He was on a mission to find and help a Seeker; a person looking to restore their soul. He's told me you are that person. Is that correct?"

Estelle looked at her crow, and it nodded. She fixed on Supernova as he carelessly stared across the room.

"You have to forgive our secrecy," Theo said. "We had to be sure we could trust you. We've been on the lookout for the elusive Seeker during our time here."

"Did you say he had a girlfriend?" Estelle asked, picturing Vileena.

"She's the love of my life," Supernova said, his voice like a razor.

Mae shot him a glance just as sharp and he avoided her gaze.

"Theo and I are from the Blue Key Club," Mae said. "We came here to cultivate a relationship with Sherman Manor, but…"

"They don't know where we came from," Theo said. "The BKC carries a certain- negative reputation. With things being so hot with Bleedstar, we haven't had a chance to tell Nona."

"Another plus of coming here," Mae said. "Was the hope that you'd come here, looking for safety. And here you are."

Supernova stepped forward.

"We need to get started as soon as possible," he said. "I'll go to the museum and get your key for you."

"And what am I supposed to do?" Estelle asked. "Sit on my ass?"

"That's exactly what you do. Stay out of the way so we can make this quick and painless."

"You really like to tell me what to do, don't you?"

Estelle clenched her jaw and narrowed her eyes.

"It must be nice," Supernova said. "Doing whatever you want when you want. Remind me- how did sneaking out of this place go again?"

"It went by me saving your sorry ass, you-"

"Kids! Kids," Theo said, stretching his arms between the two. "This is definitely not a productive attitude. I don't know much about the Seeker thing, but I feel like if it's her soul, she should be part of the journey."

"I agree," the crow said. "Doing the work for her deprives her of growth, which would defeat the purpose of her trials."

"You all know what's out there," Supernova said. "You

want her to die in a horde or get ripped apart by Demella? Being a Guardian is about protecting her, isn't it?"

Theo and Mae looked away as Supernova's black eyes dwelled on Estelle.

"Has she not already survived the Pale Lady once?" asked the crow.

"That was luck."

"I understand she's acquired power. Power which you can teach her to use, but refuse."

"Again." Supernova's voice dropped. "I'm trying to save her life. She could wind up destroying herself. It takes years to master the art. I told her once and I'll tell her again: she needs to give them up for her own good."

Frustrated, Estelle squeezed her hands into fists. She felt a surge of electricity rush through her bones.

"Hold on," Mae said. "I get what you're saying, Nova. But there's something to be said about stumbling onto something unexpected and dangerous. The people who founded this manor came across the shield tech. I'd guess they didn't know how to use it at first- but here we are in the safest place in Web Obsidia. I've even tampered with it to create the bullets in Theo's gun. I didn't know what I was doing at first, but we're all better off because of it. Couldn't the same principle apply to Essie?"

"Yes," he said through gritted teeth.

Estelle remembered her conversion with Vileena.

"Nova?" Estelle said as gently as her fury would allow. "I have to be honest: I have no intention of giving my power up. You said I hadn't earned it. How can I?"

"It takes years-"

"I know. But there must be something small I can start with?"

"She has a point, brother," Theo said. "You're one of two

master Storm Casters in the whole city. Sometimes you have to look at the glass half full, you know?"

Supernova stared at Estelle for a long while, his lifeless expression making it impossible to tell what he was thinking. He gave a grunt that Theo and Mae took for agreement. Estelle craned her head upward when he approached.

"Let me see your letter," he said.

She handed it to him. In his fingers, the paper took on a violet sheen before completely vanishing. In a blip of light, it returned, and he handed it to its owner.

"Accessing the 'other place' is a low level skill, so you shouldn't injure yourself. You infuse your powers into an item, slipping it through spacetime until you're ready to claim it again. Maybe start with something that isn't made of paper."

"That's it?" Estelle asked.

"That's it. Learn to calm your mind and it'll come easier to you."

Mae stepped between them.

"Since that's settled," she said. "We've got a meeting to get to."

"What sort of meeting?" Estelle asked.

"The sort where the manor guards decide if they want to help you."

"Didn't Nona say I had to contribute to get a vehicle?"

"She's way passed that," Theo said. "After you rescued us from Bleedstar, she thinks it's necessary."

"Not everyone sees it that way."

*The girl who brought war with Bleedstar.* The thought of those words made her stomach turn, but it was true. If she had not snuck out with Raphael- who she had not bothered to think about- then she would have never antagonized the Pale Lady.

"Don't worry about what they say," Mae said, giving her shoulder a light shake. "This city makes it real easy to do the wrong thing. The right thing gets harder and each day and fewer of us do it. Estelle, you did the right thing by saving them. Fuck what anyone else says."

~

The manor's second level theater had been a room Estelle visited on her first morning there. Now the high glass chandeliers were ablaze with somber light and fifty soldiers sat packed into the red cushioned seats, with Sue and Mike leaning against the stage. Estelle, Supernova, Theo and Mae traversed the red carpet down the center to the front row of seats, the crow flying in after and perching on an armrest. After a couple of minutes Nona strode through the door, a brisk pace driving her. She greeted Mike and Sue, then climbed the stage stairs to face her guards.

"I want to thank you all for coming," Nona said, hands clasped at her waist. "As you all know, things have been hectic as of late. The misadventure a couple of nights ago brought unwanted attention from the Pale Lady and her army. We've captured their scouts on the manor outskirts so we know they're looking for us. I want to be clear when I say this: Despite what Mike and Theo did, the Pale Lady would have found us, eventually."

"But it'll happen a lot sooner now, won't it?" a voice from the back asked.

"And we don't have the manpower," said another.

"We cross that bridge when we come to it," Nona said. "There is a silver lining; our newcomer, Estelle, was directly responsible for freeing ten people that night. Our soldiers did their part, but without Mike and Estelle, innocent lives would have been lost. I know you have mixed emotions, but she's asked for a vehicle to get to the Kern Museum. I believe the lives of ten people are worth more than an old truck."

The crowd murmured and watched Nona intently.

"I'm looking for volunteers to go with her. Sue and Theo have already offered their services."

"You're crazy if you think I'll die for her!" The voice came from the other end of the theater and laughed as though someone had told a joke. "You sure you want to lose Sue and Theo over this?"

Several others nodded in agreement. Theo stood and faced the audience.

"I was one of the people she saved," he said, his face hardened and his eyes fierce. "Helping each other is how we've made it this far. This manor is predicated on assisting the weary survivor. I won't beg for anyone's help, but Estelle saved my life and I owe her a debt."

"I don't like this," a woman said.

"You don't have to like it," Sue said, casting sharp, grass green eyes at the speaker. "You just got to respect it."

Some soldiers laughed while others shouted obscenities. Half the crowd grew belligerent in mood while the rest attempted to calm them. Sue and Theo took on several opponents in shouting matches, and there came the point when no words could be discerned. Estelle stood to get a better view of the chaos.

*Pop!*

The piercing crack of a gunshot rang out through the theater. Everyone gasped and ducked as several more shots fired off. Two men disguised as soldiers in the rear seats attacked, armed with pistols. Some up front spun around to locate the assailants while others took shelter beneath the seats. Ralph, who sat at the rear, struggled with a large man clad in dark glasses with a bald, scarred head. A comrade jumped in to help quell the imposter.

To the right, the second fake soldier wrestled with a real one. This attacker was thin with the sides of his head shaved. A mop of stringy black hair flung around in the quarrel. At first, the stranger seemed subdued, but three pops from his handgun reignited the danger. The ally soldier fell dead and Estelle met the man's black eyes. He raised his handgun and fired a shot at the Seeker.

Though the bullet was not slow by any means, her heightened perception allowed her to visibly see the projectile exit the barrel. Her reaction time left much to be desired, as for an instant she was sure it would tear through her. She was moved out of the way in the blink of an eye, lying on the soft carpet. Supernova's form extended in front of her.

The stranger in the crowd continued to fire, hitting several people. In the end, it was Sue who shot and wounded the man's shoulder and he was seized.

Nona stood upon the stage, frozen in shock, hands clenched at her sides. Theo and Mae ran to her, giving consoling words. The woman took a deep breath and steadied her nerves, but still trembled. Several soldiers scanned the theater, weapons drawn. Mike and Sue shouted orders, attempting to keep everyone from panicking. Estelle and Supernova joined the leader on the stage.

"What the hell was that?" Nona asked. "Why? Who?"

"No one recognizes them," Sue said, coming up the stage steps. "They each had one of these in their pockets."

In Sue's gloved hand was a pair of small stone tokens. They each bore a pair of red circles. One filled dot surrounded by a red ring with jagged flames. Ralph and Mike detained the two men, binding their hands and forcing them to their knees.

"The Sanguistella," Supernova whispered.

"Does this mean what I think it does?" Theo asked.

"They've infiltrated the manor."

"How?" Sue asked. "When?"

"Maybe when we fought the snake," Theo said. "We lost a

few people that night. It's possible they stole the uniforms and came back with us."

"Get them out of here!" Nona screamed.

Mike and Ralph dragged the men through the door. Before they went out of sight, the black-haired man turned his head to look back at Estelle. His soulless eyes squinted as his mouth curled into a smug smile. All around them, the soldiers were moving the bodies of their fallen friends and families. Whimpering, crying and angry shouts filled the room.

# CHAPTER 18

## AMMUT'S NECROPOLIS

Two men descended a flight of concrete stairs illuminated by white fluorescent tubes. The iron rail felt cold to the touch and the pale gray walls were cracked and faded with age. After a second set of stairs, they came to a heavy steel door that slid open, extending into a system of corridors.

The slate colored walls rose two stories above them and a forest green carpet lined the icy concrete floor. Theo explained to Supernova that these rooms were bomb shelters and storage areas. Some contained crates of old artwork, some had freeze-dried and canned food, others lay empty for planned uses in the future. One room contained a cache of weapons used to arm the manor soldiers and a sub-basement existed where the laboratory was located. That area produced and maintained the shield.

"You're really going to make her wait outside?" asked Theo.

"Of course," Supernova replied. "You've seen how bad it gets. She shouldn't be part of it."

"I can also see that even though Estelle frustrates you, she makes you more human."

"Come again?"

"We've barely heard from you in two years. Every time we did, you were always quiet, curt and illusive. Shit- that came out wrong. I'm just saying it's better to see you arguing with Estelle than knowing you're brooding and alone. Ever since what happened with Leena, you've lost yourself."

"That isn't true."

The Guardian kept his head straight, his face nestled in his cloak.

"You don't think so? Man, you used to do things that made you happy. Meditation, calling your thunderstorms, telling us stories about the places you've been. You were a man of peace."

"She brought that out of me. That peaceful man is gone with her." He sighed, his breath like a rumbling wind. "Every second that passes is another moment she suffers. It's my fault. I brought her here."

"Have you been sleeping?" Theo asked.

"Nightmares."

Even as the two traversed the bunker, shapes of shadows danced at the corner of Supernova's peripheral. They followed him ceaselessly, sometimes manifesting as either a half decayed human or a shimmering visage if they were bold enough to face him. Angels and demons. Occasionally he would turn to catch one, but they mostly vanished before he could fix on them. Two or three slid into black corners as he turned his head.

"Room's up ahead," Theo said.

They arrived at a long section of small bunkers. Two manor soldiers were posted outside the first three doors. Each one held a rifle or shotgun close to their chest as they conversed. Supernova and Theo came to the third set and gave a nod to the guards- two men, both large in size, with hardened expressions like the side of a mountain.

"Let's find out what he knows," Theo said to the men.

"Who's there?" said the first guard they passed. "Show yourself!"

The six men drew their weapons and pointed to the entrance. A pair of hands emerged, then Supernova's Seeker. The Guardian's eyes narrowed as she approached.

"This section is restricted," the first guard said, relaxing his weapon.

"I want to see the man who attacked us today," Estelle said, an edge of sturdiness to her voice. "I want to see the man who tried to kill me."

"You can't be here, miss," the fourth guard said.

"I think we can make an exception," Theo said.

"But Nona told us-"

"Oh, I know. Trust me. But wouldn't you want to confront the guy who attacked you? What if it was your sister or daughter? What would you guys do?"

The first set of guards whispered something to one another before waving Estelle over. Supernova cast a disappointed glare at his friend, and Theo shrugged.

The soldier with the keys unlocked the door and pulled it open. Supernova, Theo and Estelle entered a medium-sized room lined in faded yellow and brown floral wallpaper. The far left corner had a small bathroom with the door removed and in the right was a small cot and a blanket. Upon the cot lay the man with stringy black hair, his shoulder bandaged. His demeanor was relaxed, and he ignored the interrogators entering his cell. Supernova and Theo looked at one another before Theo gave the signal to close the door behind them. They approached the unconcerned man, Supernova remaining a few steps behind with Estelle.

"I hope your stay has been satisfying," Theo said. "I know

it gets drafty down here. I could see about getting you some more blankets. Or warmer clothes?"

Looking briefly at Theo, then closing his eyes again, the man said nothing. A comfortable smile made him look at ease, even though he sat in enemy custody. Theo frowned, looking over his shoulder at his friend, but Supernova watched the prisoner in deep contemplation. He continued to appeal with humanity and kindness.

"Look man. You and your guy killed six people today and tried to shoot my friend." Theo pointed his thumb over his shoulder. "Our people want to lynch you, but I've convinced them you could be useful. That's not such a bad deal, right?"

"Like the four others next door to me?" the man laughed. "You're pathetic and desperate. I'll never tell you anything. Stop wasting your time."

"Listen to reason. Please-"

"Why did you shoot at me?!" Estelle asked, stepping forward. The man laughed to himself.

She growled and raised her fist. Theo grabbed her arm, a spark shocking his fingers. When she realized what she had done, she apologized profusely. The prisoner cackled, slapping his leg as Supernova approached the bedside.

"I know his kind, Theo," Supernova said, eyeing the man with a stare as cold as the grave. "His reason is suffering. His logic is cruelty. His mantra is to kill. If you want information from him, you need to speak his language."

"You're going to do something spooky, aren't you?" Theo asked insecurely.

"This is cute." The man let out a small laugh, pleased at their efforts to shake him. "I've seen every kind of hell this city has to offer, and there are two kinds of people. There are those who adapt and survive by any means necessary- and then there's the weak and worthless. People who lie to get what they want because they have no real power. Like I said before: I'll never tell you anything."

"'Never' is an interesting word," Supernova said. "At no time in the past, present or future... infinity's twin sibling."

"What bullshit are you rambling about?"

"The only thing equally monumental as always having existed is never having existed. That's what I'm going to do to you if you don't talk."

"You think I'm afraid to die?" The man asked, offended.

"Dead men won't answer my questions. Screaming ones will."

The man's face twisted with confusion. Supernova closed his eyes and filled his lungs with air. As he exhaled, the temperature in the room fell and fog materialized on the ground.

"I've seen shit like this before," the man said, folding one leg beneath a bent knee. "You know where I came from, right? The Lady's powers are unmatched."

"There are beings far more powerful than either of us," Supernova said. "Eve's Hollow is in a pocket outside of space-time, cut off from the Gods and their justice. In a normal universe, Demella could not compare... You said you've seen every hell in Eve's Hollow? Allow me to show you a hell you've never known."

The Guardian turned and glanced at his friend, at which point Theo crossed his arm in front of Estelle to step her back a few feet. Supernova walked to the chamber door and the air in the room became frigid. Wispy puffs glided from their mouths and nostrils. Supernova dropped to one knee and bowed his head.

"I invoke the mighty Osiris," he said. "I humbly request access to the necropolis of Ammut."

The lights blinked twice before leaving them in darkness. Thin streaks of purple illumination filtered through the cracks of the door. A star encased in a circle burned itself on the surface of the metal, glowing brilliantly. A beam shone through the window, casting Supernova in shadow. The Guardian opened the door and the sensation of wailing misery spun through the room like a tornado. The prisoner's eyes widened, and he pressed himself against the wall. Theo and Estelle stood close together as they sought the source of the voices.

"I will show you 'never.'" Supernova's voice was low and layered in echoes and whispers. "Come, now."

"Unless you're afraid?" Theo asked.

The infiltrator slid off his cot and rose, clutching his shoulder. He walked toward Supernova, with Theo keeping watch from behind. The four stepped through.

Torches lined walls made of sand colored stones the size of cars. To Supernova's right was the large arch of a tunnel flanked by pillars carved into the likeness of seated lions with the heads of crocodiles. To the left was an ascending set of sandstone stairs that led to an altar. Upon it, lit by a brazier, was a replication of the crocodile headed lion sculpted in pure gold.

Embedded in the walls and set out across the chamber in large even spaces were heavy rock hewn coffins, each with carvings of names. There were at least a hundred. The prisoner froze as his eyes fell upon them. Theo nudged him forward as Estelle watched every dusty cranny. Supernova brushed the top of the coffins as he passed them and stopped in the center of the grid. He faced Theo, Estelle and the prisoner.

"This," Supernova said, raising his hands. "Is what 'never' looks like. Ammut is an ancient entity. You see, her purpose is to devour the hearts of the truly wicked. If you are as I suspect, she would find you ravishing. This is where her sacrifices are laid to rest. The sacrifices *I* make. If I took your heart back in Eve's Hollow, you'd have just died. Dying in the necropolis means your life, memory in others, your very essence gets trapped here. Everyone you know would forget you; even your own parents."

The stranger remained silent and unmoving. Theo tried to maintain a relaxed demeanor, but the otherworldly realm felt like hands grasping as his arms and legs. Estelle shivered, watching the dark tunnel. They, as well as the prisoner, jumped when low growling came from the darkness beyond the pillars. Shining orange eyes waited just out of the light.

"Those are undead jackals," Supernova said, peering toward the arch. "These underground chambers are full of them." The growls grew louder. "So you have a few choices: I take your heart and sacrifice you. I let the jackals have you. Or you tell us everything we want to know. I promise if I leave you here, you will *never* get out."

The would-be assassin remembered to breathe as beads of sweat formed on his forehead. He cleared his throat and worked up the nerve to look Supernova in the face.

"Go fuck yourself."

"I would say the same thing."

With the snap of his fingers, Supernova summoned the jackals. Three rushed into the tomb, swift as storm wind. They surrounded the man- beasts the size of tigers with hulking shoulders and blade-like claws. Empty eye sockets held points of hell light focused on the man. Their flesh was dry and peeling from exposed bone. The largest, yet thinnest, of the three wore a golden collar around its neck with an amethyst pendant. That one sat next to Supernova.

One jackal bit into the man's leg and he fell, screaming for his life. Another bit down on his arm and the two pulled him in different directions, snarling.

"HOLD ON!" he cried. "Please!"

"Rashma," Supernova said.

The watchful jackal with the golden collar barked and the other two immediately fell back, blood dripping from their teeth. He pet the creature, caressing its dead face. It offered a playful growl to its master.

"What- do you want- to know?" the stranger asked, panting and nursing his bleeding arm.

"Let's start with something simple," Theo said. "What's your name?"

"Ress." He panted. "Before I say anything else, all I have to do is answer your questions and you'll take me back to my cell?"

"You have our word. Supernova would be fine with leaving you here, but I actually give a damn. Even if you helped kill my friends."

"Well, Ress," Supernova said, nuzzling the jackal. "We have a lot to talk about. Let's get started."

# CHAPTER 19

# UNCHARTED TERRITORY

Estelle was awoken from her sleep on the morning after the theater incident- not that she really could rest. Her mind tortured her with the screams of disembodied voices and the ancient skulls of her Guardian's pet jackals. She was grateful when Mae roused her to depart for Kern Museum. Baron Ransley had been in his bed when she went to sleep, but at some point he left. Estelle's crow flew to Mae's shoulder, who scratched his head.

The time was four-thirty in the morning and when she and Mae stepped into the Manor's backyard, the dark orange at the horizon already began its transformation to scarlet. Ready for departure, two large, van-like vehicles sputtered to life. Where Estelle figured she would have three companions, seven awaited her arrival.

The woman forced back a smile when she saw Ransley leaning against the vehicle beside Theo, Sue and Supernova and she embraced him. Ralph waited at the next van, were two men in yellow hazmat suits loaded heavy duffle bags in the back seat. Andrew gave her a wave before turning to his companion, a man who bore "K4" on his chest, but Owen was his true name. Mae would remain at the manor, continuing her support role.

The eight piled into the vans with Estelle, her crow, Theo, Sue and Supernova in one and Ransley, Andrew, Owen and Ralph in the other. The team left the manor grounds and headed west through Serenus Acres. Turning South to avoid a series of collapsed buildings, they continued through Irontown until they came to Kollektra and stayed on its east side to avoid the courthouse. They used the tall buildings for cover, and Estelle admired the long bridges connecting them.

Sue and Theo conversed in the front seat, with Estelle and Supernova in the back. Her Guardian's head tilted back and his eyes closed as if he were sleeping, the crow in his lap. Estelle held her oval sapphire in her hand, concentrating on putting her energy into it. She made a fist and tried to will the item away, but it shone in her palm every time she spread her fingers again.

"You're thinking too much," Supernova said, motionless. "You'll overcharge and destroy it. You need to relax."

"I can't," Estelle said. "Ever since I saw your monsters tear into that man."

"You feel bad for the man who tried to kill you?"

"Yes- I mean no... I don't know. I just don't think anyone deserves that."

"He deserved worse."

"What is wrong with you?"

"Nova," Theo said, stressing the last syllable. "Come on, man."

"Didn't we get the information?" The Guardian turned his body to face Estelle. "Didn't we learn a dozen of those rats are scouring District 5, looking for the manor? Didn't we learn their locations so your friends can hunt them down? You might not like my methods, but they get results. This is how I do business, so if you have something to say..." He leaned toward her. "Speak your mind."

His eyes widened and his brows rose, and Estelle knew he smirked beneath his cloak. She imagined throwing her fist into his face and wondered if she would hit his mouth or nose.

"Nothing," she said, turning to the window, thinking of Vileena. Her head snapped back to him. "You're an asshole. A self-assured, gloomy, insouciant jackass who I can't believe is supposed to help me."

"I've got a question for you," the Guardian said. "Seekers come to this city for redemption. I don't mean giving attitude or running around with boys. What truly wretched thing made you recite the Hymn of the Hollow?"

Estelle spoke, but her scowl held like plaster. "I don't know what you're talking about."

"You must have some idea. Research is rare for what we are, but most Seekers seem to be antagonistic, mistrustful and violent- all the things you are."

"Says the man who can't be bothered to say anything unless it's an insult... *Violent?!* You set those dogs on that man, and I wonder what would have happened if he didn't submit."

Supernova laughed. "You really have to wonder?"

Estelle knew. She struggled to fathom the kind of person who would feed a living man to monsters- bloodthirsty beasts like the ones prowling Web Obsidia. What was worse was that he wore Marcel's face.

"What even are you?" Estelle asked, dumbfounded. "Are you even a person?"

"Listen, you cocky little bi-"

"SHUT IT!" Sue screamed. "Both of you!"

"Now you've done it," Theo said, sucking air through his teeth.

"We're out here on an important task and you two are giving me more of a headache than the damn Punished. Ralph is trying to tell us something, and it'd be wonderful if I could hear. Theo, please."

Estelle glared at Supernova, and he squinted in return. Theo held a black radio and turned the volume up.

"Something's wrong," Ralph said. "Pull over up here."

The vehicles came to a stop in the center of the street, with Sue pulling up alongside the first van. Rolling down the windows, Ralph pointed ahead. At first glance, nothing seemed out of place. The longer Estelle stared at the surroundings, the more she realized the slant of the buildings. Several lobbies and lower floors had been broken and beaten out, giving them the appearance of trees about to fall.

"At first I thought it was the demon," Ralph said. "I don't know. Something doesn't feel right."

A loud series of pops came from overhead and behind them. Theo stuck his head out of the window and looked for the source. Soon came a blaring explosion. It multiplied, shooting in a line from the path they'd taken. The shrunken bases of the buildings detonated in fiery chaos, sending ash, rock and flame into the streets.

Sue sped away, with Ralph right behind her to get ahead of the explosions. The hot plumes continued passed the vehicles and to the buildings down the road. Already several of them fell into one another before they crumbled and hurried to the ground.

"Go north!" Sue shouted.

The mini convoy swerved on to a highway ramp that brought them to a raised stretch of road. As their speed increased, the explosions continued in the direction they had chosen. Building tops and screaming glass shards rained down on the team.

"*Tempus*," Supernova whispered as his eyes turned a mixture of blue and gold.

The Guardian's cosmic clock appeared on his wrist and he

pointed upward. The clock face expanded and oriented itself horizontally. It quickly grew and spread out, disappearing after a few seconds. The meteor-like pieces gleamed the same color as Supernova's eyes. They fell slower, as if being lowered by invisible strings. The explosions ceased and, with the time given by Supernova, the drivers made it to a safe, yet impassable place on the highway. The stretch before them deteriorated too severely.

Once the time spell concluded, the heavens landed with a thundering crash behind them. Dust shot through the streets and into the sky. The air trembled with shockwaves, repeating across Web Obsidia. The crew found themselves on a tall overpass that cut through the center of District 2. Dozens of plundered, rusted cars sat sadly all along the beaten asphalt and the buildings that framed it cast a deep gray shade. Making haste, the vans made way down a curved ramp to their right, bringing them back to street level.

Ralph followed Sue, winding around obstacles and finding a parking garage beneath a gargantuan skyscraper. Supernova was first out of the car and he walked directly to the entrance. The rest broke into small groups. Theo and Sue conversed while Estelle, Ransley, and the rest waited by the second van. Andrew and Owen removed their heavy bags from the back and began digging into them.

"What the hell was that about?!" Estelle asked Ransley.

"I wish I could say, love," Ransley said, awestruck by the scattering dust between the sky bridges. "I couldn't be more thankful we made it, though."

"Are you holding up okay?"

"I'm a bit tired, Estelle. Unfortunately, I'm not as used to these trips as I wanted to hope."

"Just take it easy. I won't let anything happen to you."

Estelle patted his shoulder and smiled before leaving with Ralph to join Supernova. Andrew and Owen pieced together a small machine that appeared to be a gasoline generator. Tall electrodes jutted from the top with metal balls fixed to them. They connected it to a pack of car batteries and when they flipped the switch, the electrodes generated a miniature shield with a thirteen foot radius.

"How could it not be her?" Sue asked Theo. "The moment we leave the manor, we're attacked? I've only seen explosions like that in Bleedstar."

"If it were her," Estelle said. "I feel like she'd have shown herself by now. Maybe they're bandits trying to rob us?"

"There are easier ways to steal that don't involve leveling half the city. I think something else may be going on. I got no idea what."

"Nova?" Theo called. "Thoughts?

"I didn't detect a surge of electrons," the Guardian said. "That doesn't mean it wan't her, but I agree with the girl. She's not one to hide."

"'The girl' has a name!" Estelle shouted.

"Maybe we keep moving?" Ralph suggested. "Hopefully they haven't followed, but we can't assume we're safe. How much farther do we have to go?"

Estelle drew her map, handing it to Theo. He held it for everyone to gaze at. Sue pointed to a block of buildings at the northeastern edge of District 2. She drew her finger to a spot on the northwestern edge, near District 3.

"Here's where we need to be," Sue said.

"That's what," asked Theo. "Twenty? Thirty miles? We can make that."

"We're in uncharted territory now. We knew what was ahead before the buildings fell. How should we proceed?"

There was a moment to ponder their next move. Estelle noticed Supernova's back remained turned to them, her crow perched atop his shoulder. She stood next to him and scanned the dark alleys, but saw nothing.

"What's out there?" she asked.

"The Punished," said the bird. "Lots of them."

"Crow," Supernova said. "I want you to get an aerial view. See what you can see."

"I am hesitant to leave my Seeker," it said.

"Don't worry about me," Estelle said. "If anyone can be a little spy for us, it's you. I promise I'll be okay."

"If you're sure... I'll return as soon as I can."

The crow clicked its beak before flying off into the crimson sky.

"What's going on over there?" Theo asked Supernova.

The swordsman's cloak flourished as he drew his arm back and threw a punch, sending a jet of violet lightning between two buildings. It connected with something and exploded. A thin whistle sounded, screaming louder as it approached. Before they could react, a flaming rocket sped between the garage pillars and hit the shield. It momentarily fractured before it came back together, the force throwing everyone to the ground.

Estelle rolled on to her side. Her vision blurred and a deafening whine played in her ear. A hand gripped her upper arm and Supernova pulled her up. He spoke, but the throbbing in her ears cancelled him out. She forced herself to hear through the shell shock.

"-came from higher up! We need to get inside!"

Another rocket screamed toward them, hitting one of the vans. The resulting explosion tore the shield apart, sending them back as fire and smoke washed over them. They coughed and crawled as pieces of the vehicle burned around them. Over the crackle of the fire came the sound of deranged shouting. A hundred voices or more closed in on them.

Supernova was first to his feet, and he attempted to rouse Theo and Sue. While the golden-haired woman rose, Theo could only sit up. A long shard of steel had become lodged in his left thigh. Owen, who had been closest to the van, took significant damage to his left arm; so much that the rubber sleeve melted from his suit. A sickly bruised discoloration marred his arm, the skin stretched taut over a network of blue veins, prominent as if lit from beneath.

"To the elevator!" Ransley called, helping Andrew up.

Sue and Ralph carried Theo toward a service elevator deeper into the garage. He winced with each painful, bloody step. Andrew and Ransley helped Owen in the same direction. Supernova pushed Estelle forward, keeping his hand on the back of her neck to keep her head down.

At the spot where they'd just been, another rocket made impact. Scorching air rushed by them as they ducked to avoid shrapnel. They used parked cars as cover and peeked around them. Bullets pinged off the ground, forcing them to remain in place. The rabid cries of the Punished drew closer as Ransley readied his rifle and attacked.

"We have to get inside!" Ralph shouted, pointing to the elevator across the lot.

Theo and Sue mounted their rifles on the cars and picked off the orange-eyed beasts as they stepped through the flames. Supernova whipped bolts from his fists, protecting the center line. As they fought, Andrew made a desperate sprint to the elevator and pressed the button, diving behind a pillar before he could catch an invisible bullet. Once the door chime sounded, he rushed in.

"Let's go!" Andrew said through his helmet, waving his arms.

Estelle grabbed Theo with Sue's help as Ransley and Ralph helped Owen. Once they were all in, Sue pressed a random button; the 10th floor. Enemy shots continued to echo and the faces of the Punished became clear as they rushed toward them. The doors closed before they would make contact.

O nce the elevator came to a stop, the team flooded out with Ralph and Sue training their assault rifles on the shadows. They came out in a large lobby with white tiles and black walls. Opposite the elevator was a semi-circular desk made of black marble. Behind it was a tall white wall framed by two obsidian pillars with hallways on either side. Upon the wall was a black outline of a maiden with the words "*Virgo Corp*" splayed in neon white.

They spread out, taking a few minutes to regroup and recover from the ambush. The wounded were tended to and while Sue despaired at the injuries she witnessed, Supernova consoled her.

"This is officially out of hand," Theo said, wincing.

He nursed his left leg, gripping it around the shard of metal, a splotch of blood staining his pants. Sue treated Owen, whose arm hung limp by his side, the outer edge charred and bloody.

"What are we going to do?" Sue asked as she ripped fabric from her own shirt to bandage the arm.

"The streets aren't safe," Ransley said.

"What about the sky bridges?" Estelle said.

"That might work. It'd be hard to pin us down in those mazes."

After removing the metal shard from Theo's leg, the silent Guardian healed the wound; not fully, but enough for Theo to hobble on his own. He also reduced the degree Owen's burns, but whatever curious malady changed his skin and veins was beyond his ability to fix. Ralph puffed on a cigarette while Ransley took a generous gulp of his supplement.

"Careful on that leg," Supernova said to Theo. "The cut could still reopen. I wish I could do more, but that time spell took a lot out of me."

"I'll take this over the gash," Theo said, managing a weak smile.

As the group recuperated, Estelle ensured no one was looking as she slipped down the right-hand hallway. It lead to a large office room. Cubicles stretched from wall to white wall with beige dividers between them. Long black shades met the ground, obscuring the tall windows on this floor. Several panes of glass made up the far wall, with two side doors leading to the next room.

Estelle gasped when faint gray images of people wandered in and out of view, oblivious to her presence. The specters' heads hung low and their glazed eyes were sad, lost and empty. They made no sound and harmlessly phased through solid objects. As the woman ran her fingers through her hair, she pressed her back against a cubicle and slid to a seated position, staring ahead with exhausted eyes. Glancing to the side, her Guardian appeared a few feet away.

"If I wanted company, I would have asked," the Seeker said.

He said nothing.

"Is this how it's going to be? You and me hating each other while strangers try to kill us? It's not good enough that I can't go home. It's not good enough that I have to go on some dumbass scavenger hunt. People have to try to kill me?"

"Listen-," Supernova said.

"I just want to go home!" anger danced in her voice. "I miss my world. I miss my life. I miss my boyfriend..."

Estelle buried her head between her knees.

"I... don't hate you." The swordsman sat beside her.

"You could've fooled me."

"I admit I've been-"

"A jerk?"

"-rude." When she looked at him, he averted his eyes. "And I do feel... somewhat apologetic."

"Is that supposed to make me feel better?"

"I can't make you feel better." Supernova scratched his chin, his hand slipping through the shroud. "Demella was right about me. I am a puppet of the gods. I am a weapon."

Estelle searched for signs of feigned emotions in his face, but he seemed robotic; trance-like.

"What are you?" Estelle asked. "Really?"

"I'm dead," he said. "Reborn in the Underworld and bound to a primordial spirit. I serve the gods of the under-earth as their agent in order to earn my freedom."

"What does an 'agent of the underworld' do?"

"Promise you won't be scared?" Estelle rolled her eyes. "Sometimes when it's people's time to die, I'm that shadow that passes over them. Sometimes it's one person. Sometimes it's a civilization.

"You're a killer?"

"I'm a reaper- among other things. Everyone dies one day and beings like myself usher them to where they need to go."

"What about your hundreds of sacrifices?"

"Sometimes you're forced to do things you don't want to do. No matter how strong you think you are, sometimes you're not allowed to say 'no.'"

Estelle found it difficult to remain angry.

"I understand that better than anyone," she said. "My family is wealthy where I come from."

"Is that why you're such a brat?"

His voice rose, and for the first time, the anguish and darkness left him. Estelle had become used to his cynical, inflamed attitude, but it was not present. They shared a laugh.

"Yes, that's why. Most people think it's expensive vacations and buying anything I want. Really, it's the footsteps of a tall, angry man who watches everything you do and everywhere you go. One misstep off of his path... Let's just say rich men can get away with anything; especially when it comes to their daughters. I had to become someone I don't like to protect myself."

"I'm sorry. I didn't know."

"Almost no one does. Even when I try to tell them, I'm lying or being ungrateful. Only one person ever really listened to me- Marcel."

A pair of ghost walked through one another and a third passed through Estelle, making her shiver.

"You called me that name when we first met," Supernova said.

"You... look like him. You could be his twin."

"I suppose there are only so many faces in the cosmos. What's he like?"

"He's wonderful." She smiled as she thought of his gentle face. "He's smart and always relaxed. I can admit I have an attitude problem- but he never cared. Never yelled or swore at me. He just wanted to understand me and love me regardless of how much of a basket case I can be. If I could have one wish, it would be to return to him. He must be so worried about me."

"He sounds like a good man. He reminds me of Vileena."

"Mae said she came here with you. What happened to her?"

"Demella possessed her." Supernova tilted his head back and stared up at the ceiling. "A Void spirit so strong, Vileena can't expel her. She took her body, her powers, her voice... I have to get her back, no matter what it costs me."

"What kind of woman is she? Vileena?"

"Everything a man could ask for; gorgeous as a clear night sky, intuitive, graceful and strong when she needs to be. In a century and a half, I've never met anyone like her. I love her and I can do nothing to help her."

"Is there anything I can do?"

Supernova shook his head. "The best way you can help is to focus on getting home."

"Sick of me already?" Estelle asked.

"Since day-one."

She raised an eyebrow and glanced over at him. He nudged her arm and chuckled, shaking his head.

"I have a lot riding on your trials. I can't fail."

Estelle's Guardian drew a shining scroll from Other Space tied with a thin, black ribbon. He untied it and straightened the parchment, extending it to the woman. The ink glistened red, as if made of polished steel.

"*'By decree of the Underworld Three,'*" she said, reading the heading.

*"The clock ticks closer toward certain fate.*
*Eve's Hollow holds this labor, numbered eight.*

*Free your Seeker and guide her way.*
*Wickedness redeemed, for this, she prays.*

*Walk through treachery and step very carefully.*
*Keep mind to be kind and behave respectfully.*

*Find the five keys, they've scattered so far.*
*And guard the soul who's named for the stars."*

She reread it. "'Wickedness redeemed?'" She scoffed. "Is this how it works for all Guardians?"

Supernova shrugged. "I've never met another."

"The Underworld Three. Who's that?"

"The gods that oversee my contract. Osiris, Izanami and Hades. All rulers of their own specific land of the dead."

"Sounds lovely... What will they do if you fail?"

"I don't like to take their names in vain, let alone talk about them."

"Come now," a beautiful male voice came from the shadows. "Your Seeker is curious."

As if stepping into reality, a man slid from the darkness, casually approaching Supernova. The two stood to meet him. The stranger wore a deep bronze cloak that hung to the floor, obscuring his body. Sharp features defined his smooth face. His lips were wide and thin, his nose fell at a graceful slope and his eyes were the color of fresh honey. His hair was golden like wheat and wavy like the tides of the sea.

"You, of all people, should know how important it is to pass on knowledge."

"Serafim," Supernova said, looking away. "To what do I owe the pleasure?"

"Oh, I'm just checking up on you. It's been over five years and we've heard no advancement in your labor. Do you need help?"

"Time works differently here- I figured you'd know that. It's been two years for me. Not to mention I just met my Seeker."

"Speaking of, it is rude to forget proper introductions, apprentice."

"I'm your sister's apprentice-"

"Serafim of the Aurum Isles," said the man, stepping between Supernova and Estelle.

The cloak flourished in the Guardian's face as Serafim

offered a gold bangled hand to the Seeker. He wore a purple-colored exomis that hung over one muscular shoulder, completed with a golden belt. A short sword hung from his hip, its sheath crafted of scarlet leather with golden accents. Estelle took his hand, and he pulled it forward for a soft kiss. His tantalizing eyes held contact with hers and heat rushed to her face.

"E-Estelle," she replied, her heart thumping as she studied his face. She laughed nervously. "If I didn't know any better, I'd say someone turned the heat on in here."

"I like this one." Serafim chuckled. "She's got a sense of humor, unlike your other friend. Don't get me wrong, she's a piece to look at, but kind of dull in personality."

Supernova's eyes narrowed. "Don't you have better things to do? Like chasing maidens or sucking up to a famous relative?"

"Is that any way to speak to your handler?"

"Again- your sister is my handler. We're fleeing from gunmen at the moment; so if you don't mind, I'm in the middle of doing my job."

"Say no more," said Serafim with a cocky shrug. He walked away a few paces and faded from sight. Before he did, he left them with a warning. "Speaking of gunmen- I saw some on the way up. They're almost here."

# CHAPTER 20

## THE REAPER'S WRATH

Estelle's heightened senses allowed her to hear the rough stomping of boots up a nearby stairwell. Outwardly, the Virgo Corp building seemed safe and their locations secret. How could they have found them?

"Guys!" Sue yelled from down the hall.

Estelle and Supernova's attention snapped toward the elevators and when they looked back, Estelle held her breath. A shadow emerged from the room beyond the glass, shining a flashlight across the cubicles. Supernova ducked down beneath the barrier with Estelle.

"You guys in here?" Sue called again as she entered the office.

"Watch out, Sue!" the Seeker called.

A shot rang out, zipping passed Estelle and missing Sue by an inch. As she dropped to the floor, an eruption of gunfire blasted the room. Estelle's heart skipped as she plugged her ears, shut her eyes and gritted her teeth. The stench of gun smoke filled the room and the rustling of clothing neared them. A small flash of purple in Supernova's hand appeared and suddenly he was clutching a bronze dagger. Shots came from the direction of the landing.

"Leave us be!" came Ralph's voice.

His projectiles left behind light blue streaks. Fire exchanged between the two parties for several minutes. Material from the office disintegrated as bullets ripped through the walls and desk computers. Estelle looked to her Guardian, but he was gone. During a lull in the firefight, Sue and Ralph came by, using the ghosts as cover.

"You alright, kid?" Ralph asked. She nodded.

"I think they're coming from the next room over," Sue said, watching the shadows between the specters. "Something's happening in there."

She knelt and focused. Estelle peeked over the cubicle wall and trained her eyes on the glass. Alarm spread through the room as the people rushed around. The door at the back left burst open, with three masked men entering. Two of them shot at Estelle, Sue and Ralph while the third man pursued someone they could not see.

"Wait!" a muffled voice said. "Wait! WAIT! I'm with-"

His voice ended with a gunshot, followed by a second that felled the assailant. A few more bursts finished the remaining two enemies.

"We're good over here," Theo yelled from the opposite side of the room. "Sue? Essie?"

"We're clear!" Sue said.

Ransley crept with Theo, his old rifle in his hands, and Andrew came up from beneath the wall, a pistol clutched in his rubber hand. Each member of the team was cautious as they regrouped. The wandering spirits stood in the gun smoke, their facial features becoming more prominent.

"You guys alright?" Sue asked.

"They got Owen," said Theo in a low tone. "If only I'd gotten here a second earlier. Andrew got the guy."

Estelle, Sue and Ralph made their way across the room to join the others. Sue knelt and removed Owen's helmet, revealing a sickly-looking man with those dark veins spread around his lips and empty eyes.

"I was too late," said Andrew. His muffled voice was barely audible between his pants. "I failed to save our friend. If he hadn't shouted out, I would be in his place."

"What was he yelling that got him killed?" asked Ralph.

"We figured we'd try to appeal with the truth. 'We're with a group that has safety and medicine.' Seems so stupid now."

"I could have told him that," Sue said. "What were y'all thinking?" She gave an uncomfortable sigh. "One down already."

"I should have been here," Theo said.

"You can't blame yourself. We've met our share of people like this; people who take what they want by force. Good people aren't responsible for what they do."

"You're right- as always... You alright, little sis?" he asked Estelle. "You look well for someone just being shot at."

"The Dreamer was worse," the Seeker said with half a smile.

"Let's get moving," Ralph said. "We need to get ourselves together. Where's your friend, Estelle?"

"You guys go. I'll get him."

The team returned to the elevators as Estelle stepped over the bodies of the fallen, covering her mouth and nose. A whisper came from the room beyond the glass. She could not discern what it said, but it rose and fell in volume, accompanied by a whimper. Through the drawn shades of that room, a dim red-orange light peeked through. When Estelle entered, she found one shadow standing over another.

The overwhelming scent of blood hit her in the face, the carpet wet and sticky beneath her boots. She clutched her stomach.

Estelle held her breath when she saw her Guardian. Supernova stood among a pile of deceased enemies at the far facing wall. He loomed over a wounded man and gave off a wispy red aura. Short groans and labored breathing came from the kneeling person.

"Is there anything more you'd like to tell me? Soldier of Crius?" Supernova asked through echoing voices.

Estelle remembered that name spoken from her would be captors in Garnet Grove. This man was silent and cowering. He was lifted from the ground and pressed into the wall so hard it cracked. The bands on Supernova's arms illuminated the grimy, terrified face.

"His name is Kill Corner!" the man said, on the verge of hyperventilating. "He's an old friend of our boss! They made a deal to go after some girl."

"Who is this 'Kill Corner?'"

"I s-swear I don't know... we never even heard the name until last year!"

"Tell me why they want her," Supernova demanded.

Sweat poured down the man's face and his eyes frantically shot from side to side. For a moment, he caught Estelle's gaze. The Guardian's grip tightened.

"What do they want with my Seeker? Do not lie... I hate liars..."

"I swear I don't know! B-but the reward was a way out... a way to a better world."

"Impossible. No one escapes the Hollow."

"He said he found a way!"

"How!?"

"I swear to God I don't know!"

Supernova gripped the man's throat with such strength he could only gurgle and gasp. The Guardian drew his dagger back. Estelle rushed forward, leaping across the room to grab Supernova's arm. His head snapped toward her, fury and rage brimming from fire-born eyes. Estelle froze, but she resisted his urge to pull free.

"What are you doing?" Estelle asked. "You can't kill a man in cold blood."

"He will tell the others," said the Guardian, thin red smoke falling from his shroud. "Then they will bring ruin upon us. I won't let him."

"Look at him, Nova! He's too scared to talk."

The man's smooth face was bright red, and tears fell in streams from hazel eyes. A red beanie cap topped a mess of black shaggy hair. These men had little to nothing in the way of armor or well-kept gear. They were dressed in jeans, sweat-shirts, overcoats and bandanas. Even the Torchbearers wore plates of cut sheet metal for protection.

"I have seen him," Supernova said, his eyes like magma. "I have seen him and a million like him. Selfish. Lazy. Privileged. Killers for hire where a human life is a commodity to be traded."

"That's not what this is!" Estelle shouted, pulling at his arm again. "Didn't you hear what he said? They were offered a way out of Eve's Hollow. Not money. Not food. A better life. Isn't that what we all want?"

"These men tried to kill you! They didn't think about the life *you're* supposed to have! They ambushed us on the street. Set bombs off. They didn't give us a chance to surrender."

"What it *him* though? Did he do all of that? Or is he just a frightened man who feels like he has no options?"

Beneath the mask of his cloak, his eyes gave away contem-plation. He looked at the man clutched in his fist, but Estelle's hand guided him to her stoic gaze. Staring into the Guardian's blazing, red eyes was like swimming in whirlpools of fire that didn't burn but could if they chose to. Though her throat tightened and her heart raced, she saw passed the Supernova

Swordsman and pictured Marcel, saying once more. "You can't kill a man in cold blood."

Supernova turned to the pitiful man.

"If I ever see you again, I will kill you."

The reaper released him. He fell to the ground, scrambling away into the darkness. For a short time, the Guardian stood still. His red eyes dimmed until they shone no more. As the scarlet aura dissipated, he fell to one knee, holding his head in both hands. He took long, deep breaths, as if he'd just sprinted uphill. Estelle knelt beside him, holding his shoulder.

"Nova? What's wrong?"

"I'm fine," he panted, pulling away.

In an instant, he walked out the door. Estelle chased him, nearly yelling for him, but Theo and Sue returned to the office in search of them.

"Thank goodness," Theo said. "I was getting worried."

"Good news," said Sue. "They cut the power to the damn elevators."

The four traveled back to the lobby, where the rest of the group sat in silence. Ralph was the exception, who fiddled with the elevator panel.

"More of them are probably heading this way," Ransley said.

"I pulled some information from one of them," Supernova said. "There's close to a hundred-fifty men on this job. A group called the Arm of Crius. They set the bombs off to herd us into a kill zone."

"What do they want with us?" asked Andrew.

Estelle's Guardian pointed to her.

"Well, they can't have her," Sue said, her nose scrunched.

"Still, *one-hundred-fifty*? We can't stand against that!"

"What about you?" Ralph asked Supernova. "I thought you were supposed to be some kind of an expert warrior with powers. Where's all that lightning from before?"

"Storm Casting is ill advised," Supernova said. "The Pale Lady knows my powers and I've already risked it twice."

"Estelle mentioned the sky bridges earlier," Sue said. "Might be the best chance we've got."

"I agree," Theo said. "Ralph, what floor is the next bridge?"

Ralph read a rectangular chart next to the elevators. "Level 20. We have to assume they'll be waiting for us. What do we have for firepower?"

After a quick council, the soldiers were equipped with Mae's modified rifles and two magazines for each soldier. Andrew kept his handgun close and Ransley had his rifle, but few bullets left.

The stair door was located around the corner of the left hallway. Sue took the lead, with Theo and Ransley right behind her. Ralph and Andrew went next, with Estelle and Supernova bringing up the rear.

The landing of the sky bridge was spacious, with several rows of benches and stools. The broken ceiling high windows let the frigid breeze to pass through. The elevator doors sat next to the stairwell entrance and across the room was the beginning of a steel and glass bridge that extended from the current building to one on the next city block. Its frame was rusted and worn, with brown film covering its windows. Supernova joined Sue, Theo and Ralph at its beginning.

"They're waiting for us on the other side," said the man in the cloak. "A couple dozen. They haven't seen us yet."

"Can you handle it?" Sue whispered. Supernova responded with a shallow nod and she turned to the others. "We've got heat ahead, everybody. Theo and the Guardian will handle it. We'll hang back until they're done."

Estelle knew what was about to transpire. With suffocating anticipation, she watched Supernova and Theo walk down the bridge together. Sue, Andrew and Ralph sat on a bench, chatting to lighten their moods while the Seeker turned away to read the building glossary near the stairwell with Ransley.

"What's the matter, dear?" Ransley said. "I know it hasn't been easy of late."

"I just-" she thought carefully about her words. "I was ready for the Punished. For the Pale Lady. But these are people! We have to kill human beings. Am I going to have to do the same? I thought I was supposed to be doing good things? It shouldn't be like this."

"It's an unfortunate and sad truth of Eve's Hollow. It's untamed, and plenty of people will take from you what they can."

"We choose what we do with our lives," Andrew said, turning in his seat. "I learned very young what it took to survive and instead of murder, I dedicated my life to science."

"That's noble of you," Ransley said. "Not to sound cowardly, but I became adept at hiding. Especially in my older years. Estelle, what you're feeling is perfectly natural. It isn't weak to value human life. Difficult experiences have hardened people like Mike or Sue or your Guardian. That's why they do what they do."

"We have people to protect," Ralph said. "I picture Raphael and Bianca. I hate to say it, but it's us versus them. Simple as that. If I don't protect myself and my team, I might not make it home to my family. The thought of them living without me is why I fight so hard."

A sudden sequence of flashing lights caught their attention, and the wind carried fearful screams. Guns blazed like strobe lights and they were unsure of the outcome.

Booming voices and heavy footsteps from behind them brought panic as several people rushed up the stairwell. Their heads whipped to the door as it hung open. Sue and Ralph rushed to close it while Estelle, Ransley, and Andrew searched the landing for debris to put against it.

They brought chairs and unbolted benches. Pieces of fallen concrete and wood from the walls and wires from the ceiling to tie the knob down were the best they could do as a force of angry men crashed against the door. Though it shook, the barricade held.

"Get going everyone," Sue said.

Ransley escorted Estelle onto the sky bridge, with Ralph and Andrew right behind them. Sue pointed her rifle at the stairwell until her friends could gain enough distance. The men roared, throwing their weight with such force that parts of the barricade fell away. Sue paced backward until she was fifty yards from the end.

The blocked door burst open with masked men flooding the landing. Sue dove behind a mass of stone and glass as shots burst on the floor. Estelle and the others had just reached the door on their side when the Seeker turned to see Sue taking cover from a hail of bullets. Theo attempted to aid her, shooting at the small army. Even when Ralph joined, it was not enough. An enemy threw a grenade onto the bridge, tearing a hole in its frame. Sue covered her head as flying shards shot at her.

"We have to get her out of there!" Theo said.

A blade attached to a chain flew down the hall, striking a Crius soldier in the chest. For an instant, he looked at the weapon lodged in his heart. Then he fell, dead. A streak of black and red flashed by like a ray of light. In seconds, the bullets ceased flying down the bridge and became concentrated at its beginning. Men groaned and choked as Supernova slew each one of them with mathematical precision.

The men, once so confident and dominant, were reduced to frightened, anxious children who fired wildly just to stave off their respective fates. Supernova cut through each attacker, too fast for them to perceive, but Estelle took in every gruesome detail.

Her Guardian held a kopesh; a medium length sword, starting straight at the hilt, then curving into a shallow sickle. Its handle was gold with lapis lazuli stripes. Oddest to the Seeker was the chain attached to the hilt, disappearing at Supernova's wrist. Every few moments, Supernova would throw the sword, swinging to slash before pulling it back to his hand. It took less than sixty seconds for the silence to return.

The stalwart man returned to Sue, offering a hand of friendship to her. She accepted and brought herself to a stand. She and the Guardian exchanged words as he held her shoulder. The two rejoined the group at the new landing.

"You good, Sue?" Theo asked.

"Just a through and through in the shoulder. If Nova hadn't come in when he did, I might not be here. Wound's already closing thanks to him."

"Your eyes, Nova," Estelle said. "They're red."

"I finally feel the scythe's power," the swordsman said. "As we near the museum, I hear its song. My most powerful weapon: Temcindus."

Supernova held his sword up, the chain glowing as if fresh from the forge. Estelle took a few steps away from him. The rest of the team could not sense the deep, dark aura manifesting around him. He exhaled the miasma, and it reached out, surrounding everyone but Estelle.

Theo, Sue and Ralph went to examine another map of the sky bridges. After a brief period of planning their new route, the seven were off. They crossed three more glass bridges and buildings, taking stairs up and down when needed. The final landing took the whole floor and was a display of vibrant fluorescent colors. The tiles were an amalgamation of green, pink, blue, yellow, black and white. Round white pillars lined the windows, looming two stories in height. The area was void of enemy personnel, allowing a sense of ease to fall over the party. It was then that Estelle's crow came fluttering through an open window.

"I was getting worried about you," Estelle said.

"I apologize for my absence," it said. "I headed toward your last altercation, but you'd gone by the time I arrived. These men have multiple teams spread through a dozen building lobbies. Including this one."

"How?" Theo asked. "We must have covered two miles of sky bridges!"

"What are we supposed to do?" Ralph said. "We can't turn back."

"The exits are definitely being watched."

"What about the sewers?" Sue asked.

"All kinds of nonsense is crawling around down there!" Theo's eyes grew wide.

"That's sort of what I'm hoping for. Between you, me, Ralph and the Guardian, we might be able to take them. But I bet those thugs wouldn't go down there."

"That's a hell of a gamble, Sue."

"It's that, or walk into another ambush."

As the team discussed the next course of action, Estelle joined Supernova at a window. His head slowly swiveled, scanning the scenery. His eyes widened as he stared at a particular section.

"There," he said, pointing to a city block to the West. "The museum is there."

"How can you tell?" she asked.

"The red dome. The power of pure chaos."

Estelle relaxed and focused. The black and gray matte of the city looked alike in all directions, but as she quieted her mind, a faint crimson sphere became visible to her.

"We're so close," she said. "It feels impossible with these people on our backs."

"I could change that."

"How? Run through the buildings and kill them all? Like animals in a slaughterhouse.

"Do you take issue with that?"

"Just because we're in a place with monsters doesn't mean we have to be one."

"I'm doing my job."

"What is that, exactly? Somehow, I doubt you told me everything. Lady called you a puppet of the Gods. What does she mean by that? What do they make you do?"

"You really want to know?" By this point, everyone in the room was staring at the two. "The gods use me to do work they're too busy for," he said. "Hundreds of realms fall out of balance and chaos reigns supreme."

"Aren't you into that sort of thing?"

"There has to be balance! When there is too much chaos, myself or others like me are sent in to reestablish order. The means by which we do are up to us."

"And coating the floor in blood is yours?"

"What do you think is going to happen if they catch you?! A tea party? A picnic? Wake up, girl! There are evil people who do gruesome things and they do not deserve the life they've been blessed with."

Estelle felt heat rise in her face.

"Who are you to decide that?! You might work for the Gods, but you're not one. So stop acting like you're above everyone else! So much so it doesn't even bother you to take a life!"

"I hope you never have to find out from the other side. There may come a day when that's your only way to survive. Cold-blooded murder is different from fighting for your life. You haven't even begun to fight."

"You know what I've been through! How could you say that?!"

"You're two weeks into this," Supernova said, coldly. "I've been in the fight for over a hundred years. I promise it's going to get far worse before it gets better. When your back is against the wall, we'll see what you choose to do."

"There are other ways," she said persistently. "You don't have to end so many lives. Once we sin, there's no forgiveness. You're forever tainted."

Supernova studied her, and the lazy look in his eyes manifested.

"Demella was right about one thing," he said. "Those who know nothing should say nothing."

## CHAPTER 21

# RICH GIRLS DON'T FIGHT
# LIKE THAT

After the assault Estelle and her team endured, they weighed each unfavorable option, and descending beneath the streets was the best choice. The elevator shaft in the neon room lacked its vehicle, so Supernova resorted to using an extra-dimensional power. The sword chained to his wrist cut through spacetime, leaving red rifts behind. He created an improvised pulley system and each member of the party grasped the chain, each descended into darkness.

"Must be the subway station," Sue said. "Maybe we can take a train to Kern?"

A beam of light glided around the room thanks to a flashlight at Sue's disposal. Rats scurried away from it and, as far as she could tell, they were alone. Catching Estelle's attention was the fact that she had a much clearer night vision than she expected. From her perspective, a thin translucent outline represented each surface.

Scattered tile littered the cement floor, each piece a jagged shard. To the right was a long ticket booth behind a dusty pane of glass. Pairs of square brick pillars repeated five times before coming to a row of turnstiles. Just beyond them, the floor dropped to a set of stairs. Five large broken screens hung above the turnstiles, two of them suspended by overstretched wires and the air smelled of stale mildew.

Ralph entered the ticket booth and, after a heavy *clunk*, the light tubes on the ceiling blinked before giving them much needed sight. Sue took a moment to check her shoulder wound and Ransley assisted. They convened before the turnstiles.

"What are the chances the rails still work?" Ralph asked with an optimistic smile.

"What are the chances any of us know how to operate it?" Sue replied. "If we can't figure it out, it's a long walk down the tracks."

"We'll figure it out. What's down in these tunnels that we can't handle?"

"A hoard," Supernova said. "Praeformae, an ogre, a Basilisk, a couple of Amphiphtere. Really, the list goes on. Our only advantage is that whatever is down here isn't actively seeking us."

"I feel less certain about this now," Sue said with a playful scoff.

"Don't worry. I have a few ideas. My Seeker doesn't want me to kill homicidal mercenaries, but hopefully, monsters are fine."

"Don't be so harsh," Ransley said. "We've lived this life. We've all had to do terrible things just to make it to the next day. I can't say killing people is right, but I won't just forfeit my life either. Estelle is trying to be repentant. As her Guardian, I believe you should be more understanding."

"Agreed," said Estelle's crow. "Redemption is the point of her trials. If she thought more like you, she may be destined to fail."

Supernova thought on the words. He gave a nod before

turning to look down the stairs. In silence and alone, he descended the steps until he was no longer visible.

"Thank you for that, Ransley," said Estelle with a sheepish smile. "It hasn't been easy for me. For any of us."

"I know he can be a little dark," Theo said. "But he's lived longer than a normal person. Everything we've gone through, he's gone through two or three times. Don't get me wrong, he can be an asshole at times- and I know he heard me say that. But his heart is usually in the right place. He just needs a softer touch sometimes."

"I don't like it," Ralph said. "But I agree with the Guardian."

"You're the most gentle person I know," Sue said.

"I've seen too many good people brought down because they didn't want to hurt anyone. How are you supposed to keep your own safe if you're not willing to cross a couple of lines? If we'd let them, those men would've killed me and Sue. We'd all be dead right now."

"That's what makes us different," Sue said with pride. "We fight when we have to. We let people go when they turn tail. We kill humans only when we're forced to."

A calming quiet blanketed the group. It was well passed early evening as they descended into the subway and the loss of Owen weighed on them. In the silence, the squeaking of the sewer rats made an ill companion to the smell of mold. Supernova broke the silence with a shout.

"I found the map!"

The group descended the stairs, ducking beneath a metal shudder to gain access to the subway terminal. Painted lines lead to different platforms, spaced in large rows and accessible by small bridges that curved over the tracks. At the right side was another booth, this one containing a series of buttons and levers. The trains themselves resembled giant, sleeping, silver worms.

"Platform Beta," Estelle said, reading the sign's heading. "The orange line."

Supernova examined a large diagram of the train's paths. Lines of blue, green, red, yellow, orange and purple stretched out on different routes. Each one lead to a separate district with several stops along the way. The first stop for the orange line was the Kern museum. Both Supernova and Sue entered the booth, fumbling with the panels to see if the trains would operate.

Estelle wandered across the tracks, taken aback by how much work must have gone into digging the station out. Estelle's crow sat upon Theo's shoulder as he and the others followed her to the boarding platform. A hum of power rushed through the floor as three of the seven train interiors lit up. The orange line among them, Supernova and Sue rejoined the others.

"Here's hoping the way is clear," said Ralph.

The inside of the train was more or less untouched, with the windows, seats and hand bars intact. With only a thick layer of dust and cobwebs populating the corners, it was more than preferable.

Theo and Andrew sat next to one another, with Estelle and Ransley on the opposite bench. Sue, Ralph and Supernova continued to the main car. Ransley's face drooped with exhaustion.

"You should lie down for a minute," Estelle said.

"Oh, no, love," Ransley said. "I'll rest when we get to our destination. It isn't wise to let our guard down."

"You don't have to worry. I won't let anything happen to you."

"You're a very kind person," Andrew said. "I've seen many crumble under the weight of this city. You seem undeterred and strong. As someone who hasn't known you long, I can tell you'll go a long way."

"I appreciate that," the Seeker said, blushing. "I'm really trying."

"My mother had a hard life. She always taught me that everyone was bad. All you have to do is push them far enough. I... actually believed her about everyone being bad until I found the manor. Everyone was helping everyone. I hear you speak of mercy and restraint. You are proof that not all people are bad. Gifts like yours shouldn't be wasted."

Estelle swallowed. She was the only one who knew his compliments were false. She thanked him and rested her eyes for a moment. When she opened them, she nearly jumped out of her seat. The crimson ghost of her father sat beside Theo, his arm casually resting behind the unaware man. Damian Grigori smirked at his daughter.

"He has no idea," her father said. "None of them know who you really are. The brat. The aggressor. The thief." A scoff came from beneath his mustache. "If you think these people are your friends, it's because you haven't shown them who you truly are. I must admit, docile looks good on you. I wish you were more behaved like this at home. Maybe being in this city is exactly what you need."

Theo took notice of Estelle's stare.

"You okay, Essie?" he asked.

"If you think they're your friends, tell them the truth. How would this man here look at you if he knew how badly you'd beaten Clara? Or how you set the dance studio on fire? Tell them."

"Shut up," Estelle said, sparks pulsing between her fingers.

"Tell them how you paid those thugs to rob the clothing store. Or how you got half your class drunk on vodka. Where's your responsibility? Accountability? Tell them. Tell them!"

"Shut up!"

A turquoise bolt lashed out, slicing a scalding hole in the train's side. Andrew pulled Theo away, and Ransley dove aside. A glowing opening of molten steel dripped down the seat a few inches away from Theo. They stared at the woman as the color drained from her face. The car door opened with Supernova, Sue and Ralph rushing in. Estelle held her hand over her mouth, turned and fled to the adjoining empty car, the laughter of her father's spirit ringing in her ears.

Estelle placed herself at the far end of the car and hugged her knees to her chest in the darkest corner she could find. She kept her green eyes trained at the door where the ghost of Damian watched her. He said nothing. He just stared her down with a smirk, arms crossed as if watching a comedy. His form vanished as Supernova came stomping through the door.

"What was that?!" he asked.

"Leave me alone," Estelle said.

"You almost killed Theo! You need to apologize!"

"I said leave me alone!"

"What did I tell you about your powers?!"

"It was an accident!"

"This is why I told you to give them up. You're obviously not mentally stable enough to control them."

Estelle's face twisted into a scowl.

"Did you just call me crazy?"

Supernova's eyes narrowed above the scarf of his cloak. "I'm starting to wonder."

Estelle jumped to her feet and her eyes burned with ice colored light.

"Say it then," she said, sneering. "Say it..."

Supernova stood over her, jabbing an index finger against her forehead.

"Crazy!"

With a roar, Estelle knocked his hand out of her face and threw a shock charged punch at his. He caught her fist and squeezed, preventing her from taking it back.

"You don't want this," he said, eyes shining purple. He spoke slowly and his voice became dark, like the tunnels. "Stand down and apologize to Theo."

With a ballerina's grace, she jumped up and wrapped her legs around the Guardian's arm, pulling her weight down and sending him tumbling over her. Estelle recovered and leaped at Supernova, launching a powerful round kick. He blocked it and pushed her away, moving in with a combination of attacks.

Estelle moved like a flower petal on the wind, evading most of his attacks while striking where she could. Blue sparks flew from her fists and feet with each punch, kick and twirl to avoid damage. The seconds melted together and time slowed as they battled from one side of the car to the other and back again. It was when she put him on the defensive and he stepped back that she ceased.

"Fight me!" Estelle screamed.

She drew her fist back and stepped in, throwing it as hard as she could at Supernova's chin. She gasped when the attack connected, his head turning with the force. He allowed himself to be struck, and he did not move an inch.

"What are you doing?!" the woman asked.

"So, this is the real you," the swordsman said, even toned.

"What's that supposed to mean?"

The swordsman did not speak.

"Answer me! Why won't you fight? You can massacre a room full of people, but you won't hit a girl?"

She shoved him.

"Where did you learn to fight?" Supernova asked.

"What? My academy back home. What does that-"

"Rich girls don't fight like that."

"Lots of other girls took the classes with me."

"No, I mean your ferocity. The elegant barbarism. The bloodthirsty determination. I could almost believe you wanted to kill me."

"'Almost?'"

Supernova chuckled, shook his head, and Estelle glared at him.

"I shouldn't have yelled at you," the Guardian said. "Theo's one of the only real friends I have. I just kept thinking: 'What if he'd been sitting a few inches to the right?'"

The Seeker sighed, and her shoulders fell.

"They must hate me," Estelle said. "Or be terrified. Or both. I really am sorry."

"They're worried." He held a metal handrail and watched the lights of the tunnel flash by. "What happened to you?"

Just as Estelle opened her mouth to speak, the train lurched, bumping as if riding over rocks. The brakes squealed, and the two held onto the seats to stop from flying forward. They hurried to the front, where the team had gathered at the windows.

"I'm so sorry, Theo," Estelle said.

"Water under the bridge," he said, eyes locked on the tunnel.

"What is it?" Supernova asked.

"You'd better see for yourself," Sue said.

Estelle and Supernova leaned across the seats and peered out the window. Thick, white roots overran the tunnel walls, crawling up the ceiling and breaking through the tracks.

"We've come too far to turn back," Ransley said.

Cold tension ran between the group until Ralph stated what the rest were thinking. "I guess we're walking then."

## CHAPTER 22

### SAY ITS NAME

The crew disembarked from the subway train, gagging on the scent of rotten, burning eggs. The white roots tore up the ground as they looped over and beneath themselves. Supernova walked ahead and watched the dark tunnel, blending with the shadows. The roots destroyed most of the lights, and particles wafted about the ceiling.

"What sort of roots are those?" Andrew asked. "I've never seen anything like them."

"I've seen them twice before," Estelle said. "They come out of a giant hole in the ground. Nova says the Pale Lady dug them."

"Why's that?" Ralph asked, slipping a cigarette between his lips.

As he opened his flip lighter to strike the flint, Supernova appeared beside the man, gently pressing it down.

"Smell that in the air?" the swordsman asked the confused Ralph. "Sulfuric gas. Very flammable. That means no fire." He looked at Estelle. "And no lightning."

"What's the plan if trouble finds us?" Sue asked.

Supernova's chained sword materialized in his hand. "This."

The Guardian began down the ruined tracks, a haze of noxious dust and gas clouding their vision and lungs. Supernova gained a thin, white outline around his body. Estelle took up the trail of his cloak and ran the material through her fingers. It was soft like silk, but heavy like leather. The pencil thin aura around it shifted depending on how she looked upon it, like the faces of a jewel.

"Can I help you?" Supernova asked, pulling his cloak from her hand.

"What are you covered in?" Estelle asked.

"A photon field. It protects my body in really bad places."

"Do you go to many bad places these days?" Ransley asked.

"I'm here, aren't I?"

Theo and Sue laughed as they shone their lights ahead. The roots grew so thick they took up most of the tunnel floor. The group came through a bend where an ominous red glow awaited them. At the bend's exit, they came to a wide space where the walls and ceiling were widened. The tracks were removed, and the ground bored into, falling away at their feet.

The pit which grew the roots stretched thirty feet across and saturated the chamber in heavy scarlet light. Its edges came against the walls with a ledge only a foot wide. Forced into the walls was the circular ring of pillars, their strange symbols appearing. Crude wooden stairs wound around its edges with pulleys holding buckets of dirt and rocks. A wooden bridge extended across the hole, but Supernova waited at its beginning.

"We must leave," the crow said.

"What is this?" Andrew asked.

"As far as you're all concerned, this is a hole to Hell," the swordsman said.

Supernova lead the team onto the bridge where the temperature spiked. Sounds of smoldering and faint cries came from below, with Ralph stopping to look down. Only after everyone passed did the Guardian return, placing a hand on his back.

"Don't stare," he said, grimly. "It will drive you mad."

Just as they neared the end of the bridge, a clicking noise came from the tunnel ahead. They froze as elongated, decomposing arms grasped the walls. Emerging from the tunnel was a grotesque creature. Human eyes stared out from a swollen, sunken head; where lips should have been were the mandibles of an insect. Below its long serpentine arms were a set of sickle-shaped claws that greedily reached at the air. Its midsection was disgustingly bloated and instead of legs, it dragged a fleshy sack behind it.

One of its arms shot forward and grabbed Andrew's leg. It dragged him forward, with Estelle and Ransley pulling his arms. Supernova's blade swung down, severing the creature's arm. A shrill scream came from wriggling tendrils between the mandibles. It slithered forward, getting its claws in range.

"Get down!" Supernova said.

As the team dropped, the Guardian's chained blade swung in a wide arc, cutting the monster's midsection and its arm again. It reeled, but lashed out, regenerating and throwing both its arms at the group. Supernova blocked the first sweep, but the second send him tumbling over the side of the bridge.

There was no time to help him as the man-bug advanced. Despite the Guardian's warning, Ralph fired on the creature, the sulfuric gas producing a burst of fire at the end of his rifle. Their enemy raised its sickles to protect its face, the bullets glancing off. Rage filled, it slithered forward, snatching Sue in its disgusting, gray hand. It hauled her in with Estelle rushing forward to grip its slimy wrist.

"You're not taking her!" Estelle said, static forming around her arms.

She struggled against the strength of the monster, with Sue caught in the middle of a lethal tug of war. With her gun pinned to her side, she could do nothing. Estelle grabbed the monster's fingers and pried them open as Andrew, Ralph and Theo held Sue's arms. The Seeker dug in with her heels and wrenched, pulling it toward herself. It responded with a belligerent screech.

Estelle opened her palm and let loose a spray of turquoise lightning. The man-bug screamed as the licks of electricity struck its chest. The air became super-heated and the sulfuric gas ignited, spreading a plume of fire that engulfed the group. Heat reaching over 1,000 degrees spread through the chamber and into the tunnels. When the flame had spent itself, copies of Supernova's cosmic clock encircled each member of the group, giving them a golden blue outline before fading.

The chained blade shot into the ceiling and drew the swordsman up. He landed between Estelle and the monster, which bore heavy burns but was no less viscous. The Realm Reaper's red aura flared with such power that it shredded his cloak. Frantic sickles reached in warning, but Supernova stepped forward regardless. The aura was not unlike the Pale Lady's, attempting to suffocate the beast.

The ugly worm turned to flee back down the tunnel, but became trapped when the chain looped around its swollen neck. With a deep war cry, the swordsman yanked the creature from its escape route. It writhed, screeched and with a commanding grunt, the Guardian whipped the man-bug against the side of the chamber.

"Go!" Supernova said.

Without hesitation, the team made for the other side. The sound of Supernova bashing their enemy shook the earth. As the group ran across the roots, Estelle stopped and Theo cast a saddened, wide-eyed glance at her.

"What are you doing?" he asked. "We've got to go."

The rest of her friends looked to her, the crow on Ransley's shoulder.

"He can handle himself. He'd want us to get somewhere safe."

As Theo called out, the Seeker sped back the way she came faster than her friends could pursue.

Upon arriving to the pit, the battle came to an abrupt, bloody end. Beaten and exhausted, the man-bug dragged itself toward the red hole, with Supernova walking beside it, transfixed on the pathetic wretch. As its head reached the edge, the Guardian raised his sword and severed it in one clean stroke. Its body convulsed as the swordsman kicked it into the pit.

Supernova approached his Seeker, his glowing scarlet eyes returning to normal. After a step, he fell to his hands and knees, panting and shaking. Estelle moved to help him.

"I'm fine," he said, pulling away and falling again.

"Let me help you, dumbass," Estelle said, baring her teeth.

As she moved to grab his arm again, a white light shone between the two. Serafim appeared and alongside him was a man dressed in long, white robes and a white hood. He wore a golden mask of a neutral expression and his white-gloved hands came together as if praying.

"Oh, Nova," Serafim said. "Such misuse of your powers!" He scratched his chin with a frown. "I'm sure we had this discussion recently."

"I was trying to save people, Serafim," Supernova said, clenching his jaw. "I had no choice."

"That might be true, but it's not up to me. You know the higher-ups. Rules and all that."

His honey-colored eyes met the Realm Reaper's.

"Why isn't Amalia here?" Supernova asked.

"Big sister is busy, so I'll be witness to your punishment instead."

Serafim tried to hide a smirk, but the lines at the corners of his mouth worked against him.

"Punishment?" Estelle said, frowning. "He didn't do anything."

"Ah, Miss Estelle." Serafim bowed. "The rules we live by can be complex at times. But misusing our powers is so clear a fish could swim in it."

"That isn't fair."

"I do apologize. But it isn't me you have to convince. It's the gods. Mercy, do your duty."

The gold faced man held his hand out and a human heart came forth from a spark. It beat steadily in his open hand. Estelle's eyes grew wide as the organ caught fire. Supernova clutched his chest and gasped for air. He grunted and raked his nails in the dirt. Every time he pushed himself up, he choked and tore at his chest, writhing like the beast he just disposed of.

"Wait!" Estelle said, bordering on a screech. "Serafim, please!"

"He can stop it whenever he wants," the angelic man said, shrugging.

"All he did was save us! Does that mean he gets tortured?"

"He used his time powers to displace you and your friends from this reality. That is a *clear* violation of Underworld Three Treaty, article four, section two: Reality manipulation is forbidden. That means removing any person or persons from their reality of origin; even for a couple of seconds."

Supernova screamed, turning on his back and breathing in small bursts.

"He can stop this at any time. He just has to call the angel's name: Mercy."

Supernova's eyes rolled beneath his eyelids.

"Nova," she said, as stern as Sue. "You have to say the name. Say its name!"

"He won't," Serafim said. "He never does."

His grunts turned to whimpers, and the rise and fall of his chest slowed. The burning heart began to wither and darken. Serafim peered at the punishment with unblinking eyes. Estelle rested a hand on his shoulder, but he only looked upon her when she traced his muscular arm through his cloak.

"He's had enough, don't you think?" Estelle asked, stepping in closer to him and linking her pinky with his. "I mean, what about his labors? As much of a pain in the ass as he is, I need him. I think he's learned his lesson. Don't you?"

Serafim raised a sharp eyebrow and gave a low grunt of curiosity. He grinned and turned to her as the swordsman twisted like a bleeding snake.

"What do you think my best feature is?" he asked with a dimpled smile.

"How could I pick just one?" Estelle asked through a coerced laugh. "You're- well, perfect. Your hair, your style, your muscles..."

The woman pressed her fingertips to his chest, and he flexed, smiling. She became lost in his stare, forgetting for a moment the shallow breaths of her Guardian.

"Do go on," the man said with a grin.

As Serafim waited for her to answer, the sound of Supernova's labored breathing ceased. The heart in Mercy's hand burned no more and lay in its white gloved hand, smoldering.

"Reset, Mercy," said Serafim.

The lump of crumbling flesh was instantly revitalized. It grew like fruit on a tree, swelling to its proper size. Mercy blew on the black heart and the burns and ash fell away, leaving it in its original state. Supernova gasped as he awoke, but before he could speak, he screamed. His heart burned once more and his punishment resumed.

"You were saying?" Serafim said, never taking his gaze from the Seeker's.

"I-"

Supernova's animalistic wails pulled at Estelle's heart. His scream was familiar, but not. Time seemed to slow as she fixed on her Guardian. *"I've never heard Marcel scream before,"* she thought.

Her eyes bulged, and she choked on her own air. She did not know if the Void pit played a trick on her or if she had truly lost her mind. For the shortest of seconds, the man on the ground disappeared and in his place was the love of her life.

"Well?" Serafim pressed. "Something wrong?"

Estelle bit her tongue as a swear prepared to leap forth.

"It's just hard to compliment you over his screams. How about you let him off the hook and I'll tell you?"

The plum robbed man looked from the doe-eyed woman to the man writhing at his feet, then nodded.

"I think Estelle is correct, Mercy. Don't you?"

Mercy nodded, and the flame around the heart extinguished. Supernova coughed and wheezed, drawing in so much air, he gagged on it. Serafim stepped closer to Estelle, stroking her hand that he still held. He beamed at her, drawing her so close they could kiss, and color flooded her face.

"Y-your eyes," she whispered. "You have the most gorgeous eyes I've ever seen. They-they're like the sun on the best day in summer."

Ear to ear, the man grinned, giving Estelle's hand a soft kiss. He then stood over the Supernova Swordsman, wrapping his cloak around his body.

"Let this be a lesson to you, apprentice," he said. "We all have our place. Know yours."

In a wisp of light, Serafim and Mercy disappeared, leaving Seeker and Guardian to bask in the red glow of the pit.

"Why wouldn't you say it?" Estelle asked, exasperated.

"Why did you have to use your lightning?!"

"We were about to die!"

"I was handling it!"

"You weren't there! I was trying to protect my friends! Do you think I wanted to blow up the tunnel? I didn't have a choice."

"Is that why you were clinging to him like that?" Supernova asked in a grumble. "You 'didn't have a choice?'"

"Are you serious?! I did that to help you!"

"He would've given up before me," the Guardian said, coughing.

"It didn't look like it to me. I've never seen a beating heart in someone's hand. Was it...?"

"What do you think?"

She did not respond. Estelle fiddled with her sapphire in her pocket as she opened her mouth to speak, but withdrew. Supernova stumbled to his feet and cloaked himself, pulling his scarf up beneath his eyes.

"Make sure you tell Marcel about your good deed here," the swordsman said, gliding through the tunnel entrance.

Supernova's body shook as the two made their way toward the party, the red walls turning black and gray again. They did not speak.

Their friends sat around the subway platforms when they returned; except for Theo and Sue, who were preparing to search for them. Supernova ignored all questions, allowing Estelle to explain with impunity. After she quelled their worries, they proceeded through the terminal and up the subway stairs.

It felt pleasing to feel the air of Eve's Hollow as they came up to a night-burgundy sky. The streets were dark with some operational lamps still working. The skyscrapers tapered as they made their way, going from cloud shrouded towers to three and four story constructions. Estelle perceived the red dome down the road; the Kern museum. Just as the group began to breathe easily, Supernova held his arm out to stop Sue.

"What is it?" she asked. "What do you see?"

"Bodies," the swordsman said quietly. "A lot of them."

The darkness made it difficult to tell, but several masses lied strewn the street, the closest about thirty-five feet away. Once their eyes became familiar with the low light, they took several steps back. Before them, spread out from sidewalk to sidewalk and as far as the eye could see, were corpses. The massacre claimed the lives of seventy or more men; their ski masks offered no protection from the onslaught, their weapons useless against a superior force. Large pools of blood made the road slick and reflective.

"These must be the men waiting for us," Ralph said. "What did this? The Punished?"

"I don't hear the screaming," Theo said. "This looks fresh."

"Beware," the crow said. "She is here."

The bloodied ground combined with the glow of the lamplight gave just enough illumination for Estelle to make out a figure among the dead. They were hunched over and to her sensitive ears, it sounded as if the person panted and growled like an animal. Just as Estelle made the realization, the Pale Lady stood to her feet, a mutilated victim clutched in her armored hand. She turned toward them with shining eyes, ablaze with malice. When she saw them, her blood-soaked mouth rose high into a grin.

## CHAPTER 23

---

# THIS DAY BELONGS TO THE DEAD

The Sherman Manor team stood like petrified stone. As their sight fixed upon the Pale Lady's blood-soaked face, no one wanted to make the first move. Though they caught her off-guard, she remained relaxed. Her feeding frenzy appeared more important to her; satiating her literal bloodlust. After a glance toward them, she brought the corpse in her hand to her mouth and bit down. Then she threw the mutilated cadaver aside, wiping her mouth, smoothing her skirt and fixing her wild hair.

"I knew it had to be you," she said. Her voice was low, yet the wind carried it in forms of whisperers that slithered in their ears. "I thought I'd lost you, my love."

"When I engage her," Supernova said to Estelle. "Make a run for the museum. I'll try to keep her busy as long as possible."

"Nova," Theo said. "You have to be running low on energy. Are you sure you can handle this?"

"I'm so close to the scythe, I can almost draw it out."

Supernova opened his hands. In the right, his curved

sword materialized. In his left appeared a bronze short sword, chained to his wrist as its sibling was. The Guardian crossed his blades before holding them up to, as if seeing an old friend for the first time in years.

"Let us pass, Demella!" he demanded, his voice booming down the street.

In response, the she-demon held her hand out, funneling red energy into a sphere. Squeezing it created a sword of her own. A long two-handed hilt made of obsidian and silver sat beneath a cross style guard dawning a small red skull. The blood colored blade was of a crystalline construct with many facets beneath a smooth, polished surface. The evil woman held the sword at her side as she hunched down. Estelle clenched her fists, her eyes glowing, but Supernova held her back.

"Still don't trust me?" the Seeker asked with a pompous attitude.

"You have an important job," Supernova said, locked on to his enemy. "She will try to attack you all as I hold her back. You must protect them if she gets ahead of me."

"You sounded confident a second ago," Ralph said.

"I can't assume I'm right. Demella is crafty and unpredictable. If you have a god, I'd suggest praying to it."

Anticipating her blitz, Supernova put all his weight on his front foot and took off just as Demella did. As their blades clashed, a pocket of air exploded, scattering dust and breaking the windows of nearby buildings. A numerous exchange of slashes, blocks and parries took place in seconds.

"Let's go!" Estelle said.

The crow took flight toward the end of the street as each member of the party followed, leaping over the dead. For the briefest of moments, Estelle's eyes met the Pale Lady's.

Supernova blocked her attempt to rush the Seeker,

pushing her away. Their blades were so fast and violent, they became silver streaks. Estelle allowed Ransley, Sue, Andrew and Ralph to push forward while she curbed her speed to match Theo, whose leg slowed him.

A shiver rushed down Estelle's spine. She pulled Theo to the ground as the Pale Lady's crimson blade cut across in a horizontal arc. Theo aimed his rifle at the demon, blue streaks splattering as she blocked the shots with her sword. Demella sped around the bullets, thrusting her blade at Theo. In a moment of instinct, Estelle took hold of Demella's arm.

"You're stronger than you were before," Lady said through her grin. "You burn brighter!"

"Why can't you just leave us alone?" Estelle asked, gritting her teeth.

Before an answer could be given, a gold chain looped around Demella's neck and dragged her back. The Pale Lady was thrown into a building, disappearing into a hole filling with crumbling bricks. Estelle's Guardian kept his focus there, his blades pouring flaming aura.

Estelle chased after her friends as a gathering of Punished trickled from dark alleys, dragging their feet after the team.

The sound of the chains rushed passed them, slicing through the Punished on the left flank. In an instant, it whipped back in time with a war cry from the swordsman. Estelle could not help but to turn to see. As the two entities applied pressure, scarlet and violet whirled together.

More Punished filtered after them, with Estelle throwing bolts at all that drew too near. She severed their limbs and knocked small groups away with such ease, she laughed to herself.

In a flash of dark lightning, the Pale Lady blocked their path. She was closest to Theo, and she swung her sword indiscriminately. Theo's eyes grew wide as she closed in, giving him no time to react. Before she could cut him down, Supernova's curved blade caught hers. Estelle saw the opening to strike, and she delivered a lightning charged punch to Lady's midsection. The impact sent the evil queen flying back, but she was able to recover, sending a red bolt of lightning that struck the swordsman in his chest.

Supernova shot down the road, taking a heavy tumble before rolling to his feet. Estelle called to him, but her voice was drowned out by a shrill scream. The Pale Lady's giant snake appeared, breaking through the ground with a tremor. The black serpent attacked Supernova, snapping and spitting acid. Jumping and ducking, he fought back, but the serpent was resilient.

The team defended themselves with guns, knives or blunt instruments as a segment of the onslaught cut them off.

Demella pressed her attack against Estelle, swinging her sword violently. The Seeker held her breath, avoiding each slash by jumping back or bending her body. Her focus on the blade was why Estelle didn't see the punch to her stomach coming. Feigning a straight stab, Lady moved her weapon off target and buried her fist in Estelle's solar plexus.

"Stupid girl!" the Pale Lady said, cackling.

Estelle struggled to breathe as she clutched her belly. Cold armor gripped the woman's throat as she was dragged forward to meet Lady's sadistic eyes. Estelle jumped up, pulling herself backward and the Pale Lady with her. The Seeker twisted her body, grappling Lady's arm and throwing her toward the museum. As the foul demon prepared to sprint once more, Estelle charged her lightning and unleashed a wave upon the twisted woman.

The Pale Lady's power burst forth so strong it repelled Estelle's attack. Filling her arms with more of a charge, Estelle raised her hands to fire again. Lady drew the Seeker's attack around her sword. Demella wound up and threw it all back. Estelle crossed her arms before her face and took the brunt of the blast. The bolt knocked her down as it split apart, flying in different directions.

"RALPH!" cried Sue, her cracked voice carrying over the Punished.

Estelle turned on her belly to look at her friends. Raphael's father was prone and motionless, Sue on her knees trying to rouse him. Estelle moved her feet to get to them, but she was jerked back by her hair and the Pale Lady's steel arm wrapped around her neck.

"What's this?" Demella asked, reaching into Estelle's pocket.

The map fell to the ground with a flutter and the violet sapphire with a clink. The Pale Lady drew Estelle's key and pushed her away. The Seeker scrambled for her jewel, clasping it against her chest as she glared at the Pale Lady.

Demella held the key up, her pupils dilating. Black tendrils with a red sheen formed from her hand, enveloping the key. The twisting mass swallowed it and the Pale Lady gasped as her aura flourished.

"Such power!" said the demon. "Such memories?"

A blazing whirlwind of energy escaped the Pale Lady, pulling at Estelle's being. Nausea overcame her and her vision darkened, but Demella pulled her hair so she had to watch her friends struggle. Estelle's fingers grasped at the armor that was her prison. She could barely breathe, let alone speak.

"That dead man was you friend?" Lady asked. "It wasn't my attack that killed him. It was yours. His death belongs to you, girl. I can see your sins!" Estelle roared and wrenched at Lady's arm in vain. "And he's not the only one, is he?"

"Please," Estelle said, gasping. "Let me go!"

"Let's make a deal. Let me absorb you and I'll save them."

Estelle's allies fought back to back, stabbing the Punished or beating them away while Sue made continued efforts to resuscitate Ralph. Supernova continued his battle with the

Nagira, the snake cutting him off any time he attempted to reach them. Andrew became separated from the group as a Punished tackled him, knocking him away. His suit protected him from immediate harm and he was able to fight his way free. However, more of the creatures blocked his path to his allies. Andrew was forced to flee into an alley with more than a dozen pursuers. Theo went down to one knee, his leg wound having reopened, and Sue protected him.

"*Shu Nut Ra!*" Estelle screamed.

The activation of her lightning was so strong it split the asphalt. With sky blue embracing turquoise in a chaotic surge, Estelle jerked the Pale Lady's arm away. She spun around and threw everything she could muster into a barrage of punches, the sapphire clenched in her fist. Each one connected with the demon's face, chest and stomach. Her fists burned bright as if dipped in sunlight and she screamed with each connection. She topped her combination with a small energy sphere that detonated in a beam, sending the Pale Lady flying back toward the museum and causing her sapphire to vanish.

Demella's body was caught several yards away by an invisible force field rendered physical once she hit it. Contained within it was a tall stone wall with a wrought-iron gate. Out from this gate came a half-dozen men who at first seemed to be Punished. Though appearing to be dead, their past human appearance glinted in iridescent waves, their eyes alight in amethyst. The dead men, dawning military fatigues knelt down, taking Lady's arms and restraining her. They pulled her up and held her in place, as if presenting a target for the Seeker.

A violet bolt crashed down next to Estelle and Supernova appeared. Down the street, he left Nagira unconscious, but alive. He crossed his wrists, palms facing outward, and summoned his Life Lightning. The spark at his chest snaked its way between the backs of his hands.

"*Mortestella,*" he said.

The Guardian pulled his hands apart, and the spark fell in on itself, detonating in a radical, multi colored explosion directed forward. The Nova Bolt hit Demella, slamming her into the red dome, the undead soldiers seemingly unfazed. The Pale Lady screamed as the white light burned her flesh. Once the bolt fizzled out, the she-devil fell to her knees, hairless and covered in third-degree burns. Supernova froze, his hands trembling and his eyes large.

The pale-faced woman tried to stand, her legs buckling. Estelle stepped forward, holding her hands up for another attack. Before she could make a move, the Pale Lady vanished on a red bolt. It screamed across the sky to the south, and in the calamity the snake, too, had fled.

Estelle looked behind her, the Punished defeated. So too was Ralph. When she saw his quiet, still body, she shut her eyes and silently cursed herself. Theo and Sue lifted him, putting his arms around their shoulders. Feet dragging and head slumped, they brought him toward to the gates. Ransley held the crow beside them in mourning.

They came to the museum wall. Beyond stood a mass of living corpses, their lifeless, purple eyes lazy and unfocused. Some were soldiers of wars past, some were clad in black and gold robes, some were shirtless, marked in white stripes, circles and other symbols. Behind them was a tall white building. Its core was square, with three cylindrical wings attached to each side and the rear. The front face was crafted of glass and silver, with a matching clock at its peak.

"Fall in!" Supernova said, passing through the gate.

At an instant, the warriors formed ranks in four rows that spanned the distance between the gate and museum, roughly one hundred yards.

"Prepare this man for his final rest."

An eerie warble pulsed through the dome-shaped room, momentarily drowning out the constant ticking of two cosmic clocks. Estelle relaxed in a theater seat and watched her Guardian pacing back and forth before a glossy, white pedestal with a beach ball sized sphere hovering over it. Three rings of seats surrounded it, with only a single aisle leading to an exit behind the Seeker, a gold plaque reading *"J. Doyle Planetarium."*

Radiating on the floor was the golden blue clock Estelle had seen her Guardian manifest, its wheels turning slowly, ticking in unison with a red counterpart on the ceiling.

A woman stood beside Estelle. Her skin was marble white, and she wore a dark teal cloak. Star silver curls draped the sides of her face and a black cloth was wound around her jaw. The woman wore a white and silver dress, woven with pearls at her stomach and beneath her bosom. She watched the swordsman with dark violet eyes.

Thelxiope was her name and during her ancient life she was a siren, haunting seashores and misty shallows for human prey. When she crossed paths with the Supernova Swordsman, he killed her and her spirit became bound in service to him.

"You expect me to believe that crap?" Supernova asked his servant.

"It isn't up to me to dictate your expectations," Thelxiope said, her voice ringing in their minds. "I only do as I am commanded."

"Who commanded you to keep the scythe away from me?" Supernova spat as he yelled. "Izanami? Amalia? "

"You did, Master."

"I would *never* give up my weapon! For what?!"

"A place was required to keep safe the Seeker's key. The scythe worked best- you are welcome."

"Do you have any idea how hard it's been without it?"

"No more difficult than any other human, I imagine."

"That's the last time I ever trust you! You know I need that weapon for my work. We nearly died out there."

"Yet here you stand, victorious."

"Not all of us, siren. We lost two, thanks to you. This isn't victory. Victory would have been the girl allowing me to come here on my own. Victory would have been zero casualties. This day belongs to the dead."

"How about a little positivity?" Estelle asked with narrowing eyes.

"I don't want to hear anything from you!" Supernova said, not bothering to look at her. "I told you to give up your powers, but you didn't listen and now a man is dead."

Estelle bit her lower lip, her eyes glowing. "Don't you dare-"

"Don't what?! Tell you I was right the whole time?"

Estelle jumped to her feet. "Because you're never wrong?! You didn't get captured by the Pale Lady. You didn't lose your little weapon. You didn't lose your girlfriend to a monster!"

His eyes grew wide, and he stood over the woman, rings of red circling his dark eyes.

"Choose your next words very carefully," Supernova said.

She scowled. "Or what, reaper?"

Thelxiope's hands came between them, pushing them back a few steps.

"I must advise that you both recenter yourselves," the siren said. "Despite your feelings for each other, you must to work together."

"How can I help her when she won't listen to me?!" Supernova pointed an accusing finger at Estelle. "How could you let Demella absorb one of your keys?! Now her power has doubled!"

"It's not like I planned it!" Estelle shouted. "She took it from me while you were losing to the snake!"

"Every time you use your powers, something goes wrong. Ralph is dead. You almost killed Theo. You're-"

"Master!" Thelxiope said, her eyes widening. "It may not soothe your wrath, but I would reveal your weapon and the Seeker's key. If I may?"

The swordsman waved his hand and turned away. Thelxiope pointed to the white sphere and a transparent curtain fell.

Floating above the ball was a scythe. Its staff gleamed dark silver and a small projection of the cosmic clock appeared at its top. The scythe blade curved with a silver cutting edge, but the top half was slate gray with a curved tooth halfway across. Behind the blade was the bronze sword Supernova kept chained to his left wrist, angled upward.

Below the scythe, bouncing in the air, was a shining key sculpted of smooth jade. A square with a hole drilled through it sat at the top, and its smooth stem bore two sets of three collars. The bit at the end was square with jagged marks cut around it. As Estelle focused on it, warmth radiated through her body and it called to her in a chorus of beautiful song only she could hear. She took it, feeling a rush of power course through her.

"*Mori*," Supernova whispered.

The realm reaper held a hand up to his menacing weapon, and it disappeared in a pop of red smoke. That same smoke formed long and thin in his hand and when he grasped it, the scythe appeared there. The room's light faded with circular symbols etching themselves inside the clocks. Crimson light shone through, giving the observatory a hellish appearance.

Supernova held Temcindus high as reality shifted, the walls and ceiling receding. The cosmic clock glowed at their feet, one hand spinning rapidly and the other moving at a snail's pace. The shift slowed, then reversed with the scythe consuming the red, foggy energy left behind. Releasing the pole, it popped and was gone again. Supernova bathed in the energy for a short time, glancing at Thelxiope every so often.

"What is this red time spell?" he said finally. "Who cast this, Thelxiope?"

"You did, Master," said the specter.

"This is beyond my capabilities. I won't have any more of your lies."

"I have said all I can say. I forgive you."

With a formal bow, Thelxiope dispersed into mist.

"You smug, little-"

Supernova rubbed his head, appearing tired and sluggish. His facial muscles struggled to keep his eyes open. His breathing was shallow and slow and, just for a moment, his posture faltered with shaky legs. He straightened himself and left the planetarium.

Estelle and Supernova returned to the entrance where Ransley, Theo and Sue sat immersed in deep conversation, the white crow seated on Sue's shoulder. Theo sat against the ledge before the massive windows, and Sue sat on the lip next to him while Ransley paced before them.

"I know what I saw," Sue said. "As soon as he went down that alley, he was swarmed."

"Andrew was the smartest person the manor had," said Theo. "Didn't he help create that portable shield? If anyone could have found a way out, it'd be him."

"We wouldn't make it ourselves," Ransley said, exhausted. "We're running on fumes as it is. We've got no ammo. No vehicles. No backup."

"He's right," Sue said. "Notwithstanding how hard it was

to get here, the manor will still be on lockdown. I'm sorry Theo."

Theo threw his head back, and his lips pursed, but he nodded. His face lit up when Estelle and her Guardian returned. Supernova walked with his eyes shut, as if sleep-walking.

"Did you find what you were looking for?" Ransley asked.

"I did," Estelle said, holding her jade key up. "But, I lost my first key to the Pale Lady."

"I'm sure we can get it back."

"Easier said than done," Supernova said. "After she took the key, her power grew significantly. She can absorb energy, and she's taken a liking to Estelle's soul. We may have defeated her today, but she'll be back. When she wants something, she's relentless."

"What are we supposed to do, then?" Sue asked.

"You leave it to me. The further away you all are from this, the safer you'll be."

"What?" Theo furrowed his brows. "We're not leaving you guys- right everyone?"

"We're here," Ransley said. "We may as well be useful."

Supernova shook his head. "You'll be of more use to her than us. If she knows we have loved ones, she won't hesitate to use you as leverage. The best thing we can do is keep her attention on myself."

"That's stupid," Estelle said. "Why would we willingly put ourselves in harm's way?"

"Because that's the only way they'll stay safe. Otherwise, Demella may tear this city apart to find you. You still have three keys to find, and that *thing* has one now."

"We should be very careful with how we proceed," the crow said. "I had hoped we could complete her trials in secret."

"Agreed. We need a new plan. First things first, though. Gather around, everyone."

The remnants of the team formed a circle around Supernova. He summoned his scythe and held it at a right angle, tapping the end of the pole on the ground three times. He mumbled something and magic circles burned around them. Beneath each person appeared a glowing outline of a lotus flowers and within the petals they felt a deep comfort as it healed their wounds. Theo's leg, Sue's shoulder, multiple cuts, bruises, scrapes and bites- all repaired.

"*Tempus*," said Supernova.

Eyes aflame golden blue, the ticking of his cosmic clock washed through the museum. With a fling of his wrist, its projection fell to the ground and expanded, bordering the walls. The inner wheel was near a radiating 3 and when Supernova held his hand out, it wound backward. It spun slowly at first, but with each rotation, it sped up. In time with the clock, the museum transformed.

Kern's environment became less worn with each rotation. Dust disappeared, and the fractured windows fixed themselves. With each second, numerous shades of past people entered and exited their vision, walking in reverse. The museum returned to its former glory; the floor shining and the walls pristine. Floods of civilians reversed through the halls in triple time until no one remained. Streaks of glorious sunlight spread through the windows as the ticking ended. Supernova's scythe dematerialized, and he took a deep breath, exhaling slowly.

"Welcome to Web Obsidia," he said. "Circa fifty years before the Great Inversion. If any of you ever need a safe place..."

A look of panic came over the Guardian's face. His breathing slowed, and he knelt, feeling his own heartbeat. He doubled over, coughing, each draw of air sounding like it was being forced through a pillow. Wounds opened on his body, splotches of blood forming on his left thigh and right shoulder. The skin of his left arm sizzled away, leaving his hand and shoulder glossy and withered. He fell forward, wheezing.

"What's happening to him?!" Sue asked.

"Have to rest," Supernova said between breaths. "I... need my..."

"His sarcophagus," said Theo. "He needs to regenerate."

"Where?" Estelle asked Supernova. "Where is it?"

"Planetarium," said the Guardian.

The group helped Supernova to his feet and returned him to the room with two clocks. Already waiting for them near the white sphere was a long gold coffin that was not there before. Its bulky frame came up to Estelle's waist. It was the same coffin the Deep Witch put Marcel in.

They struggled to move its heavy lid and budged it just enough for the Guardian to climb in. Just as Supernova's hand touched the top of the face, he fell unconscious, tumbling headfirst into the sarcophagus. Without assistance, the lid slid back into place, sealing itself.

"I've seen him do this before," Theo said. "He'll be a few days, so we should get comfy."

As the team watched in silence, Estelle approached the shining box. She traced the relief of a man resembling Marcel but wearing an ancient Egyptian crown. He crossed his arms, holding the chained swords with a far off look in his intense eyes. The blue, green, purple and sand-colored gems glinted under the low ambiance.

"Crow," said Estelle. "I want you to take a message to Sherman Manor. Tell Nona what happened."

"I will tell them the objective has been completed," it said.

"Be kind when you tell her of the lost."

"It shall be done, my Seeker."

The crow's wings clapped as it flew away. Theo sat in one

of the observatory seats with Sue on at his side. Ransley approached the Seeker, gazing down at the coffin before looking at his friend.

"Are you alright?" he asked.

"I wish I could say I was," Estelle replied. "I can't stop thinking of who we lost today. Can't stop wondering if those men are still after us. It's just been a long day."

"Perhaps Supernova isn't the only one who needs rest."

# CHAPTER 24

# ESTELLE'S FIRST MEMORY

For three days, Supernova slept, and peace and grief made its home with Estelle and her friends. Estelle found herself unable to free her mind of the lives lost. With the museum restored, she and the others explored. A security guard barrack off the foyer equipped with showers allowed them to bathe away the grime and blood. As well, a section of the main building opened to a small cafeteria with three fully stocked kitchens.

On the first day, Estelle and the group paid their respects to Ralph. Venturing beyond the doors of the museum returned them to present day Web Obsidia. Black clouds full of despair floated through the red sky and Supernova's undead army stood guard, three or four approaching the gate when a Punished would wander too near.

The group found Ralph resting peacefully atop a stone bench. A black silk cloth covered his body and his weapons rested on the ground nearby. Sue stepped forward and pulled back the cloth with a catch of her breath. Ralph looked as if he were sleeping and the sullen clan honored him with a moment of silence.

"We'll miss you," Sue said. "You were a good man, a loving husband, and a caring father. You always went out of your way to help others. You always did what was right."

"He was a phenomenal friend," Theo said. "One of the best."

"I'm sorry this happened to you," the Seeker said. "If I had been stronger, faster... smarter. I'm responsible for what happened to you."

"No, Estelle," said Ransley.

"This ain't on you," Sue said. "The devil did this and mark my words- she will pay."

"These things can happen," Ransley continued. "It wasn't you. It wasn't something we could have predicted. It could have been any of us. What's important now is that we honor him the best way we can."

Estelle could not meet Sue's eyes. She pulled herself away from her friend, consumed by guilt, and left to be alone. She would isolate herself for the next two days. During this time, Estelle's friends dispersed to the exhibits. Theo investigated the technology wing while Sue and Ransley explored what biology offered. On the third day, Estelle's crow returned as she made her way to check on Supernova.

"I was getting concerned," the Seeker said, the crow hopping along the guardrail. "How's the manor?"

"There are developments," it replied shortly. "After Nona allowed the leaders to leave, there was much unrest."

"Is she okay?"

"She is stressed, but healthy. I warned her of talks of a coup. She wanted me to tell you- 'escape, live your life. It was worth it.'"

"What's going to happen to her?"

"Her fate is uncertain."

Estelle entered the planetarium, stopping a few feet from the sarcophagus. It remained sealed, humming low as it blinked on and off with a shimmering light. The crow flew to its lid when the Seeker sat with her back against it. The two clocks ticked away with the glowing second hand passing over her legs.

"Wherever I go, bad things happen," said she. "Getting Theo caught, the fight at Bleedstar. And Ralph... Now the woman who helped me get here could be in trouble. That's all I need; another town of people who hate my guts."

"Don't think of it that way," the crow said.

Estelle stomped her boot. "Is anyone even helping Nona?"

"One of the scientists," said the crow. "A man named Riggo Raimi. He seems logical and has worked closely with her for years."

"Do you think he's a good man?"

"It would be easier to tell if he didn't wear the hazmat suit. He's one of the few who supported your cause if it makes you feel any better."

"It wouldn't be the first time I got someone in trouble." A dazed look came over the woman. "There was this family- the Boyles, who worked for mine as groundskeepers. I was friends with the oldest son, Aidan. I'd known him since I was just a girl and when we were older- well, you know. Young love and all that."

"That doesn't sound so bad," the crow said.

"It was great at first. Secret midnight dates at the gazebo. Having wine by the river. It was magical- at least until Father found out. Then all of a sudden the Boyle family decides to move back to Scotland after three generations in Hiemson. Aidan stopped talking to me and I never saw him again."

"What makes you think your father had anything to do with it?"

"He got tired of my sobbing after a week. Then he burst into my room to tell me to stop weeping over a poor man's son. That I'm destined for greater things and I'd only ruin my life by spending it with a gardener." She scoffed. "I'd heard rumors that he made people 'disappear' and I put it together on my own. I bring misfortune to anyone I come in contact with. Just like Aidan Boyle. Just like Nona."

"You did not directly hurt these people," the crow said. "You cannot be blamed for what others do."

"What if the same thing happens to Marcel? What happens when Father finds out about us? Will he be sent to prison? Will he vanish in the night without a word?" A lump formed in her throat. "Like I did?"

"Estelle..."

"I'm more trouble than I'm worth," the Seeker said. "No matter how hard I try to stay out of the way, trouble has a way of finding me and people get hurt."

"What are you saying?"

"Nova was right. We'll have to finish my trials without our friends. No one else can die for me. Not Theo or Sue or Ransley. No one."

"What about what they want?" the crow asked.

"I don't care!" her voice was sharp like her Guardian's swords. "As much of a headache as he is, it should be just you, me and the grumpy cloud."

The sarcophagus gave off a magic pulse, a golden ring expanding like a ripple on a pond. The stone ground against itself as the lid shifted and slid open.

"I guess I'm the expendable one," her Guardian said as he emerged.

"It's been three days," she said.

"I expended an atom bomb's worth of energy. You're lucky I lasted as long as I did."

～

The Seeker, Familiar and Guardian found Theo, Sue and Ransley seated at a table in the cafeteria, having just finished a meal. After a curt discussion, Supernova would send everyone where they desired to be. Though Ransley and Theo wanted to continue to help, Estelle made a vehement argument that it would be too dangerous. She would have no more lives on her conscience. After their farewells, Supernova summoned Temcindus.

Supernova slashed at the air three times, forming a doorway of sorts. Each cut in reality burned like iron in an open flame. It filled itself in with an golden-orange glow and the Guardian instructed them to think about where they wanted to go, then step through. With hugs and words of encouragement, Theo and Sue disappeared through the veil back to Sherman Manor. With a tired smile and a warm embrace, Ransley departed for the Catalina. Once the party was gone, the portal closed.

"Well?" Estelle asked. "Now what?"

"You must use your key," the crow said.

"Say 'I summon the Dimension Door,'" Supernova said, looking to the Seeker.

She repeated the phrase. Waving into existence came a tall, white door. It was close to ten feet tall with an angled, pointed top. A gold frame encased it, and a snowflake of silver adorned its face. Where the knob should have been was a circular cutout filled with jade, leaving a thin keyhole in the center.

As Estelle inserted the key, the lock trapped it, pulling it from her hand. It disappeared within, becoming a solid piece of green stone. The locks slid, and the door cracked open. The Seeker pulled it, revealing a reflective wall. She touched a finger to it and it felt like water, cool and leaving ripples with each little disturbance. With her Guardian and crow, she passed through.

Reality shifted as Seeker, Familiar and Guardian arrived into an ever moving continuum of glass shards. Some were monstrous, and some were tiny, like grains of sand. They traversed a marvelous bridge of glass and gold, just one of millions that criss crossed above, below and to the sides, each one extending for an eternity. Countless razor fragments danced weightless before them, breaking down to dust. They then constructed an arch with another mirrored portal.

"What is this place?" Estelle asked.

"The crossroads of space-time," said Supernova, tracing the banister. "The bridges of parallel realities. This one must be connected to your home world."

Burning characters appeared in the mirror, instantly crystalizing and turning black. *December 25, 1994.*

"Is this day significant to you?" the crow asked.

Estelle looked away.

"Let's get this over with," Supernova said, disappearing through the silver shimmer.

The Seeker readied herself, taking her crow into her arms. She crossed the threshold, and they came out in a patch of forest that had been cleared out to make room for a small plaza. Covered in a layer of snow, it consisted of a blue instrument store, a red clothing shop, and a hub for souvenirs. Christmas lights hung in all of the windows, accompanied by stockings and shiny garland. Whatever building sat at the end had been reduced to a pile of charcoal and ash.

A dozen people stood several yards from the burned heap, cut off by yellow emergency tape. The eldest of the group, a woman dressed in a tan wool coat with graying brown hair and bright brown eyes, stood at the front. Behind her were young boys and girls from the ages of thirteen to eighteen, and Estelle's apparent younger self was among them. Beside the woman was a taller girl, bearing blue eyes and auburn hair and, a younger, heavy set Nina stood beside her.

Time slowed to a halt for the Seeker and her companions, holding the world in a snapshot. Still faces mourned over the destroyed building as the trio observed them. Estelle fixed on Nina and the taller girl at her side.

"Why are we here?" Estelle asked, wide eyed. "That's the old dance studio- well, it used to be."

"You tell us," Supernova said. She avoided eye contact with him.

"Something important must have occurred," the crow said. "How does this relate to your trials?"

"I don't know," the Seeker said, looking away.

Supernova eyed her. "You said that pretty quickly... And you keep staring at that girl. What are you not telling us?"

Estelle bit her lip and glanced at her younger self. Supernova did the same, but stepped closer, his face inches from the past version.

"What are you doing?" Estelle asked. "Get away from her- me."

"The end of your hair is burned," Supernova said. "There's ash on your neck; trace amounts, but I can see it." He turned to the Seeker. "You're an awful liar."

"I..." Estelle stepped back.

"Do not fear," the crow said. "We are not here to judge you. We are here to help you. Just tell us what happened."

The Seeker's voice failed to come forth. She hugged herself, shaking her head and shutting her eyes so tight a vein arose in her forehead.

"Look at me," Supernova said.

When she refused, he grasped her shoulder, and she flinched. His grip burned her skin, though not enough to injure and images flashed in her mind of the day she disappeared. The radiant purple eyes. The glowing chains. The hulking shadow that took Marcel's place and followed her into the nightmare. There he stood.

"If I wanted to," he said. "I could will the truth from you with Temcindus- invade your mind and force you to betray yourself. It's cruel and easy and I don't want to do it."

Estelle searched his face for the hints of falsehood. He held a far-off, sleepy gaze and his mouth was relaxed, without so much as a twitch. The heat on her shoulder spread down her arm and across her chest, and she knocked his hand away.

"Why not?" Estelle asked. "You've been more than willing to take your anger out on me- like I'm your verbal punching bag."

The swordsman sighed. "I wish I had never taken this job."

"Then just go!" The scream hurt her throat and her Guardian stared. "Why do you stick around since you obviously don't like me?! I never did anything to you except ask for your help and you treat me like a stray dog. So please, tell me what I did to deserve it!"

Estelle felt the light in her eyes as she scowled.

"She has a point," the crow said. "No one doubts the weight you bear, Supernova. And none of us can hope to understand it. But your frustration is tangible and we all feel it. Theo led me to believe you're a man of wisdom and compassion. Was he incorrect?"

Supernova gave a half frown and dwelled on the white bird.

"Theo thinks the best of everyone," he said. "He overstates my graces while downplaying my flaws." The swordsman laughed to himself. "You think you're here for redemption, Seeker? You can't fathom the things I've done- why I lost Vileena and the fact that I fucking deserve it. You think you've seen me kill? I've wiped entire continents away! Billions and billions of deaths on my hands! And for what? 'The will of the gods?'"

Supernova paced in a circle, his breathing heavier and louder.

"Nova-" Estelle said.

"You're wrong," the swordsman said. "I should have never taken this job because I'm the worst possible Guardian you could have been saddled with. I'm arrogant and problematic. I dwell in darkness and obsess about what I want until I go mad. You're not the problem. I am."

He became still again, peering at the snow covered ground. Estelle gazed upon the people frozen in time, then at the blackened pile of wood.

"The fire was my fault," Estelle said, facing the auburn-haired girl. "Natasha and I never got along. We got into a fight when we were ten and we've hated each other ever since. You could say being in the same dance studio was trench warfare at best."

The form of Estelle's past life took on a golden aura.

"The Regional Ballet chooses a handful of dancers to go on their world tour every year and three would come from our studio. I tried like hell... but Natasha was better. She was chosen for the world tour and I'd have to stay behind. My one big chance at getting away from my life- gone."

"So you burned down the studio?" Supernova asked.

"It was an accident. I broke in early Christmas morning to... redecorate. I shattered a case of apple cider bottles against the mirrors and an outlet caught fire. I wasn't thinking about what came after. Just how mad I was that Natasha got what I was working so hard for. I didn't mean for it to happen like that."

"We've all been in that place," the crow said. "Acting on emotions or impulse. We make mistakes."

"Most mistakes don't cost people their lives."

"Someone died in the fire?"

"No, but they did for me to get to Kern... I was so focused on getting here, I didn't consider what would happen after. I can't stop thinking of Nona and how I cost her the leadership position. I didn't think about Theo getting caught when I snuck out of the manor. I cost my dance class our studio and I got three good men killed. Who's the real problem?"

"Neither of you are problems!" the crow shouted, spreading its wings, startling the Seeker. "I know little of your struggles, Estelle, and less of yours, swordsman. What I do know is that you're both trying your best. I see a lost woman trying to reclaim her life and a man shaking under the weight of the world, but still holding it up. Both of you need to focus on your victories and learn from your mistakes. That's the only way we'll make it through Ever's Hollow."

A wisp of light left the past version of Estelle, wafting to the Seeker before circling her head. She inhaled, and the light flowed into her nose and mouth. She relived Christmas of '94 in her mind, feeling the disappointment, rage and sorrow from that day. Where she had hoped to feel some sense of completion for finally reclaiming a portion of her soul, she only felt hollow.

Reality around them shattered and fell away, swirling in a storm of white dust. It enveloped Estelle, unlocking doors in her mind and binding to her spirit. Once again, they traversed the golden glass bridge. As she was left with new knowledge, she realized the shards of glass in their vicinity featured a myriad of her own memories. They all showed her life ranging from her day of birth to young adulthood as well as two or three with an older version of herself she did not know. Both happy and traumatic windows circled them, but Estelle could not access them. They returned to the museum via the dimension door. Once on the other side, it faded from existence.

"Well?" Estelle asked. "Now what? How do we get my key back from Lady?"

Supernova stared with lazy eyes. "Oh, no. We're not there. Not by a light-year."

"Then... find my other keys? The letter says I have to find five."

"They'll have to wait. I need to check something first."

"Seriously? My life is riding on this and you want to run an errand?"

"I'm bothered by the time spell in the planetarium. I need to find out what it is, who cast it and why."

"I've been working toward this since I woke up, and now it's in front of me. You want to stall on my trials for some research?"

"I couldn't begin to explain what my life is like outside of this job. All you need to know is that something isn't right around here and I'm not making any moves until I have some kind of idea what it is."

"The all-powerful Supernova Swordsman is really so afraid?"

Supernova's brows furrowed, and he glared at her. He approached the museum's front doors and knelt.

"I pray to the mighty Osiris. The Supernova Swordsman, your humble and trusted liaison, requests access to the Bygone Atheneum."

The glass of the doors changed, becoming matte white. Warm light slipped through the crack beneath and the sound of birds chirping came muffled from the other side. Supernova opened the door and faced his Seeker.

"I will be back shortly," he said, carefree and shrugging.

"What the hell am I supposed to do?" asked Estelle, hands on her hips.

"Do what you want. You don't approve of my methods and I understand why. You challenge everything I say and it infuriates me... but I would do the same in your place. Come or don't come; I don't care."

Supernova turned and walked through the light. Estelle stuttered as she chastised him.

"Who does he think he is, walking away like that?" Estelle asked her crow.

"You insulted him," her familiar said. "Some men seek company when their spirits are down. Some seek solitude."

"His ego can't be that sensitive?"

"I don't think it has to do with ego. Perhaps he truly is afraid of something."

# CHAPTER 25

# THE BYGONE ATHENEUM

The Bygone Atheneum was a massive building with a quartz floor glazed with gray striations. Elegant bookshelves that stretched twelve stories up to the atrium's glass dome hid the walls. Intricate wooden stairs and wide walkways lined the towering shelves in rising, repeating levels.

Ancient trees stood between the bookshelves, embedded in the walls, their thick branches sprawling out overhead. Birds of red, yellow, orange, aqua and white danced among emerald, ruby and golden leaves.

"Look at this place," Estelle said to herself, searching every surface of the atrium.

"It's an enormous library!" the crow said.

Numerous hallways lined spaces that broke the bookshelves apart. Upon and betwixt them were stone balconies where vines, flowers and greenery overflowed. The occasional waterfall poured down natural rock and into pools that disappeared beneath the floor. Tables and desks dotted the wide room with a tall square bench in the center made of white wood. Several elder men and women sat on its inside. In the center, a short rise above the others, sat an old man with an enormous gray beard. He wore small circular eyeglasses and wrote feverishly, lost in conversation with the Supernova Swordsman.

Estelle weaved through what felt like a hundred people as their chatter washed over her. The crowd pressed close, a kaleidoscope of unfamiliar fabrics and dazzling colors. Robes of red and gold baring jewels on the sleeves, armor clad men and women draped with vibrant, patterned cloaks, ethereal women in white dresses adorned in silver. With her crow, the Seeker approached the tall bench.

Excitement and joy emanated from her Guardian's conversation. He spoke of space; stars, planets and galaxies. She had never seen the swordsman so happy and did not know he could be so. The storm cloak shook on his shoulders with laughter as he painted a verbal image of his favorite nebula. When the old man saw Estelle, he waved her over.

"Questa è Stella?" he asked Supernova.

"My new pain in the ass," he replied.

"I'm sorry," Estelle said. "My Italian's pretty rusty."

The old man motioned behind his bench as he bent down to search. When he returned, he brought with him a coin-sized piece of aquamarine with the small depiction of a door. He offered the totem to Estelle, who took it and rubbed the polished surface.

"What does it do?" the woman asked.

"Reciprocal translation," said the man in a raspy voice. "I hope you find your stay here enjoyable, young Stella."

Estelle looked from the man to the stone, her mouth dropping.

"I'm heading to my study," the Guardian said. "Please let me know if you find anything about the time spell."

"Worry not, old friend. Wisdom be with you both."

"Farewell Signore Galilei."

Estelle bid the gentleman goodbye, and they traversed the lengthy halls beyond the benches. Rows of trees embedded on either side segmented the walls there. Their bushy branches concealed the roof until they came to a four-way cross with a curved ceiling bearing dimly lit stars. Taking the right-hand path, they entered a corridor with silver doors set between each tree. Supernova approached one with golden stars fixed at the top. He let himself in and closed it behind Estelle.

The woman marveled at a two story room the size of a house, stepping on shiny obsidian tile. The second floor was open with a silver banister following it around the room and down the staircase in the center. Bookshelves lined both floors along with pedestals of mystic artifacts, stands fully clad in armor and strange weapons mounted on racks.

A tall, thick tree sat merged into the wall on the left, beginning at the floor and stretching through the balcony, covering a large bed draped in purple silk. Just behind the stairs and out of sight was a long glass desk with a large wooden chair at its edge. The desk sat before a great circular window that overlooked a glorious, booming city ablaze with neon signs.

"What is this place?" Estelle asked.

"Home base," Supernova said.

The swordsman lowered his hood and scarf, breathing in the earthy scent of the tree. A fluttering came from above and a raven with a two-foot wingspan descended to land on the Guardian's shoulder. Its purple eyes looked like deep, grape colored pearls.

"Hello Daiona," said Supernova, petting the bird. "Welcome to my home, Seeker. We won't be here long. A day or two so I can try to figure out what that spell is."

"What about my trials?" asked Estelle, stepping toward Supernova. "And our friends? You want to spend a day reading while they're suffering?"

Estelle's brow furrowed when Daiona spread her wings and snapped her beak. Estelle's crow tilted its head.

"She means no disrespect," the white crow said to the raven, who replied in a series of clicks and squawks. "Yes, she does question everything, even Supernova's wisdom. But how do we attain wisdom without inquiry?"

Daiona acquiesced with a caw before the Guardian sent her back to perch in the canopy.

"Time works differently across the realms," Supernova said. "Once we're back, hardly any time will have passed. Probably a few hours."

Supernova swept through the study, stopping at every other display to take a book or two. It appeared as if he had little attention to devote anywhere else. Estelle recalled Vileena's words about the swordsman's obsessive tendencies.

"What am I supposed to do?" she asked. "Sit around like a cat?"

"What do you want to do?" he asked, setting his books on the desk and staring at her with half-open eyes.

"I want to go home."

"Are you so eager for monsters and mercenaries that you can't wait a day?"

"I have a life to get back to."

Supernova neared a bookshelf packed from side to side with varying tomes. He eyed each one, his index finger searching. He drew one and set it on his desk, littered with parchment and texts already, and opened a marked section.

"*Come here,*" he gestured with his eyes. "Read that."

"*'Chronicles of Eve's Hollow Seekers, Chapter 3,*" Estelle said. "*Emeline Maylus began her trials in Seis Regina in the year 322 of the Dark Peace. Five queens ruled the Six Points city, and it was foretold the 6th queen would usurp them all. The 6th queen came in the form of Miss Maylus. Accompanied by her owl, Mira and Guardian, the Shadow Horse,*"

*Emeline brought peace to Seis Regina for the first time since the Fall.'"*

Estelle flipped through the pages, glancing over the details of Emeline's journey and coming to another Seeker named Derek.

"That's the only book on Seekers in the whole library," Supernova said.

"You want me to do homework?" Estelle placed her hands on her hips. "Really?"

"How many things are as important as knowledge and information?" He organized the scrolls on his desk. "I thought you were a learned woman? How did you get through university?" Estelle glared at him and Supernova raised a suspicious eyebrow. "The point is, we can be more prepared."

"I thought we were doing fine."

"If you call Demella ambushing us 'fine.'"

The Guardian's gaze remained focused on his research. Heat rose in Estelle's face and without thinking, she cleared his desk of its content, sending the papers scattering across the obsidian floor. Estelle stood back, waiting for him to rise. Waiting for him to turn his dark fury on her. But he did not. He simply knelt and began collecting the pages without so much as a glance toward his Seeker.

"Estelle," the crow said. "Maybe we should go for a walk? This place seems lovely-"

"Don't you care?!" Estelle said, slapping the papers out of his hand.

Supernova watched her, his cloak covering his body.

"People died so we could get to the museum! And you want to sit here in this quiet, comfortable place so you can ready your dirty scrolls and ignore me? Did Ralph and Andrew and Owen die for nothing?!"

Her Guardian searched her face.

"Have you ever been in a war?" Supernova asked.

"Of course not."

"When circumstances are greater than the people, there's one thing that matters as much as the army you put forth: knowledge. Knowledge is why the Spartans died at Thermopylae. Knowledge is why Napoleon lost at Waterloo. If we want their deaths to mean something, we need to be as prepared as we can going forward. We mourn, but we keep moving."

"But-"

"I did my best to keep Demella's attention focused on me. To spare the people the worst of her wrath. It worked for a while; especially when she captured me. But all that changed when she got a taste of your soul. Now she knows *you*. She'll hunt *you*."

"I'm pretty sure we won the last fight," Estelle said. "Why don't we just finish the job?"

"You're not ready."

"Then why did she run?!"

Supernova stepped forward, looming over her and baring his teeth.

"We caught her off guard," he said, the edge of a cliff in his voice. "She wasn't even close to death. There's not enough power between us to finish her for good. We could have tried until we passed out. She'd have been hurt, she'd have been incapacitated, but she'd be *alive*. I've seen her regenerate from a pile of ash."

"I don't believe you." Estelle shook her head. "I don't believe you."

"She showed you a percent of a percent of what she's capable of. Don't let your accidental victory fool you into thinking you can kill her! Demella would rip you apart piece by piece just to hear you scream!"

The Pale Lady's words rang in Estelle's memory. *I can see your sins. He's not the only one, is he?* Ralph's face flashed in her mind. Then the subway incident and Theo's petrified face.

"How can I become ready?" she asked, her face relaxing.

"To kill Demella? Last time you said you couldn't face her. What's changed?"

"Nothing. I hope I never see her again, but I'm not dumb enough to think it won't happen. When it does- how can I be ready?"

Supernova backed off. He pulled a scroll from a glass case near his desk and brought it to Estelle. She untied the string and let it unravel. There were diagrams of a person performing different positions, along with a visual guide for manipulating energy into various shapes.

"*'Proper technique for materialization,'*" she read. "*'Warriors of the War of Elements developed several techniques to summon weapons on the battlefields. The Sky Dwellers harnessed their Life Lightning, transmuting their souls into steel and iron. Beginners of this technique should not see battle until at least six months of practice.'* Six months?"

"Have discipline," the swordsman said. "*Shu Nut Rah.*"

"It's a start," the crow said. "You can do it, Estelle."

Supernova's umber eyes shone purple as the star appeared at his chest. Working its way outward from his feet, the energy gave off a strong violet aura. It pushed past Estelle, and the obsidian floor shimmered like dark amethyst. The Guardian was still, fixed as if in a trance, but he watched her, unblinking. The aura shrank back as the pillar of power rose a short way above his head. The star sparked and the white lightning appeared, snapping at the inside of the pillar.

"*Shu Nut Rah,*" said Estelle, her power rushing outward.

The power nearly spilled freely from her body. Estelle held her electricity back like a rabid dog on a chain, her Life Lightning whipping around the room. Fists clenched, she shook as the energy threatened to assert its will over her.

"Breathe," he said. "Fill your lungs and your belly, and draw the power toward yourself."

Estelle expanded her diaphragm and exhaled at half the speed. She allowed herself to relax and her lightning followed suit, gradually drawing closer to her. Her pillar rose to an appropriate height and her Life Lightning steadied to a graceful dance. Though the pressure was difficult to bear, she stood erect.

"Materialization is a simple concept," her Guardian said. "You can wield a bolt of lightning like a sword. The more your refine yourself, the more detailed and intricate your weapons become. It will take after you. This is also how you get your sapphire back."

Estelle inhaled sharply at the mention of her gem.

"I never told you about that," she said.

"No, you didn't."

# CHAPTER 26

## SUPERNOVA'S PROPOSITION

Estelle practiced her new art for two hours as Supernova remained at his desk, his head encircled by white smoke rising from his black wooden pipe. She began with a bolt no larger than a dagger, holding its form for less than a minute before her energy overwhelmed her. Once rested, she continued. Within the first hour, the Seeker gained enough control to form a staff sized bolt.

Fatigued, Estelle took a break and admired her Guardian's collection of mystic treasures. She thumbed through old, wrinkled books on martial arts, mythology and philosophy. After reading, she carefully inspected some of the items on pedestals and shelves. She found a crystal pyramid with a human eye inside, a gold necklace with a skull shaped pendant, a small statue of a man with horns and more.

There were items hidden by discarded papers and unraveled scrolls. A glint on a bottom shelf caught her eye. She knelt to clear it and found an impossibly beautiful iridescent conch shell. She held the smooth object, watching the light travel across its blue, pink and white streaks. How could something so glorious be kept buried? She replaced it, deciding not to disturb her Guardian's possessions.

A weapon rack caught her eye next. Four poled weapons decorated it, polished and well-kept. One was a spear with a long, thin tip. Next to it sat a two-pronged trident, then a glaive with a sweeping curved blade. The final piece, made from a simple wooden pole, held a blade longer and wider than the spear, but with a simpler curve than the glaive. She reached out to touch the cold, smooth metal, amused by her reflection in the blade.

"The Japanese naginata," said an enchanting woman from behind. "A clever choice."

Estelle whirled around to meet the gaze of a tall, olive-skinned woman. Her facial features were soft, with full lips and a short, thin nose. Her long brown hair draped down her shoulders in wavy locks with blond highlights, beaded braids mixed in. Her soft silver eyes peered through Estelle as if she could spot her every atom. Dressed in a simple white cloak that hid her body, she bowed her head in greeting. A golden clasp in the representation of an owl sat just below her neck. Estelle was speechless; she had not heard her approach and Supernova remained engrossed in his studies.

"My name is Amalia," said the woman. "A pleasure."

"Estelle," the Seeker said. "But I feel like you already know that?"

Amalia smirked. "Why don't you pick up that weapon?"

It felt like more of an order than a suggestion, and Estelle complied. She took the naginata in her hands. It dragged her arms down and she buckled, trying to keep it upright. Amalia took a stance in the center of the room, exposing a single arm adorned in silver bracers and bands. White light appeared in her palm and she squeezed it to summon a Greek short sword. Holding the tip toward Estelle's heart, she smiled.

"*Shu Nut Rah!*" Estelle said. Her powers allowed her to lift the weapon in a meaningful way and she readied herself.

"Go easy on her," Supernova said, keeping his focus on his work.

The woman in white disappeared and swept Estelle's, appearing behind her. She swung her blade at Amalia's feet, but the skilled fighter jumped over it. Estelle scrambled up in time to avoid a slash at her throat. She stepped back as the warrior applied pressure. As a downward slash came, Estelle blocked it using the pole. She parried the attack and threw her own blade in Amalia's direction.

Supernova appeared beside the staircase, watching them spar. The exchange of steel quickened, becoming silver streaks. They locked weapons and pushed each other in opposite directions. Amalia stood upright and bowed, with Estelle following suit.

"You have passion," said Amalia. "But also great rage. You may want to practice clearing your mind. With discipline and wisdom, you'll make a fine warrior some day." She turned to the Guardian. "Have you been training her, Nova? It is your final test before your promotion."

"You guys told me I had already surpassed that level."

"In skill. Not in rank. You'll never be a true master until you've taken an heir."

"Why would I want to drag anyone else into this shit show? All we ever do is fight."

"We fight for those too weak to fight for themselves. I consider myself a protector first, a scholar second, a warrior third. It's the gratitude of the people that makes it worth it."

"You can say that. You and your brother are used to being heroes. You kill a few monsters and the whole country sings your praise. That has not been my experience. I see fear in their eyes. They bow and give offerings in hopes I will spare them."

"Well, you're not very personable," Estelle said. "Most of the time, you don't seem like you want to be bothered."

"She's not wrong," Amalia said. "It isn't enough to kill a beast. You have to show the citizens that even with all your power, you're still one of them."

"I'm closer with the beasts. With nature. A lot of those 'monsters' we kill are just animals trying to protect their homes. People move into the forest and start cutting it down. Or overfishing, leaving the seas barren. When nature fights back and people get what's coming to them, we show up to save them and they learn nothing."

"Then why not educate them? If you have this unique insight, why not share it?"

"I will the day they put their weapons down. Regarding Estelle, I'll tell you the same thing I told her: she needs to give up her powers."

"Don't you think that's for her to decide?"

"She has her own life to live. Do you think I'd be irresponsible enough to set her up with these powers and let her do god-knows-what with them? I know she wants to keep them-"

"That will never change," Estelle said, smirking at Amalia.

"It's not a lifetime commitment," Amalia said. "You just have to train her enough so you can get your promotion. There's more to be said if she does good things with her powers. You could be the cause of that."

The swordsman sighed. "Even if I wanted to- and that's a big 'if'- we don't have the time or the freedom."

"How long would you need?"

"To be effective? Years. We're supposed to be on a mission. We don't have time."

"I think you're looking for reasons not to. Why did you come here if time is such a factor?"

"That's what I said!" Estelle scoffed.

"Come see," Supernova said, rubbing his temples. "I need your assistance."

"You never ask for help." Amalia followed Supernova to his desk. "Least of all from myself."

He pulled two pieces of parchment from the messy pile, pushing everything else aside. The first page bore a twelve-pointed star within a circle. Three rings with strange symbols were within, oriented at the edges to create a triangular formation. In the margins, Supernova sketched his two swords. The second page displayed an ink rendition of a scythe simpler in design than Temcindus. Around it were dozens of markings, phrases and symbols with three circled: an hourglass, a sickle and a star.

"While in Eve's Hollow, I lost access to the scythe," the swordsman said. "I found it in a museum, and the entire building had two powerful spells cast upon it. My cosmic clock was on the floor and another on the ceiling."

"These are the symbols you saw?" Amalia asked, resting her hand on the page.

"Among others. I saw them in one of the time spells. The red one."

"I've never heard of a red time spell. They're normally gold, blue or white." She picked up the page with the twelve-pointed star. "This Underworld spell resembles one I learned about when I was assigned to you. Hades allowed me to use his library, and I saw something like this. It was called *The Well of Might*. It's a channel to the Underworld's power. Very few would have the access to cast this. Even you."

"Is it possible someone like me is in Eve's Hollow? Another vessel of the void?"

Amalia shrugged. "I know they exist, but in 200 years of travel across the globe, you are the only one I've ever met. I don't know anyone aside from a god that could have cast that spell."

"Do you think Hades or Osiris could be helping me?"

"It's not unheard of. In my time of need, Athena gifted me the Aegis to protect myself. Eve's Hollow is an awful place to be. Perhaps one of your patrons took pity? Perhaps it is best not to question a gift?"

"Perhaps."

"Nova," said Estelle. "Your friend- Thelxiope said that you cast the spell. What does that mean?"

"I have no idea," he replied. "I couldn't even summon Temcindus, let alone cast a spell like this."

"I'll see what I can dig up." Amalia turned to Estelle. "Would you please excuse us for just a few minutes? I must speak with your Guardian in private."

The Seeker exited the room with her crow perched on her shoulder. The hallway was cool and the sound of the birds soothed her. A low purr caught her attention as she felt a soft body nudging her leg. A gray cat with black stripes and striking green eyes wrapped itself around her boot. The woman knelt down and scratched it behind the ears. It was only once the cat hunched down and fled, did Estelle realize Serafim was leaning against a tree down the hall, watching her.

"Serafim," she said. "I didn't see you there."

"I know," he said with a smirk. "How go the trials?"

"Slowly. We suffered losses before we got to the museum."

"I'm terribly sorry to hear that. If I could have helped, I would have."

"You stayed long enough to torture my Guardian," she said with a raised eyebrow.

Serafim smirked and looked at the ground.

"That wasn't my fault. We all have rules to live by."

"You sure enjoyed it enough." She rolled her eyes.

"It isn't that." Serafim said. "He can just get a little big for his status. A little arrogance peppered with a lot of ego. Am I false?"

She looked away and shook her head, and the glowing man approached.

"How do you like Summom Scientenia?" he asked.

"It seems like paradise," Estelle said.

"Oh, it's just another one of the many. Home to many deep thinkers and wisdom hunters."

"Then why does Nova get to come here?"

The two shared in a laugh before Serafim answered. "His job title allows him special privilege."

"I know he works for gods. Where I come from, they're myths, but you guys say they're real."

"Very much so. Maybe you'll meet one some day. When people complete great feats- sometimes the gods make them what we call Divine Heroes. Supernova is on the cusp of graduating. His final test is to take an apprentice."

"Amalia said something about him training me. She thinks I can be like you all."

"How do you feel about that?"

"It sounds wonderful the way your sister talks about it." Marcel's face flashed in her mind. "But I really just want a quiet life with someone I care about. Besides, I'm not special like you."

"Many heroes start out as normal people," Serafim said. "When Amalia and I were barely adults, a boar the size of a boulder terrorized the western isles of Aurum. Amalia, with three of her friends, sailed there to do battle with the beast and save the villagers there. They were so thankful they named their island after her. Afterward we became servants of the Gods. Your Guardian can perform miracles and slay beasts too, but his methods are visceral to behold."

"I'm aware," Estelle said. "I can't say I'm a fan."

"I don't want to speak ill of the man, but you should be careful around him. Sometimes the spirit in his head gets to him. He becomes detached; irritable. I don't want to say I fear for your safety."

"You think Nova would hurt me?"

"Sometimes he is not himself. I've heard tell of an incident where he was charged with protecting a small coastal city. In fighting off a beast, he caused the deaths of several civilians. This is just a rumor, though. Even if it were true, I'm sure he did not mean for it to happen. Still, carelessness can be its own punishment. My sister would agree."

"Speaking of- I wish I knew what they were talking about. They're like my father, making choices about my life without me being there."

Serafim grinned. "Arachne's Gift."

The sunlit man held an open palm up and in it appeared the iridescent conch shell. He held it to his ear and listened before giving it to Estelle. As she angled its point toward the door, whispers slipped through the shell's opening.

"Wasn't this in his room?" Estelle asked.

"He never thinks of this old thing. Probably had it stashed in some crate."

Estelle held the conch to her ear and aimed it at the door. The sound of ocean waves crashed within the item and voices rolled over it.

"Who are you to decide that for her?" Amalia asked, raising her voice. "She was blessed with a gift."

"It is a curse!" Supernova said, agitated. "One she cannot handle. She's already screwed up using them. She's responsible for at least one innocent death and my friend could have met a similar fate. Would you go to deal with her if she gets out of hand?"

Estelle pulled the shell away from the door, her chest tightening. She wanted to stop listening, but curiosity brought the conch back to her ear.

"The best way to avoid that is by preparing her," Amalia said. "I think you should give her a chance."

"Even if I trained her," Supernova said. "She's reckless, and she thinks she knows everything. What good are my lessons if the brat won't listen? She's more likely to destroy herself than master Storm Casting."

"I refuse to believe she's that foolish. She may be head-strong, but she's not suicidal. Serafim tells me she's more than eager to return to her home. Am I correct?"

"You are. But what happens when she attracts the wrong attention in her world? She already burned down a dance studio. Police? Military? You think she'll go quietly? Or do you think she would bring chaos?"

"I understand your concerns. I really do. But more knowl-edge is always better. Estelle is her own woman, and she needs to make the choice on her own."

"If she becomes an issue?"

"*If* that day comes, you won't be alone." There was silence for a moment. "How long do you need?"

"As much time as you can get me," Supernova said with a sigh.

The voices fell silent, and Estelle hung on Supernova's harsh words. She offered the shell back to Serafim. He put his hands up and shook his head. The conch vaporized, turning to ocean mist.

"Hold on to it," he said. "What did you hear?"

"I'd rather not talk about it," Estelle said in a slump. "Thank you, though. I guess I heard what I needed to. I'm just going to focus on getting stronger so I can get back home."

"That bad, huh?" Serafim locked eyes with the Seeker. "Listen, I don't know what you heard, but you're witty and determined. There's nothing you desire that you can't have. When you want that conch again, ask for 'Arachne's Gift.'"

The door to the study clicked open, with Supernova and Amalia stepping out to greet them. The Guardian made eye contact with Serafim for a moment before looking at Estelle. Though she saw him from her peripheral, she kept her eyes trained on the glossy floor.

"What have you decided?" Serafim asked.

"Supernova will train the Seeker," his elder sister told him. "Providing I get them time and permission. It would be better to allow her to acclimate to her powers before sending her off to a new life."

"You agree with this, Nova?"

"It isn't my first choice," Supernova said. "But her powers are dangerous without proper instruction and she won't give them up."

"Are you sure you're up to the task?"

Supernova's eyes narrowed. "You have doubts?"

"Certainly not." Serafim put his hands up in a defensive wave. "I just understand the weight on your shoulders. You haven't had a chance to rest in how long?"

"I can handle it," he said through gritted teeth.

"It's just-"

"Serafim!" Amalia said sharply. "Leave him. Go wait with the elders."

With a smile and a deep bow to the Guardian, he started away, but not without a sly wink to Estelle. Serafim rounded the corner and was gone. Amalia sighed, rubbing her forehead.

"I'm going to speak with the elders," she said. "Estelle, normally visitors can't stay more than three days in this realm, but you'll need longer than that to grasp Storm Casting. I'm going to try and get you as much time as I can."

"Of course," Supernova said. "The choice is yours. We can head back right now if you'd prefer?"

"I have a question first," Estelle said. "You've told me that time works differently between the realms. So when I get home, how much time will have passed? Will I wake up in the hole I fell down? Will it be weeks later? I need to know if I'm spending all this time in other places."

Supernova and Amalia frowned at one another.

"We don't know," the woman in white said. "No successful Seeker was heard from after they escaped."

"As far as Summom Scientenia," Supernova said. "Time beyond this realm turns much slower. We could spend years here and barely scratch a month in Eve's Hollow."

Estelle weighed the options as she ran through her Guardian's words in her brain. She could not free her mind of his cruel voice.

Estelle had a way of dealing with teachers who tried to make an example of her. She would put all her focus into mastering their class while simultaneously undermining them. Be it sleeping in class, obsessing over her makeup, or talking with her friends, Estelle's response was to claim the class was too easy. Supernova would be no different.

"I'd like to train as long as I can," Estelle said confidently. "I love my powers. The more I know, the better."

"I like her," Amalia said. "Athena would be proud. I'll meet you soon. You know those mind-readers; they'll have my answer as I walk in the room."

The two watched her until she disappeared, then Supernova made his way down in the opposite direction. Estelle hesitated, but followed, comforting herself by scratching her crow's small head.

At the end of the corridor was an ivy covered arch that lead to a round balcony overflowing with shrubs and flowers. The sky was a deep orange, pink and indigo on the horizon, fading to black, high above with twinkling stars and a pale yellow half moon looked down on them. Nightingales, bluejays and cardinals flapped around the flowers, singing their bedtime songs. Estelle watched her Guardian as he breathed deeply and said not a word. The wind blew the scent of fruit and flowers over them and the Seeker filled her lungs with it.

"Activate your powers," he instructed.

"*Shu Nut Rah*," she said, her eyes burning bright blue. "What's first?"

"Calm yourself," he said. "Take in the night air. Listen to the animals. Smell the ocean blossoms. Bathe in the moon's light."

"I thought we were supposed to be storm casting."

"How can I teach you anything if you keep challenging everything I say? I can't help you if you drag your feet the whole way."

"It feels like you never care what I have to say," she said bluntly, her lightning dissipating. "Like you're the only one with the answers, and I'm only in your way. Would it kill you to listen to me once?"

Supernova gazed out over the ocean as the moonlight bobbed with the waves. Bright neon lights lined the city and spotlights beamed high from a large building somewhere within.

"She has a point," the crow said. "You are a force of nature, Supernova, and no one doubts your capabilities. But sometimes looking at the larger picture means you miss smaller details."

"That's fair," the Guardian said, turning to Estelle. "I know I'm not much for casual company, but when it comes to my art, I know what I'm doing. So a proposition: Listen to me and let me teach you. I'll give you more space to express yourself."

"No," she said, crossing her arms. "Expressing myself shouldn't be conditional. Accept me for who I am or- I'll find a new Guardian."

"That's not how it works."

"I don't care. If you want me to be little miss student, you'll accept it. And a bit more help on my trials would be appreciated."

Estelle turned away. She ground her teeth, holding in every insult she wanted to hurl at her Guardian.

"You're right," the reaper said. "I've been obsessed with saving Vileena for a long time. That will never change- it just won't. I know where this road leads for me, and it isn't above ground. Before that day comes, I will get you home."

"So if I listen to you, you'll focus more on my trials?"

"I swear on my burning heart."

The Seeker turned to him, his right hand extended. Estelle accepted, agreeing to the terms. A burst came from the other side of the atheneum and a majestic white bird flew high into the sky so fast that Estelle came close to missing it all together. The streak of light rose higher and higher until it blended with the light of the moon.

"What was that?" Estelle asked, leaning over a bed of marigolds.

"Amalia," Supernova said. "She must have our answer."

"Then where's she going?"

He pointed to the moon. "Lady Selene's realm, home to the Lunar Anchorites. *Locus.*"

Purple light spread through Supernova's irises, and he held his arm out to Estelle. She moved to question him, but held her tongue at his glare. She looped her arm through his as the white crow nestled itself in the flowers. A lightning bolt took them soaring into the sky faster than she could perceive. The ground disappeared beneath her feet and she became weight-less. She gripped her Guardian's arm and looked down, gazing at a sprawling web of lights. Clouds passed them by as the atmosphere disappeared.

The feeling was strange, having nothing to stand on or

push off of. A thin white outline surrounded both of their bodies, allowing them to breathe in the vacuum. Using his energy to produce speed, Supernova flew them to the moon.

The craters grew wider and mountain ranges came into view. Nestled within the crags and peaks was another web of lights that Estelle took for another city.

Tall moonstone towers and temples mimicked the pointed landscape. They fell toward a large circle of stone surrounded by pillars with a tall brazier in the center. They flipped right side up as they touched down.

Amalia waited for them with a twenty foot tall owl covered in white feathers that looked as if they were dipped in a sunset. Flaring pink, orange and red at its wingtips contrasted its soft cotton plumes. Its quiet black eyes watched them as they approached its mistress.

Estelle stared upward in disbelief. Away from the city lights of Summom Scientenia, the stars quadrupled in number and multi-colored light bathed the sky. Swirls of white dust and shooting stars dotted the heavens.

"You have three months," Amalia said. "It isn't much, but it's better than nothing. In theory, if Estelle progresses enough, you should get your promotion."

"I've done more with less." Supernova said. "I'll make it work."

"Are you ready?" Amalia asked Estelle. "I won't be going with you, but I'll pop in from time to time."

"I'll make it work," Estelle said, smiling. "I appreciate what you did for me. I won't forget it."

Amalia gave a nod to Supernova, who returned it. Bowing its head to allow her on its back, the owl cooed. It spread its massive wings and took off into the sky, ascending high before plunging below the lunar mountains. Supernova beckoned his Seeker, and she approached.

"Estelle," he said. "You are about to experience something

a handful of people ever will again. It will be tough, stressful and grueling beyond measure."

"Trying to scare me away already?" she asked with a laugh. "I'm ready."

"I know you think you are. I don't doubt your willingness, but have an appreciation for what this is going to be. I'm going to push you to your limits. Train your mind and body beyond their breaking point. If you push past that, you'll come out a stronger person. Though you are free to quit whenever you wish."

Supernova stared up at the heavens, lost in its infinite glory. Then he pointed a finger at Estelle's heart, bringing forth the spark of her life lightning. From it, the pencil thin outline of a cloak fell down her body, filling in with light gray storm clouds. Tiny snowflakes fell as lightning flashed within.

"Under the eyes of the divine and at the watch of the Underworld Three; I take you as my apprentice if you will have me as your Storm Casting master."

"I will," Estelle said.